DOG YEARS

DRUE HEINZ LITERATURE PRIZE

DOG YEARS

STORIES

MELISSA YANCY

University of Pittsburgh Press

The following stories, in slightly different form, have been previously published: "Dog Years" in *Zyzzyva*; "Consider this Case" in the *Missouri Review*; "Firstborn" in *Prairie Schooner*; "Hounds" in *Colorado Review*; "Miracle Girl Grows Up" in *Meridian*; "Go Forth" in the *Kenyon Review* online; "Teeth Apart" in *Glimmer Train Stories*; "The Program™" in *The Journal*; and "Stray" in *At Length*.

Cover design by Joel W. Coggins
Cover image by Todd McLellan, taken from *Things Come Apart : A Teardown Manual for Modern Living*, published by Thames & Hudson.

Published by the University of Pittsburgh Press, Pittsburgh, PA, 15260
Copyright © 2016, Melissa Yancy
All rights reserved
Manufactured in the United States of America
Printed on acid-free paper
10 9 8 7 6 5 4 3 2 1

ISBN 13: 978-0-8229-4467-6
ISBN 10: 0-8229-4467-7

Cataloging-in-Publication data is available from the Library of Congress

For Dad
For Mom

CONTENTS

DOG YEARS

DOG YEARS

THE BERGER FAMILY IS IN A BIG-BOX STORE, ONE THEY HAVE driven several miles out of their West L.A. neighborhood to find, and the cart is piled so high Ellen has finally conceded to getting another. With their speed through the aisles and the ziggurat of toilet paper, tissue, and toothpaste now cresting over the lip, the scene is suggestive of an apocalypse. Or the late great game show *Supermarket Sweep*. It is odd, Ellen thinks, that the possibility of racing through a supermarket, knocking rows of pure maple syrup, wrapped hams, and giant wedges of parmesan into a cart to compete for the highest sales total ever sounded like a good time. Was it wish fulfillment for the thrifty, this one chance to buy only the most expensive—if arguably unglamorous—items? Or was it the hope that all those hours spent in actual grocery stores, hunching to see prices, dodging mindless carts, and placating babies (who kept dropping their binkies on the floor) were training days, that there would be a moment when all of that wasted time would find meaning?

They are near the end of this trip but have come to their customary paralysis at the cereal aisle, the place where every color has its chance to compete: yellow to suggest wheat or corn; red and neon green to suggest candy; brown for all things chocolate; purple to simply say raisins; white or understated blue to attract adults; and orange, the most conflicted, which can signify honeyed wholesomeness in its more subdued hues or full-on space food in its brighter versions. Ellen has been arguing for the regular Cheerios (yellow), which are on sale for $2.28 for an 18-ounce box, but her younger son, Zach, prefers the peanut butter ones (orange for regular, white for multigrain), which are $3.68 for a 12.25-ounce box. They have a rule about cereal in their house—no more than $2.50 per box, even for the smallest size. Two dollars is better. But they've never bothered to adjust for inflation, so the options continue to diminish.

Her eyes keep drifting across the aisle to a display of melamine plates printed with blue anchors and sand-colored starfish. Summer is almost here. If she had those plates, they could have people over and she could serve—what is the least troublesome thing she could serve?—Prosecco, maybe, and some decent beer; they could do it if they make it easy enough. She begins to wander away from the aisle toward the display of plates and little votive holders wrapped in beachy rope, even though she promised herself on the way to the store—no melamine! no duvet covers! no scented candles!—and when she leans over to look at the price, she sees the red tag instead of the white, the color that would normally give her a hit of pleasure until she realizes that the plates are on sale because it is the *end* of summer, not the beginning. She knows that, of course, how can she not *know* that, but for a moment, it still seemed like there was time for summer.

Her husband Gordy calls her back to the cereal. Zach's legs are getting tired and Tyler, their sixteen-year-old, will be late for his guitar lesson. There is still no agreement about the Cheerios. They have considered other options, compared ounces, become nostalgic for Raisin Nut Bran (orange, purple, *and* white, a real crowd pleaser), which has not been on sale for many years.

"Just get what you want," she says, less magnanimous than tired. But at moments like this, she can't help but think, Zach will live a short life, and you are going to deny him Peanut Butter Cheerios? But it is the principle of the thing, of living a normal life, that includes grocery thrift.

This is why their house assistant, Jeanette, who is away for a friend's wedding, usually does the household shopping. Jeanette, who spends her free time gorging on house porn online, determined to bring beauty to their lives.

"I'm still getting these," Ellen says, balancing the box of plain Cheerios on top of the cart. "It will bring the per-box average down, at least."

"This is not going in the movie montage," Gordy says.

The watch on Ellen's wrist spells out eleven fifty-three. It was a gift from Gordy for her forty-sixth birthday, and she gasped with primal relief when she opened it: some product designer had understood how little energy she had in reserve to translate numbers into words, let alone the geometry of hands into numbers into words. The watch is actually a small computer designed to keep her even more tethered to demands, when her head is already a ball on a string, getting whacked around a pole. She ignores the zings and pulses on her wrist and enjoys the Helvetica, instead.

Eleven fifty-three means running only four minutes late to make it to north campus by noon, where Ellen has been asked to speak to an undergraduate seminar about her research. Twenty minutes of zipper talk, fifteen for questions and she can get back down the hill and review a fellow's grant application by 2 p.m. She speeds up the main walk, running her hands along the tops of papery reeds planted beside the sidewalk, reeds that look like small bamboo but are another, noninvasive species. She likes to do this, as though she is not a professor but a young girl. It makes her feel present, somehow. Like she is stopping to rest while still moving forward.

She arrives only two minutes late, good enough to make a detour to one of the powdered coffee machines that Gordy calls her transfusion centers. On south campus, she knows how they are all calibrated—some sweeter than others—and can choose accordingly. The plunk of the cup being dropped, the plastic door sliding open in its Jetsonian way, and the sight of the little froth the machine leaves at the top fills her with the deep, chewy comfort another person might get from a basket of rolls passed at a dinner table.

There are five versions of the zipper talk that scale in complexity: versions four and five don't contain a zipper analogy at all, because the transcription and translation of DNA to RNA to protein is more complex than that. The zipper is a lie, but the kind of lie that helps people understand.

"DNA replication is like a zipper," she begins, sipping at her froth. "A gene is a section of DNA that contains instructions for producing a protein. The gene is split into exons—the part that codes for a protein—and introns, the junk. Duchenne muscular dystrophy is caused by a mutation in the dystrophin gene. In Duchenne, an exon is missing, and because of that, the rest of the strand can't be assembled. Imagine the offset teeth of a zipper and a missing tooth. The rest of the zipper won't zip. So the body can't code for dystrophin."

She recognizes a few of the students near the front, overly eager undergraduates who have had summer internships in the lab and who refer to Gordy as Dr. Gordy, since no one can bear to call him Gordon, much less refer to him by last name. They do all but call him *swell*.

"The concept of exon skipping," she goes on, "is that we inject a molecular patch that hides the exon you want to skip. So, if someone were missing exon 52, the patch would hide the neighboring exon, so that now 51 and 54 will match up again. You still have a gap, but the rest can zip up. The trial that our Center for Duchenne is working on now is for a drug that enhances the effects of the patch."

At the end of the talk, one of the girls near the front raises her hand. She is a small Asian student who looks about twelve, in pink Converse and a T-shirt silk-screened with a butterfly, the kind of student Ellen often finds surprisingly formidable. She wants to know—although she asks it quietly, her head gently cocking—which came first, the research or their son?

"Is that okay to ask?" the girl says, even though she has already asked it.

Ellen is a molecular geneticist; Gordy is a clinical geneticist; their son, Zach, has Duchenne's, a genetic disorder. In the movie version of their lives, scientists scribble on whiteboards while kids in wheelchairs pull wheelies and give high fives. Two scientists born to find a cure . . . racing against the clock . . . to save their own son! Ellen likes the moment in a movie trailer when the screen fades to black and the tinkling of piano—over which the dramatic problem has been laid—bursts open into chorus, and someone driving down a country road in a convertible throws her hands up in the summer air. "Where is my convertible?" she asks Gordy.

"The genetics came first," Ellen tells the student. "But we didn't study muscular dystrophy. We both were—are—cancer researchers. But if we could devote some of our time and resources to Duchenne after Zach was born? It only made sense. There wasn't enough being done."

The gene for muscular dystrophy was discovered in the '80s, and since then, nothing: that was academic freedom for you. Now, she and Gordy run a center that has NIH funding, clinical trials, boys coming from across California to receive care, the kind of success that was hard to come by in the crowded world of cancer immunology. For a different audience, Ellen likes to say she will not cure cancer in her lifetime, but she can cure Duchenne muscular dystrophy. And that cure will lead the way for other genetic diseases. But this is a student, and she doesn't like to spin with students.

"I want to study Alzheimer's because it killed my grandfather," the girl says. "But is it bad to study something so close to you?"

"Define bad," Ellen says.

Over the years, Ellen and Gordy have run through almost every actor in *who would play me?*, one of Gordy's favorite games. The running joke is a comfort, but it also indulges a narcissistic streak that no one but Ellen sees. Perhaps, having spent so many years in Los Angeles, he can't help but frame their lives this way.

"Michael Nyqvist," he says now. It is Sunday morning, the few minutes he calls Temple of the Bed, when Ellen brews coffee right on top of her clothes dresser, where she has stationed a machine along with her computer chargers, lotion, water bottles, and other bedroom blight.

"Who's that?" she says.

"The Swedish actor. The Stieg Larsson series?"

"When did you see those?"

"Just a photo online. I like the look of him."

"Melissa McCarthy," she says.

"Oh-kay." He pauses in the way of all seasoned husbands who sense conversation hazards ahead.

"I want someone really funny to play me. I finally figured that out."

"But you're not funny," he says.

"I laugh a lot, don't I?"

"That's not the same as being funny. That's like being—funn-ied."

"Or funee—like a donee."

"See what I mean?" he says.

It is Zach's birthday. He is turning nine. This year, he has not requested a trip to Magic Mountain or the Safari Park but a backyard party with friends. They have set up a volleyball court and bought every kind of foam ball and stick game ever manufactured. Jeanette has hidden the family's hoarding from sight and bought marinated pollo asado from a Mexican grocery down the hill. Ellen's job has been to select the cake: it is the Space Shuttle *Endeavor,* in patriotic hues, the last year Zach may like something like this. As a joke, Tyler has bought the fat numbered candles for thirty-six, since Zach argues that because of his short life, his age should be treated like dog years. He gives himself four years for every one and shouts out *dog years!* when they tell him he isn't old enough to do something.

Zach's two closest friends from school arrive first so they avoid the awkward school dance feeling that can descend on a child's birthday party. Within seconds they are outside, fencing with foam batons. Zach is unsteady in the fencer's pose, easily knocked off balance by the strikes. She sees him wobble and look for a flatter space on the grass.

Zach has always had plenty of friends from school, but now that she and Gordy run the center, a few families of boys with muscular dystrophy have entered the fold. It is supposed to be good for Zach, or for them, and although it has made him less alone, it has introduced him to his future, a perverse variation on the way older children so often introduce younger kids to things they aren't yet ready for.

Ellen opens Sauvignon Blanc and the women congregate in the kitchen, drinking, while they watch the men outside on the grill. The women like to mourn at birthday parties, and the men just want to relax. She remembers when Tyler was growing up, how they would sit around and groan that their boys weren't little boys anymore. It was bittersweet, a feeling that had felt complex then. But now that she has added another dimension, a child whose health degenerates each year, the old feeling is so flat, so easy.

"Gordy is such a great guy," her neighbor Rosie says as they watch Gordy scrape the grill and hold court with the other men. Rosie has lived down the street for years; she knew them before they were *these* people.

"Is he?" Ellen asks, sipping her wine. She can't afford to get drunk, exactly. But she would like to feel that feeling that butts up right against it.

He *is* a great guy but she is bothered by how often people remind her of this, the implied commentary about equivalence. He is more exuberant than she, it is true. He is still trim and his thick beard masks the age on his face. She looks tired and, by virtue of the expectations placed only on women, more unkempt and therefore less happy. But there might be something else she fears people can see manifested in their physical forms—that inside, they are each telling themselves a different story, something they do not talk about or always talk around.

One of the center's patients, Gilbert, a twelve-year-old who is now in a wheelchair, arrives with his mom Lena. Zach greets him briefly then runs crookedly off, putting as much distance between himself and the boy as he can. Tyler gets Gilbert an orange soda and goes out to the patio with him and keeps him company. She cannot believe her boy Tyler. He calls adults Mr. and Mrs., gives firm handshakes, and puts his plates in the sink. Tyler is a muscled, pimply saint.

"When did you get that?" another neighbor asks, pointing to the electric chair lift that's been installed on the stairs.

"A few months ago," Ellen says. "We wanted to get Zach used to the idea of having it there. So it's not a big deal."

"While he can still walk?" one of the non-Duchenne mothers says. "Doesn't that feel defeatist?"

"It will be worse to put it in after the first time he can't make it up the stairs," Ellen says.

"How did he take it?" Rosie asks.

"Not well," Ellen says. "He can't imagine he'll ever need that."

"I get it," says Lena. She pours herself a glass of the wine. "He won't have to admit it this way. He can just use it—when he's ready." She turns to the other women. "You can't imagine how hard it is for them to admit they can't do something they could do the week before," she says. "They're boys."

"Oh, yes," Rosie says. "Boys and men. That is why the crown molding in my living room is hung upside down."

"And why the water knobs on my sink are reversed," the other neighbor says.

There is always someone who makes the conversation light again. Ellen has a sudden urge to take them down as far as this well goes, to squeeze the wine glass in her hand until it breaks. But she does not do that. It is her job to quip. Without that, no one will follow. People will turn away.

Before they are ready to blow out the candles, Ellen pulls Zach aside.

"You need to spend some time with Gilbert," she says. "Be a good host."

He looks away from her, over his shoulder at the boys playing. How many more days will he be able to walk, to do this?

"Are you listening to me?" she says. "He came here to see you."

He doesn't answer her, but when the cake is cut, he goes to sit by Gilbert, and when they're done eating they throw cake at Tyler who artfully dodges all but one splat of frosting.

She thought it might help to have friends who understand, but she feels like the Duchenne parents are watching her and wondering where their cure is. They volunteer and fundraise for Ellen and Gordy's research. And she can't help but think they are judging her for sitting there with a glass of wine in hand.

But in her heart she makes the opposite case. Zach may be able to walk only for another year or two. Shouldn't she spend every moment of the good years with him that she can? Or should she wait and be there for him in the harder years? It is not a race against time. They will not cure their son. They will cure an idea of their son, while her real son diminishes each day.

Dr. Stame, the CEO of the medical center where she and Gordy work, is a child psychiatrist by trade. His office is more like a tech guru's than a doctor's: in the center is a large standing desk topped with three monitors. On the wall above a large conference table is a melting Dalí clock, the kind of decoration Ellen imagines belongs in a college dorm room. There are framed quotes: from Wayne Gretzky, *Don't skate to where the puck is, skate to where the puck will be;* and from the Queen in Alice in Wonderland, *It's a poor sort of memory that only works backwards.*

Stame is known for TED talks, for believing that a story is always the solution, and his stories, in Ellen's estimation, often have little medical relevance; he will tell how they arranged for a young pregnant woman to travel across the state to their medical center to give birth so that her grandmother, who lay dying two floors up, could hold her great-granddaughter just once.

Cultivating Stame is Gordy's job. She finds the whimsy unsettling. But Gordy has a meeting with the dean and so she is here instead to ask him to be a sponsor for their annual fundraiser for muscular dystrophy. It feels like begging from Peter to pay Paul, and it is; this is how the money flows from the medical center to the medical school.

She begins by telling Stame how successful the past events have been, but he raises his hand to stop her. "You don't have to convince me," he says.

She has been told he grades people on their conversations and she imagines the deductions he is already making.

"Your husband is a good man," he says.

"So I'm told," she says.

"He's been helping me with a side interest of mine," he says.

"Oh?"

"I ask people to track moments of meaningful coincidence," he says.

Hearing those words is like smelling another woman's perfume on her husband. Lately, Gordy has been babbling about synchronicity, and Ellen has wondered if he was getting religious on her. She will catch him smile, or shake his head in a private thought, and when she asks him what it is, he says nothing. Because when he has tried to explain it—how a particular name or book or song keeps coming up—she has been dismissive. She understands the coincidence part but not the meaning: What exactly is the universe supposed to be telling him? Now she knows why he has been looking. Synchronicity is a total Stame word, juvenile and Jungian.

"And what has Gordy come up with?" she asks. The idea of his conversations with Stame feels like an infidelity, telling stories out of turn. The difference between Ellen and Gordy is that she finds purpose, not meaning. There are circumstances and she has decided to make herself of use; it is causal, linear, and does not fold in on itself in a way that is supposed to mean more.

"This kind of information is more interesting in the patterns," he says.

"Patient confidentiality?"

"He's not a patient."

Just a subject, Ellen thinks. She knows that Stame is collecting information to use them, to feature their story as one of *his* stories, which is his occupational right. It is the kind of story Stame lives for, that he would make up if he could.

Get dressed, Gordy is saying.

She is trying. She has squeezed into a stretchy girdle and has been digging through the hamper for her only thick-strapped bra that smoothes out back fat. It has managed its way to the bottom where the pilly sweaters she has not committed to discarding rest.

"I need a zip!" she calls out to him, and he comes in, one shoe on, one shoe being shimmied into as he moves across the floor.

She brushes her hair in front of her shoulder and feels his hands move the zipper up and then stop.

"What?" she demands. "What's going on back there?"

She cranes her neck around. He smells like cologne. She has not smelled cologne on him in months.

"Just hold on," he says. She feels him unzip, then rezip and stop again, tugging.

"MOM!" Zach screams from downstairs. "We're going to be late."

"I'm too fat," she says to Gordy. "I'm too fat!"

"No, it's just stuck. It's a bad zipper. But maybe suck in a little?"

But the zipper won't budge.

"I've been telling you!" she yells at him as she goes to the closet, as though if he had only acknowledged the fact of her girth, she would have been transformed. She almost never wears dresses, and fundraisers are the only time she's required to doll up.

"MOM!" Zach screams again. "Come on!"

"Your mother is NAKED!" she screams back at him. "Naked!"

She grabs her silk robe from the bathroom and Gordy stops her. "What about that?" he says.

"What about what?"

"That looks like a dress. Like one of those wrapper dresses."

"You're insane," she says. "My boobs will fall out."

"We'll tie it tight," he says. "Or we'll tape it underneath."

It is black, it is silky, and with her gold flats and a red beaded necklace, it almost looks like something that could be worn to the Beverly Hills Hotel. She dabs at a speck of toothpaste on her chest as she gets into the car.

"Why are doctors always late?" Zach says.

"Zach," Tyler warns. "They are not in the mood."

The patient who is being honored at the gala has just graduated from high school with honors. In the last year he has grown an impressive mustache, and Zach and Tyler now call him Selleck, which he loves. At the Duchenne Center, the physical therapy team has recently fitted him with a new arm-assist that helps him use his hands to type or bring food to his mouth. He gets food caught in the mustache all the time but doesn't care. He has been admitted to UCLA and begins in the fall. For people who think of college as only a preparatory exercise, it probably doesn't make sense. But what Selleck has left is the life of the mind.

A colleague once explained to Ellen, using a smudged equation on the back of a greasy lunch receipt, that if you assumed you would live to eighty, and you chose five as the perceptual beginning of your life, then twenty was the perceptual halfway point. She was thirty-five at the time, blithely thinking she had five more years to a halfway point, not that it had blown by long before she had even understood the cruelties of time. She would worry this thought like a hole in her pocket for years, the tear only widening the more she wriggled her fingers against it.

And now it is a strange comfort, her life no longer measured by her own years. To think that even if Zach dies in his early twenties, he will already have lived half a life. She understands the logical error in that but does not care. And a part of her still believes, whatever the math might say, that if only she could be more present, she could control its speed.

Ellen and Gordy skip most of the meal, splitting up and covering the room. She has perfected the art of the leaned-in interruption. She squats, one hand on the back of the ballroom chair, trying to keep her breasts tucked in. She meets strangers, friends of friends who have been enlisted in the cause. They are in the door and now she must sell: she must not let them leave without a car.

When dessert is finally served, the lights go down and they sit. The video is seven minutes long, as dictated by the fundraising consultant. That is precisely the length required to garner emotional commitment without boredom and the video must make the audience cry three times. If they fail to produce actual tears, there must be goose bumps, a prickle in the heart. There is a strict formula: it begins with a toddler at the moment of diagnosis, and then the sobering facts—*it is universally fatal; there is no cure*—and the progression with each passing year, the gait growing more awkward and slow, the wheelchair, the loss of hand use, the ventilators, and finally the heart, the last muscle that goes. There are stories of the parents, cradling their teenaged sons down into bed at night, and then the screen goes black: when it comes back up, it is stop-motion in a busy clinic. And then Gordy and Ellen are in the lab, talking about how much has been discovered in the last ten years, how they are close enough now that the toddler diagnosed today has real hope. The end of the video is the familiar punch line, the reveal that half the audience already knows. In comes Zach, their son. There are parents and there are researchers and then there are Gordy and Ellen: Is there anyone in the world who could want this more?

The grand prize of the night is backstage concert passes and a personal visit with Justin Bieber. Ellen sits there like a clerk at an airport foreign exchange as people bid on items, translating money into project costs. She has spent every dollar before it is raised. The tyranny of money would be as bad as the tyranny of time, except that she holds out hope that there is a great supply of it they are about to unearth. But to raise the money *takes* time, time that could be spent elsewhere, so the two tyrannies intertwine.

They are watching the second half of the third *Mission Impossible* movie. They don't have two hours of free time, so they watch the forty-seven minutes that remain, trying to piece together what is happening. Her sons have seen it before and Gordy is snoring on the floor, his face smashed against one of the rough couch pillows. When people ask Ellen if she has seen a movie, she shrugs. She has seen several scenes of several hundred and she is fairly certain she is not missing anything. Gordy calls this *cinemas interruptus.*

"Pulchritude," Ellen says to Tyler.

"Mom, stop," Tyler says. "Watch the movie."

"It's one of those words where the meaning doesn't match the sound of the word."

"I'm studying for the SAT," he says. "Trust me." But she is afraid Tyler is sabotaging, that he is putting off the decision that will come if he gets into the colleges he wants.

"Wait," she says, when the villain rips off his face mask. "I think maybe I have seen this before."

"I told you," Zach says.

Zach has seen far too many R-rated movies but he has claimed *dog years!* and Ellen is too worn down to object. Zach, who has always had a gift for the dramatic, is finally getting to take an acting class in school and can now add the ammunition that television and movies are research.

"Oh my God!" Zach screams out. "Oh my God!"

Gordy bolts up from his sleep. "What?" Ellen and Tyler yell back.

"We're supposed to bring, like, cookies or something tomorrow. It's my turn at school for the birthday month."

It is 9:30 at night. In half an hour, they should all be in bed.

"I guess it'll be a sad birthday this year," she says.

"Mom! We *have* to," he says.

"We don't have anything to make," she says. "You should have told me. Or told Jeanette."

"I know, I know," he says. "My bad." He gets up from the couch and walks to the kitchen. At night, his steps are a little stiffer, and she can see his left leg is bothering him. He opens the pantry and pushes aside cans of stock and old vegetables that they will eventually donate.

"Look," he says triumphantly, holding up the value size box of cereal. "We have this entire box of Cheerios that no one will eat."

"Great," she says. "You can bring that."

"We can do something with it," he says. "Like they do with Rice Krispies."

"I'll Google it," Tyler says, jumping up to the computer.

Gordy stumbles into the kitchen, his hair mussed and cheek red with upholstery stripes.

"Aren't you glad you bought those Cheerios?" he says with a dumb smile. A Dr. Stame smile. And he means it, in his everything-happens-for-a-reason way.

"Fuck you," she says. "And the universe, too."

She thinks about the perfect days—how many were there? 500? 550?—and how she hadn't known then they were perfect. She tries to remember when she knew something was wrong with Zach, but there had been no singular moment, just times they had compared his development to Tyler's. It had been so long since they'd had a toddler that they didn't trust their recollections. They were too busy and too old to worry. Her pregnancy had been a surprise, inconvenient and miraculous. They had always wanted another child but had never gotten around to it.

She remembers those early days now through the scrim of memory—stitched together moments of Zach, milk-drunk, and she, in a kind of blissed-out exhaustion. She would sit at the end of the couch so she could rest her arm on a pillow and position herself in the sun so that it warmed her back but didn't hit Zach's face. She would listen to NPR while he slowly nursed. That's what having an infant means, in her memory, basking in a warm corner like a housecat. When it was not anything like that.

Just as when she sees undergraduates gathered around a table in the union, oily faces reflected in their computer screens, she feels nostalgia for a time in her life she knows she didn't especially enjoy. She can remember being lonely, eating rice and soy sauce and obsessing that other girls were pretty. But now she thinks only of the freedom, the days stretching out like a long yawn, spontaneous trips to the beach on unexpectedly hot afternoons.

And she knows that these days now, while Zach can still walk, will be the perfect days for her future self. She will not remember the grant applications and the broken garbage disposal and the flesh that is folding over her waistband. And yet knowing this makes almost no difference at all.

Ellen is at a college fair for Tyler in a generic hotel ballroom where she can be a generic parent among strangers. At the snack table, she has found herself next to a shuffle-and-speaker, the kind of woman who must strike up a conversation as they move sideways down the line. Ellen balances her plate of carrot sticks and cheese squares on top of her plastic cup of lemonade so she will have a hand free to eat (one of the problems of the world an engineer should have solved by now), and the shuffler is planted beside her, entering full confessional mode.

"I always wanted a daughter," the woman is saying.

"I didn't," Ellen says, which is true. "I only had brothers growing up. I wasn't sure what I'd do with a girl."

The woman looks her once over, as though realizing this is probably so. The woman wears skinny white jeans that are snug in the rear, a chambray shirt artfully half-tucked and a coral necklace. She is the kind who has made enormous effort not to let herself go. Ellen was never successfully hanging on.

"But we lose our sons," the woman continues. "We have them until what? End of college, if we're lucky. After marriage, they're gone. Girls stay."

"This is true," Ellen says. And she has the strange urge to hug this preening creature. She wonders—in the most hideously Stame-like way—

if people are actually saying things to her she needs to hear or if she is just editing everything else out.

She watches Tyler patrol the room, noticing whether he picks up brochures from out-of-state colleges. She excuses herself and trails behind him, collecting those he has missed.

"Mom," he hisses. "Back off."

It will get harder in the coming years. Zach will be able to do less for himself. It would be easier to have Tyler at home. But a part of her wants him to go to New England, not just far away but to a new cultural landscape, a place where he must become his own person. Of course, she would settle for San Diego or Santa Barbara, enough distance to have his own life but only two hours away.

Some of the admission lookbooks are thin and glossy, and others are saturated with matte hues: students play Quidditch in one frame, build an electric car in the other. There are violinists and kids in lab coats, paint-splattered fun runs and Nobel Prize winners and everyone is laughing, sometimes in the rain. A bearded boy stands among llamas; a bikini-clad girl swims underwater with a sea lion. Everyone is multicultural and has good teeth. It is all real and yet in snapshots—in its omissions—it becomes a lie. Yet she loves that lie. That is exactly the problem. She loves the lies. She always has. But in lies, there is hope. And she cannot hope. She must have all the ambition, the urgency, as though there were hope, without the actual hope itself.

They have promised, as a family unit, to make the foyer their designated dumping ground, to shed the detritus they carry and keep it from creeping past the entryway into the house. Jeanette has purchased stylish linen bins in striped shades for each of them, hooks have been hung, a new console table that hides the mail assembled. And yet dirty shoes have mounded like a pile outside a sacred temple, and magazines threaten to block the door; there is a soccer ball and never-used rain gear and reusable grocery bags everywhere. It was brilliant in the magazine spread Jeanette brought home, the kind of home publication full of special lies like alphabetized spice racks and magical cord keepers.

Today, Ellen wants to walk into stillness instead of chaos for a change. She steps along the pavers that are spaced irregularly in the gravel around the side of the house, then goes to the patio. She feels like a burglar approaching her own back door, a funny kind of familiarity, like when she leans over to kiss Gordy upside down on the couch and thinks that this is what counts for novelty in her life.

She steps in through the French doors and sees the soda cans that signify her boys are here somewhere, but for a moment she can't hear them. She wonders if she is now obligated to go to the foyer and divest herself of her junk, or if she should put her computer in the office, her tote in the closet, her papers on the kitchen station they use for their nightly work. What she needs, she realizes, is a cart. She can put her things on the cart and have her cellphone, her laptop, her lab and class papers near, and then leave the cart by the door so it is all there when she's ready to leave in the morning.

Her linen bin in the entry is full but she smashes her bags on top and forces it back into the storage bench and when she turns the corner there is Zach, cruising down the stairs from the second floor on the motorized chair. It hums with electric life but moves with an almost comically slow pace as the teeth in the rack and pinion engage one-by-one. She sees his look of surprise, as though she's caught him with the bathroom door open.

"Oh hi, Mom," he recovers, and she stands there, waiting for the seat to descend to the bottom.

"I thought I'd give it a test run," he says, when he reaches the ground. He gets out and leans against the baluster, in a pose of mock relaxation that she knows is actually for balance. "Dad said maybe I should run it once in a while, like a car. For the motor's sake."

"What do you think?" she says.

"It's kind of funny," he says. "It reminds me of the haunted mansion in Disneyland. Maybe you could hang some creepy pictures and mirrors on this wall." He grins.

They tell you about the resiliency of children—they do—but what they do not tell you before you have children of your own is what they will do to *your* resiliency: how on the one hand, you will see how brittle you are in relation to them, and how on the other, you will develop a resiliency that flows from them and for them, as though taking in secondhand air from their exhalations. And how, if you will ever have to be without them, you will not be put back together again.

"I'm hungry," he says. "I can't *take* anymore string cheese."

"There are tater tots in the freezer," she says. She looks at her watch. Six forty-five. She has a deadline tomorrow morning. "I told Dad to bring home pizza."

"Pepperoni?"

"No, anchovies."

"What? Dis-gus-ting!"

"I'm your mother," she says. "You think I don't know you want pepperoni?"

She is about to sneak to the office for a minute when Zach says he wants to show her something he has learned in school that week. "It's kind of hilarious," he says, and she follows him into the living room. "Just watch."

She doesn't recognize the music at first. It sounds like science fiction, a mysterious blooming synthesizer followed by chimes. And then the heartbeat comes, a skipping pulse, and it arrives: the piano. The introduction to *Chariots of Fire* blares in the room.

At first, she thinks something is seriously wrong. Zach is frozen in space, like he's about to seize. Then she sees he is moving, running in meticulous slow motion.

Tyler comes barreling down the stairs with the thunder unique to teenage boys.

"Oh my God," Tyler says. "We had to do this in Mr. Dwight's class, too. This is total flashback." He stands next to Zach and positions himself to race. "I can go way slower than you," he says.

"Let's see you try."

Soon, both sons are in exaggerated running poses. Zach keeps losing his balance and resets. Tyler's back leg is high in the air, as though about to come around for a hurdle.

"Come on Mom," Zach says. "You have to do it, too."

"I think not," she says.

"It's a warm up. It loosens up the mind."

"They're teaching you this in school?" she asks. "What is the purpose of this exercise?"

"Mom," Zach says. "Not everything is science, okay?"

The song is the most undeniable kind of lie, a story with no words at all. She gets up and feels ridiculous, grateful that there is no one there to see, and lunges her right leg forward, her right arm back, and pushes her left leg from the ground. It is hard to move slowly, like tai chi, harder than it is to move fast, and yet why should she be surprised? If she knows nothing, it should be how hard it is to bend time, how pointless it is to muscle against.

When Gordy walks in, holding the pizza box aloft with one hand, his bag in the other, they are just reaching the treacly crescendo and mother and sons are standing, fists wild in the air, necks craning forward, and she has the stupid feeling for just a moment that she can feel the wind.

CONSIDER THIS CASE

THIS IS THE ONE DAY EACH YEAR THEY COME TO HIM, ENSHROUDED
in blankets and footed rompers, matching sets of pink plaids and blue
stars or T-shirts proudly declaring personal interests in trucks or lady-
bugs. Nowhere else do so many twins and triplets, all under the age of
five, congregate en masse. Julian, stationed with a chair and a photographer, looks something like a wasting Santa Claus. He scoops them up—
one in each arm if they are small enough—to smile for the camera. The
babies rarely cry. They touch his thick eyebrows, his prominent nose.
They have to be coaxed to look at the photographer.

The reunion is one of Julian's favorite days each year. It is the only time
he works in the sunlight, when he can allow himself to relax. When he is
not in the operating room, he is in the clinic or in his lab. The lawn
between the hospital and the parking garage has been set up with rental
tables and a tent, and a food truck stationed in the entry drive serves
burgers to the families. Older children, now four and five, race around

the perimeter with blades of grass stuck to their sweaty faces, waving their sticky Popsicle fingers—exhibiting their dominion over this place, their right to be.

He first encountered these children as fetuses. The same jokes get told. From him: "I knew you when!" From the parents of the triplet toddlers: "Did you have to save *all* of them?"

After lunch, the photographer sets up for the annual group photo, positioning Julian in the center of the crowd. She perches high on an A-frame ladder, directing the dozens of children. More tables have to be cleared to fit everyone.

They are nearly in position, ready for the group wave, when the telephone in his pocket vibrates. It is his sister, Liv, calling from London. She never calls just to talk to him: everyone in his family has this uncanny ability to call at the worst possible moment, usually to deliver bad news.

"It's Father," Liv whispers through the phone, as though their father hovers nearby. "It's time. He can't be in-de-pen-dent anymore."

"Why are you whis-per-ing?" Julian mimics. "I can barely hear you." All around him hips bob, pacifiers are offered. A few toddlers are chased down at the fringe.

"I can feel his anger from across the Atlantic," she says.

The photographer gesticulates like a conductor. It is time to wave, time to smile.

He misses half of what his sister says, but he knows what she's asking of him. He tells her to hold, smiles for the camera. Then he excuses himself and squeezes through to the edge of the lawn.

"He only has a couple of months," his sister says. "It's not like a permanent situation."

"Life is not a permanent situation," Julian says.

Liv is an actress, currently on the West End. Their mother is long dead. Their younger brother Jay is also dead, from an overdose that may or may not have been accidental. Their father is still at home in Virginia, which makes Julian, all the way in Los Angeles, his nearest relative. Julian offers to pay for in-home care, but this is not what his sister has in mind.

"He needs to be in hospice," Julian says.

"You could get a nurse to come to your house every day. And you have the space."

"He'll try to redecorate," he says.

"So what?" she says. "The place could use a woman's touch."

At the airport, Julian parks the car and goes to wait in the cordoned-off area near the baggage claim. He can't remember the last time he has gone to the trouble to do this.

"They don't let you come to the gate?" is the first thing his father says. "So much for welcomes."

He is wearing a seersucker blazer and tan slacks and a tie with a tiny sailboat print. His loafers look brand-new. His father looks around at the abundance of flesh, flip-flops, and bedazzled sweat suits.

"It's like the apocalypse," his father says. "As though they were all looting, and this was all they could find to wear."

"It's the West Coast, Dad."

"It's something, all right."

He has brought only two bags—a matching leather set—and tells Julian that he has sent his other belongings through "the United Parcel Service." He has a lifelong aversion to acronyms and abbreviations.

Perhaps his father will be impressed by the location of his house, if nothing else, Julian thinks. Some people are taken with Malibu. But the weather hasn't entirely cooperated. When they arrive at the beach, it is dull and brown outside. Like its neighbors, Julian's house is unimpressive from the street, just a simple clapboard square wedged between the highway and the ocean. But when you step through the front door, the highway seems to recede, and the water extends in front, giving the sensation, as the enthusiastic realtor had called it, of "having stepped off the continent."

But the ocean view from Julian's living room might as well be of a cinder block wall for the impression it makes on his father. It's cold like a Rothko out there.

His father eyes the floating staircase in the modern house. Julian has almost forgotten that his father is truly ill. His hair is white but still thick, with the soft sheen of old age. His posture is erect, too, but the footsteps are smaller, nearly a shuffle. Julian has rearranged things so the space he uses as a downstairs office can serve as his father's room. He goes to help him unpack, but his father pushes his hand away hard.

At dinner, Julian tries to remember ever having sat alone like this across from his father at a meal. When his siblings were in college, there were times his mother went out to play bridge with her friends. But had they sat together or retreated into their rooms? Julian only remembers how hollow the house had felt in his mother's absence. Even though his father selected and arranged most of the décor, he never seemed to inhabit the house in the way Julian's mother did. Without her, none of them knew how to behave as family members. Like children, she had to keep reminding them to share, to set a good example for their siblings, to call on each other's birthdays.

"I didn't know you could cook," his father says. Julian has made penne with sausage and greens and French bread. He remembers his father's weakness for the tang of fresh bread.

"Mom taught me in high school," he says. "So I could fend for myself in college."

They talk of Washington. His father chronicles the current First Lady's fashion in great detail. A glimmer comes into his eye. Her style is classic, he tells Julian, but fresh and bold. He is particularly pleased with a recent mint shell paired with a coral pencil skirt. There have been missteps, too, he reports. He did not care for an ombré evening dress. "It looked like she had been wading in mud," he says.

He stares at his son, as though he too will feel sufficiently worked up about ombré. Julian does not know what ombré is.

"You know," his father says, pushing himself back from the table and eyeing the open floor plan, "modernity is all about poverty. Cheap reproduction and delivery to the masses. Like that case study house the Eameses lived in. That house looked like a rabbit's warren."

Julian knows that it is not so much his taste that bothers his father but his disinterest in taste, his failure to take a position. Julian has delegated the furnishing of the house to friends. He knows his father associates this disinterest with his career, with a predilection for science, when in fact it was cultivated in childhood, a path of least resistance to his father.

"A warren has mounds and tunnels," Julian says. "It hardly looks like a box."

"I was speaking metaphorically of the specks of junk everywhere. And the terrible use of textile."

Julian wants to laugh. But his father is deeply serious about the "terrible use of textile," whatever that could mean.

"How are you feeling?" Julian asks. He begins to think his sister has tricked him, that his father has years more to live.

"Quite well. Physically, I mean. Aesthetically, I am suffering at the moment."

Despite his father's protests, Julian takes him to see one of his colleagues in oncology at the hospital. Walking in through the sliding front doors with his father beside him—when he usually enters from the staff entrance at the rear—he no longer feels ownership over the place. He feels almost out-of-body, as though he's never worked there at all.

His friend confirms that the lung cancer is stage IV, the kind that, to his father's great pleasure, will kill him quickly. His father is the sort of man who will gladly choose death over loss of dignity. He is known, in fact, for pronouncing death as a preference to many things: American cheese, West Texas, and prime-time television, to name a few.

The oncologist prescribes pain medication and says they can get an oxygen tank for the evenings if Julian's father gets short of breath. The oncologist keeps telling Julian how lucky he is. The cancer is killing his father softly. Julian thinks that's a strange way to put it. He pictures the cancer kissing his father all over his body, spreading until its lips cover his, until it snuffs out his breath.

To get out of the house, Julian agrees to attend a political fundraiser at the home of a wealthy philanthropist. One of his nurses, Terri, has convinced him that a few eligible bachelors will attend. Julian's nurses, all women, are like a tribe, and he has given himself over to them completely. Most of them have known him since his residency, and even though he is only forty-three, they treat him like a helpless old man, picking out his car, his furniture, and arranging his kitchen cabinets. For the fundraiser, Terri has picked out his clothes; Julian spends his days in scrubs and is always at a loss when he approaches his closet.

He wears a tapered suit and a skinny tie that strikes him as too feminine. The house where the party is held is indiscriminately ostentatious—what a realtor might call Mediterranean—and with his cocktail in hand, Julian feels like an extra who has stumbled onto a bad set. He keeps catching glimpses of himself in the large gilded mirrors that fill the home's foyer. Some of the mirrors high on the wall are strung by wire and angled, giving a birds-eye view of the guests. He sees that he is getting balder on top. He has hair everywhere except his head. Why hasn't he noticed this before?

Terri introduces him to an architect, a handsome man with the confidence of the newly, rather than perennially, single. Julian feels himself shrink beside him. On the subject of his work, the subject that should give him confidence, he falters. He always calibrates his professional specificity to the listener, calling himself a doctor or an ob-gyn or a fetal surgeon, depending on the kind of conversation he wants to discourage or engender.

He settles on doctor.

"Is it too cliché to ask you about health care reform?" the architect says. "Normally I wouldn't talk politics, but I suppose that's why we're here." He smiles. He is one of those men who age well, Julian thinks; he undoubtedly looks better than he did fifteen years ago. His teeth are so tidy and white. Sometimes Julian feels angry at those men.

"I'm for it," Julian says flatly, "if that's what you want to know. Although it doesn't impact my patients. Fetuses. They don't really have a status." His patients, in fact, are the mothers, but he spends his days in the womb.

He waits for a reaction. The word "fetus" carries a charge for anyone who is not a physician. And yet he throws it out there like smut.

He sees the architect formulating a question, wondering if he is a quack or an abortion doctor or just being funny.

"I imagine it's hard to bill and collect," the architect says. "Fetuses tend to have a weak credit history."

Julian actually smiles. Why has he been an asshole? "I'm getting another," Julian says. "Would you like me to bring you anything?"

But the architect shakes his head.

At the end of the night, Julian goes out back to get some air. One of the caterers is smoking a cigarette. He is scrawny and fey, and Julian feels more comfortable out there with him.

"What's this party about?" the boy asks.

"Politics," Julian says.

"I got that much. For what?"

Julian is a gay man who saves fetuses and performs medical research on sheep: he is always an abomination to someone. He is accustomed to strange political company.

Julian shrugs. "Our side," he says.

He has a new triplet case referred from one of the status hospitals in town. Many of the families seem impossibly young to Julian, but not this one. The mother is an executive in her forties, pregnant with triplets through in vitro fertilization. "An embarrassment of riches," she says to Julian, as they sit waiting for the father to arrive. He is a television producer, she explains, and it is difficult for him to get away during the day. When the father arrives and takes a seat, he keeps his cell phone balanced on his knee.

Terri sits beside the family while Julian tells them what is happening. He explains that even though the babies are in their own amniotic sacs, they share the placenta. Two of the babies aren't sharing the placenta equally because of a problem in the connected blood vessels. One baby is providing too much blood to the other. On the ultrasound, Julian points out the donor and the donee. The donor is dangerously small and can't urinate enough to make amniotic fluid. The baby could become shrink-wrapped in its own sac. The donee has too much blood, too much urine, and its tiny heart is working far too hard.

"You mean they pee in there?" the father says.

"Well," Julian says. "As the pregnancy progresses, more of the amniotic fluid is made up of urine."

The man looks over at his wife. "I guess that makes sense," he says, but seems repulsed.

"What about the third one?" the mother asks, running her hand over her stomach.

"He's an innocent bystander," Julian explains. "Off to the side doing his own thing."

If they do nothing, at least one and maybe both of the twins will die. The parents understand, so they agree to the surgery.

"Three," the father says. "We're going to need a bigger house."

Julian and Jay and Liv had been three, but they came in a trickle instead of a flood: Jay two years after Liv, Julian two years after Jay. His brother had been the reckless one, the one who gleamed—not onstage or in the darkness of an operating room or in Washington but in life, with real people, when intimacy was actually required. Jay's death had broken their hearts. When Julian thinks of his father as a father and a husband, his mind always goes to Jay's funeral, which stands like a wall between the father of his childhood and the one he now knows. At first, his father refused to attend the service, but his mother wouldn't allow it; in her usual way, she forced them to behave as a family. But he wouldn't comfort their mother. He wouldn't lay a hand on her at all.

At the time, Julian had hated his father for his stoicism, what had felt like a rejection of each of them. It was his sister who had explained, "He's ashamed, Julian. You don't see that? His son died from addiction."

As an actress, Liv spent her life inhabiting people—not invading the body, the way Julian did—but gaining entry in ways that led to different understandings. He was envious of that sometimes.

"Jay was sick," Julian said. "He can't treat this like an affront to his *manners.*"

If their father acknowledged that shame, Liv told him, if he allowed himself to live in it, he would expose himself to deeper shame, shame he would not be able to manage. His was a fragile little carapace, she said.

Carapace, Julian thought. Like a crab, like cancer. He had never thought of it that way, how emotion could explode that shell, letting what was soft and rotten inside metastasize throughout the body.

"But what's he got to be so ashamed of?" Julian said.

Liv only put her hand on his shoulder and shook her head.

The surgery does not go easily. Julian cannot insert the scope in the usual place because of the innocent bystander. He will have to work around the third baby.

The procedure begins as it normally does. His nurses stand off to the side of the operating room watching the monitors; they help him find the vascular equator, to build the roadmap of large and small veins that he will ablate. But it is cloudy in the uterus, the turbid amniotic fluid like watery milk speckled with mucus. Just finding all the connections takes him twenty minutes. He can often finish a surgery in that amount of time.

He has to pump in Ranger's solution for visibility, then use the diagnostic scope to get a look at the spot he is going to laser. But when he pulls the scope out and slides the laser into the cannula, the landscape has already gone cloudy again. It feels like he is walking down a dark hall, brushing cobwebs out of his face all the way.

The babies won't stay where he wants them. When the solution rushes in, one of the babies raises his hand up to feel the water moving against his palm. He closes his fingers to grab on to the scope. Normally, Julian finds this cute. Sometimes he will even point this out to the mother if she is alert enough.

"I need you to scoot over, baby," he says.

He has to find a rhythm, and the rhythm is fast: he has to add the solution, put the diagnostic scope in, find the next connection, then whip out the scope and get the laser in while he can still see. But he keeps getting lost. He gets a large vein that should have been adjacent to two smaller ones, but the smaller ones are not there.

"How many are left?" he asks Terri.

"Three large, five small," she says.

"Scope," he barks. "Scope, scope, scope."

"How many are left?" He asks it a dozen times. He needs to hear Terri's voice telling him that he is almost there.

"We're winning," he finally says. "Did we get them all?"

"Last one," Terri says.

It doesn't feel like the last one. It still feels like new veins are proliferating, swelling with blood when his eyes are closed.

When he gets home, the house is empty. He goes to his father's room, where antique whale-oil lamps and Canton vases now cover the midcentury dresser. At the far end, closest to the bed, his father has set out a series of frames—photos of himself with American presidents and visiting shahs and kings. In the largest photo, he and Pat Nixon stand in the Green Room, one of dozens of rooms they had rescued, in his words, from Mrs. Kennedy's handiwork. His father spent almost thirty years redecorating the State Department's diplomatic reception rooms and then curating the White House, but it was only Pat who really let him have his way.

His eyes go to one photograph of his father alone. The photo is more recent, yet in it he looks more youthful than he does in the older pictures: he wears a yellow-and-green floral blazer with creased cream pants and black-and-brown saddle shoes. He is leaning back against a wall of black-and-white Moroccan tile in what looks like an exotic locale. The photograph looks professional.

"Excuse me." His father has propped himself in the doorway behind him.

"Where have you been?" Julian says.

"For a walk."

"On the beach or the highway?"

"I found a little tributary," his father says, making his way slowly to the corner chair. "Who lives in a place where there's nowhere to take a walk? Private beaches. Hmmph."

"Where's the nurse?"

His father leans back and closes his eyes. "I let her go, I'm afraid. She was supposed to be a nurse, not a warden."

"But she was in *my* employ," Julian says.

"Please. It's a service. They'll send a new one tomorrow."

Julian stands there, waiting for his father to open his eyes.

He phones the nurse. "I'm so sorry, doctor," she says, before he has even begun. "He wanted to go shopping for antique furniture. He said he was going to have a mover come and take your furniture out of the room. He had a list of the furniture he needed to buy. I told him we couldn't go, not until we spoke to you."

Once, when Liv was eight and away at summer camp, their father had redecorated her room. She'd wanted a princess room—in the pedestrian pink sense of princess—but she'd returned to find a room that was practically Elizabethan. Julian hasn't thought of it in years—the big reveal, his sister squealing, dancing through the velvet drapes that hung from the four-poster bed, gesturing as though about to give a monologue. He always thinks of his father as a disinterested figure hovering at the edge of their childhoods. But perhaps it is Julian who wasn't interested in him.

"You did the right thing, of course," he says. "You're not fired. You should come back tomorrow."

"They've already reassigned me. I think it's for the best," she says. "He requested a male nurse."

The architect calls. Julian has so excluded this possibility—they had not exchanged information, for one thing—that he sits there dumbly on the phone, wondering if his father has called an architect to redesign his house.

"It's Wesley," he says. "From the fundraiser. Do you remember me?"

"Of course," he says. He didn't remember learning the man's name. He has thought of him only as the architect. "I didn't expect to hear from you. How did you find my number?"

"Terri."

"Oh, yes. I must not sound too resourceful."

"She also told me you're more charming than you came across."

"Is that so?" Julian says. He should just admit to having been intimidated by the architect's good looks. But he can't manage it.

"I thought I'd give you the opportunity to redeem yourself," he says.

The architect wants to see Julian's house, so he invites him over for the date, with the reassurance that his father will keep himself entertained. The housekeeper has just come, but Julian patrols the house for anything to straighten.

His father comes out of the guest room. "I thought you were having company," he says.

"He should be here soon," he says.

"Then why do you look like a farmer?"

Julian has put on a thin denim button-down and tucked it into his khakis. He does not look anything like a farmer, but he does not feel like himself, either.

"It's unstudied gay," he says to his father. His father hates it when he says the word "gay" aloud.

His father comes over and lifts his reading glasses up.

"This look is neither happy nor what I would deem homosexual," he says. "So it fails both senses of the word. Why don't you put on a nice striped shirt?"

So Julian does. He looks like a junior professor, but he feels more comfortable. When he comes back, his father has poured himself a drink.

"Let me give you a word of advice, son." He pauses for effect. "You may live in California now, but nothing about you will ever be unstudied. This house, your clothes, your gait. It is not in your blood."

The architect arrives, wearing a light blue V-neck sweater, linen shorts and loafers, his salt-and-pepper hair effortlessly combed back with natural wave. Apparently the look is in *his* blood. Julian feels an unexpected charge, seeing the man on his doorstep like that. Perhaps it's because he brings so few men home that it makes him feel familiar, as though their relationship has already progressed past awkward beginnings.

When Julian brings him into the kitchen, his father has thankfully disappeared. Julian opens one of his best bottles of white wine—he knows nothing about wine, but one of his tribe has stocked the cooler with the cheap ones on top, ones for entertaining on the bottom—and pours them both a glass.

The architect has wandered off and is showing himself around the living room. "Occupational hazard," he says when Julian brings him the wine. "I tend to help myself around other people's homes."

"You probably think you can tell a lot about a person by their house and what's in it," Julian says. "But not me. I haven't picked any of this."

"What could be more telling than that?" he says.

They sit on the couch that faces the ocean. It is dark already, and Julian has left just one lamp on in the living room. He apologizes for his behavior at the party. "I can't imagine what would have made you call. Was it my incredible charm, my sense of style? It must have been my body."

The architect just smiles. Julian can smell ginger and amber on his skin. It makes him want to lean in.

His father emerges, claiming he needs a glass of water, and the architect gets up to greet him. A consequence of being well-bred.

His father picks up the bottle of wine. "And what are we having, Wesley?"

Wesley falls for it all. He offers to pour. He insists that Julian's father join them for a drink, and suddenly Wesley and Julian are not knee-to-knee on the couch but outside on the deck chairs because his father thinks they need some ocean air. Julian goes to fetch blankets for them, and when he returns, his father and Wesley are laughing like old friends. He stands in the living room for a moment, watching. His father leans in, the way he does when he approves, when he wants to know more.

"Your father was just telling me about his career," Wesley says. "About a certain naughty First Lady who kept gilding the silver fixtures."

"I thought an architect could appreciate my stories," his father says.

"I think most people would," Wesley says. "Everyone is fascinated by first families."

"And did you share your thoughts on architecture?" Julian asks his father. "The modernism-poverty-communism speech?"

The architect frowns: Julian is being mean again. So Julian wraps his father in the cashmere blanket and prepares himself to endure.

He knows the stories. His father's favorite is how he swindled collectors by asking to borrow their favorite pieces of art and furniture to have them reproduced, only to place the originals in the White House and slyly suggest that it was the more fitting home. Some of them—either too stunned to protest or flattered to see their belongings take residence in the White House—had agreed to give the original up.

Wesley looks charmed. He asks about the first ladies, the marriages, the changes in what constituted formal entertaining. His father could have rivaled Emily Post in social graces; it was the intimacy of domestic life behind closed doors that seemed to paralyze him.

"This is fascinating," Wesley says.

"You really think so?" his father says. "That's nice of you to say. I didn't suppose we would be discussing all this this evening."

"Nor did I," Julian says.

"Could you top me off?" his father asks Wesley.

"I'll get it," Julian says, but Wesley is already up, leaning over his father.

"Wherever did you meet my son?" he asks now. "Do you run in the same circles?" He says this as though that couldn't possibly be the case.

"It was at a political event. Although he didn't seem interested in the politics. Or in me."

"Oh, never mind that," Julian's father says. "See his face right now? That's interested. That's what a surgeon looks like skydiving."

The wind is coming through Julian's blanket and reaching his toes. He has been hiding them not just for warmth but out of vanity, too. He almost has more hair on his toes than on his head.

"Dad, aren't you cold?" Julian says.

"Who cares? I'm dying. I should enjoy it. Maybe I'll never feel wind like this again."

"How about we not accelerate death?" Julian says. "The wind will still be here tomorrow."

It is a long good-bye. His father shakes Wesley's hand in both of his, grasping onto him like a railing. Wesley kisses his father's cheek.

It is a chore to get his father back into his room. He wants water from the kitchen, then a magazine from upstairs. With his father in bed, they move back into the house, onto the long gray sectional again. But Julian can't completely relax. This is what it must be like to have small children. Even once they are in bed, the parent is still spring-loaded, ready to go into action.

"Is he very ill?" Wesley asks. "He looks so healthy."

"Either that or my sister lied to me," Julian says.

"It must be interesting to have a father who's gay," Wesley says. "I've always kind of wondered what that would be like. How it might have made me different."

"He is not gay," Julian says.

"Oh. But—" Wesley sits back against the couch with a strange smile on his face.

"What?"

"I misunderstood."

"He's Southern," Julian says. "He's deeply Southern."

His father has no complaints about his new nurse, although Julian comes home each day in fear of a remodel. But his father no longer has the energy to coordinate an attack. His health is diminishing in a quiet, almost invisible way not noticeable day to day; yet it's markedly worse than when he arrived.

The nurse gives Julian thorough reports, even sharing news from Liv, who calls a few afternoons a week, just after her evening show is over.

Julian supposes the time zone is to blame, but she never calls when Julian is home.

Julian tries to sit with his father, but he rarely looks up from his biographies. "What does he do all day when I'm gone?" Julian asks the nurse.

"Reads. And asks me to talk to him. He seems to think my life is a telenovela. He wants to know all about the romance."

At work, Julian has a breakthrough. For a year, he and his collaborators in engineering and cardiology have been trying to implant a fetal pacemaker onto the tiny heart of sheep fetus, spending long afternoons at the research barrack at the edge of the medical center. They've been working with a small intramural grant from the hospital's research institute, an award that covers the cost of the sheep, the anesthesiologist's time, and not much else. The team uses sheep because of the ewe's paper thin uterus, the way it lights up like a zeppelin, all the ramuscules and arcades easy to trace. Today, for the first time, the prototype of the pacemaker has stayed put. It is the kind of career news a person wants to share, however difficult it is to explain. He drives home thinking of telling his father, how he could relay its significance, if he wanted to.

But when he arrives, the architect, the nurse, and his father are all having drinks in his living room.

"Join us," his father says. "We were just getting started."

Wesley turns to Julian apologetically. "I was down the street visiting a client. I thought I would stop in."

"Stop looking so scandalized," his father says. "We were just swapping stories of Rio."

"You've never been to Rio," Julian says.

The nurse gets up and comes to him, wrapping an arm around Julian's shoulder and pulling him into the kitchen. Julian flinches at his touch.

"It's happening," the nurse says.

"He's never been to Rio," Julian repeats.

"Listen to me," the nurse says. "It'll be fast, now."

"Should he be drinking?"

"The drink is weak. A little is fine. It'll help the pain."

"He's in pain?"

"Why don't you join them?" the nurse says.

But when the nurse heads home, Wesley gets up, too. It is only later that Julian realizes this is because his father wants a moment with him. He wants to show him the outfit he'd like to be buried in. "I already showed it to them. Both approved."

"Dad."

"It's happening soon enough. And you think I'm going to let you pick it out?" he says. "You'll dress me like it's my first dance."

He follows his father to the bedroom, where he rolls open the left hand side of the closet. On a wooden hanger is a cream-colored evening suit. His father lifts the hanger off the rod and pulls it out, gently running his hands along the back of the suit to show it to Julian. Next, he holds up a light teal dress shirt with French cuffs.

"When have you ever worn that?" Julian asks.

"If you can't be yourself when you're dead, when can you be?"

His father maneuvers past the bed to the dresser. From the top drawer, he pulls out a pocket square, then sits down on the bed.

"This is the most important piece," he says, fingering the cloth. "Come look at this."

Julian sits down on the bed beside him. His father holds a small printed square of teal, cream, and coral. He is staring at it as though looking at a photograph.

"This is a medallion print," he says. "That's a man's word for flower. They didn't used to use the word flower for anything for men."

The medallions are lined up in neat military rows, rimmed by a teal border. He holds it up to Julian. "See this? These are hand-rolled edges, not machine finished. See how plump they make it? This is what you're looking for."

He lays the square out across his knee, and Julian sees how slim his father's leg has become. "I haven't taught you these things," he says. He folds the square neatly. Julian rises and opens the top drawer for him. "Perhaps the architect can attend to these things when I'm gone," his father says.

Julian is washing up from supper when he hears his father cry out. He almost doesn't recognize the sound at first—it is high and muffled, like a cat's scream. He runs to the bedroom and, finding it empty, realizes his father must be in the bathroom. The door is locked.

"Can you unlock the door?" he asks.

His father moans. "Leave me be," he says. His voice is coming from a low point; it sounds as though he's on the floor.

"Did you fall? Can you reach the lock?"

"I must have eaten something that disagreed with me," he says. Despite his father's best efforts, Julian can hear the high pitch of pain. "Call the nurse," his father says.

"He's gone home. I'm here now."

"He'll come back if you ask."

"I'm a physician, Dad." Julian presses his ear to the door.

"I don't have a uterus," his father says.

"Jesus Christ." Julian bangs on the door with the side of his fist. "Can you reach the lock? Let me in." He listens through the door but hears nothing. "I'm a doctor," he says.

The hole on the outside of the doorknob is very small, so Julian gets an ice pick from the kitchen, comes back and drops to his knees to get a better view of the outside of the privacy lock. He threads the ice pick in and feels around for the groove, but the pick won't catch. He tries a few different angles with no luck. He is a surgeon, and he cannot unlock a privacy door. He jams the ice pick in lazily, like a child without a strategy. He needs a tiny screwdriver, the kind used for eyeglasses. His father might have one in the dresser. He is about to go searching for it when the lock clicks.

Julian opens the door and stands there with the ice pick still in hand. His father is wet, prone on the floor between the shower and the toilet; there is a smear of feces across the floor in front of him, and Julian cannot quite piece together the order of events. Without his clothes on, his father looks more than naked—he is a sea creature yanked from its shell.

The intensity of residency is meant for moments like this; it leaves a muscle memory that is more like a scar. Although the son wants to scoop his father up, the doctor knows better. He assesses him first, and only when he finds nothing broken, no signs of internal injury, does he carefully lift him up and set him down in the shower chair, where he can wipe off the feces with a warm rag. The son doesn't really see his father—only the doctor sees. It is not until later, after he has dried his father and put him in his proper pajama set and gone to sleep out on the couch so that he can come to him in the night, that he closes his eyes and finally sees his drooping breasts, the last tuft of hair sprouting proudly on his concave chest, his skin so translucent it's a roadmap, a surgeon's dream.

He cancels all his work except for surgeries. Those cannot wait. The next closest fetal surgeon is in San Francisco, and, like Julian, he is always at capacity.

At home, his father sleeps most of the days. He calls Liv, and she arranges to come to Los Angeles for a three-day trip in two weeks. Julian wanders and waits. He edits a journal article he has been putting off. He cleans his home office. He works in a hospital, yet he knows nothing about illness, not really.

One morning, his father wants to take his tea in the living room and watch the morning light on the water. There is no fog, and the ocean looks lit from within. Julian sits with him. They are both wearing robes and slippers as if it were Christmas morning. His parents always wore matching robes, which, as a child, Julian interpreted as a symbol of deep love. It is hard to clearly remember his parents on a holiday morning; the memory of his own anticipation is stronger. He remembers running downstairs without using the bathroom, trying hard not to pee on the floor by the Christmas tree. He can see the extravagance of the house, perfectly decorated with old-fashioned ornaments his father liked: lace snowflakes, golden orbs, wooden Santas carrying trees. He can see his father leaning forward in his high-backed chair that he positioned near the tree, while his mother sat with her legs tucked up beneath her on the end of the couch.

"I can't complain about this view," his father says. "Although it could get lonely looking out at this."

"It does," Julian admits.

"Trees make me feel insulated," his father says. "You and your sister always had a higher tolerance for loneliness. In different ways. She's surrounded by people, of course. But there's no lonelier life. Jay was always more like me. Looking for something to fill it."

His father never speaks of Jay and certainly not in relation to himself. "I hadn't thought of it that way," Julian says carefully. "As you two being alike."

"Unfortunately for Jay, I'm afraid so," he says. "But you—the work you do. I don't know what kind of person one has to be to do that. It frightens me. I thought it was crazy enough when you decided to study gynecology."

Julian tells his father about the pacemaker, about the federal funding he could get. He does not fill in the gaps or explain that he researches on sheep. He tells him instead what it could mean for the babies.

"The lengths a person will go to bring a child into this world," his

father says. "It's the only thing that still astonishes me. People are so pre-
dictable in other matters. But not this." He is looking out at the water, the
rim of the cup grazing his lips. Julian feels he has stepped into a private
moment that perhaps he shouldn't be witnessing.

"Look at me, for example," his father says. "Consider this case."

"Yes?" Julian asks.

His father turns to face him. "Look at me," he says.

Julian is looking. His father is a shrunken man, skin now barely hiding
what lies beneath. And yet somehow he still looks royal.

Julian has always believed he and his siblings were a nuisance or a
social obligation to be fulfilled. He has been telling himself a particular
story for so long—has had, in physician terms, a cognitive disposition to
respond, the kind of bias that leads to errors in diagnosis. As a boy, he
could identify the symptom: a coldness that swept over their home. But
the only cause he could attach to it was his father's preoccupation with
his work. He had understood the work to be the cause, but what if it had
been the compensation, instead?

"It's been worth it," his father says. "You and your sister and Jay. I know
that you're more than a doctor. I've understood that all along. But that's
exactly what I'm afraid of. When all I want for you is a great love. That's
all I want for your sister, too. That's what I wanted for all of you. And yet
I suspect I did the thing that has made that impossible for you."

In medical school, Julian thinks, they would call his blindness "anchor-
ing": the tendency to lock on to salient features in a patient's initial presentation and fail to adjust in the light of later, contradictory information.
Julian reenvisions his father's life now—a life, as he's always understood
it, of sacrifice—but with different bargains than Julian has previously
understood.

He says to his father what he says with great intention to every patient
he encounters: "It is not your fault."

Terri briefs him when he arrives. They have done an ultrasound, and they are missing one heartbeat. This mother is at the follow-up visit alone; the father was unable to get away from the studio that day.

Sometimes the nurses are wrong. Sometimes a shift of position changes the scene. But not this time.

"We are missing a heartbeat," he tells the mother.

She does not need to ask him what that means. He takes her hand and watches her face. She blinks slowly, her eyes rimmed with laugh lines he doesn't see in most of his patients.

"We have to run some tests," he said, "but it appears the ablation was successful. But the donor's bladder is still very small. It would indicate that the kidney failure was already too advanced."

"Will I have to deliver now?" she says.

"No, the vessels are severed, so the donee is safe," he says. This is, technically speaking, good news. But he has always found this the hardest news to share. "Eight more weeks," he says. He squeezes her hand. "You can do this."

He is lucky. Days with bad news are fewer and further between. He is not entitled to ask why this woman must now live for two months with a dead baby inside her. If things happen for a reason, he has not figured that reason out yet.

What makes him saddest about his work is not those he disappoints but the shame his patients feel. Some of them are young and superstitious; others have gone to great lengths to get pregnant, but no matter the level of education or circumstances, they feel a deep responsibility. This is why he has learned to absolve them out loud. They need to hear it said explicitly, more than once, and by him. It is not the same when they hear it from someone else.

He thinks of his patient in the months ahead, of the baby shower, of strangers touching her belly in the supermarket, of the innocent questions people ask. Of how some people can bear hidden knowledge inside them, buried under skin and muscle, half-formed, something they will never betray.

The nurse warns Julian that there may be a little burst of energy near the end. The light doesn't just dim; the switch has to be turned off—and that takes a final push of spirit. Julian remembers this phenomenon mentioned briefly in medical school, but he is skeptical, as there is no real switch, no physiological need for this burst. But there may be evolutionary reasons, he thinks, the energy to pass on one final piece of survival knowledge—*Watch out for bears near the far ridge of the mountain!*—that comes straight from the cavemen days.

So when he finds his father making breakfast one Saturday morning, he has forgotten. He is so surprised to see him there that he just smiles. Only the night before, his father seemed half-conscious. He wasn't eating or drinking and wouldn't tell Julian the last time he had had a bowel movement. Julian sat at his bedside like a doctor on a house call, taking his temperature, listening to his heartbeat. The beat was irregular, his father's eyes glazed.

Now his father is in the kitchen making chocolate chip pancakes and scrambled eggs. The house is filled with the sharp sourness of real buttermilk. "I can't stop thinking of chocolate," his father smiles. "I had to have some."

Before the pancakes are ready, Julian is called in to work. There's an urgent case from Arizona. It is his father's nurse's day off. He would call Terri, but she is at work, of course, waiting patiently for him with the couple.

He calls the only person he can think of: the architect. He considers for a moment what favors of this kind usually mean, how advanced a relationship must be to call one in. But Wesley doesn't hesitate. Julian wonders if it is his father's illness or his father himself or something about

Wesley that has allowed them to bypass so many preliminaries and what, if anything, this portends for their relationship.

When Wesley arrives, he is a weekend-morning beauty, hair tousled, tan feet in flip-flops. His father delights at the sight of him, smoothes his own hair back with a quick gesture.

"I hope you haven't eaten breakfast," Julian's father says. He pulls another mug out of the cabinet and places it next to the coffee maker.

"I can't thank you enough for coming," Julian whispers to Wesley. He wants to hug him but settles for squeezing his elbow instead. "This is a real gift."

Wesley goes to the kitchen, helps carry the plates and the mugs to the dining room. He goes back for the syrup and the juice, then pulls out a chair for Julian's father, who sits at the head of the table. His father's hands just graze the beam of morning light that slices across the dining table. It will take only a couple of hours. Julian quietly backs out of the room, leaving the two to their breakfast, smiling over their mugs like old mates.

FIRSTBORN

THE TRIP HAD BEEN POSTPONED FOR SEVENTEEN YEARS. THAT was how Laurie thought of it—as merely a postponement, never a cancellation. Matters of life kept springing up like nasty carnival moles demanding to be whacked: there were protracted deaths, seasonal colds, trips to the veterinarian for the Russian Blues.

The trip to Paris was meant as an eighth-grade graduation gift for her niece Paulette, who at the time had been a slight girl in braces with feathered hair and high-waist jeans. Now Paulette was thirty, although she lived at home and had never traveled, so the trip would still be an orientation of sorts. Laurie had imagined it differently with a young girl, of course: she would dress her, selecting scarves and showing her how to tie them in European styles. She would teach her basic French and introduce her to her first tastes of Burgundy.

The thirty-year-old Paulette was scheduled to arrive at Laurie's apartment in San Francisco within the hour and Laurie had not quite put things in order. She wanted to get the apartment in better condition, but there had been other priorities preparing for the trip. This was Paris, after all. She had needed at least two new silk blouses and had decided to invest in a fresh pair of black pants, as she'd noticed her favorite pair were threadbare in the rear. Normally, Laurie preferred polyester blouses to silk for the ease of maintenance, but this occasion called for something finer. Silk proved to be considerably more expensive than she recalled but she managed to find a couple of suitable options at the resale shop down the street. They were not exactly the Kenzo prints she had envisioned, but they would do.

Her niece was spending only one night in the apartment before they departed the next morning for Paris. She'd never been much of a cleaning lady—mistresses generally didn't need to be—but had managed to straighten up. Now, she was rushing through the apartment, from bathroom to kitchen to living room, wiping every surface she could find with a rag that had been soaked in Pine Sol and water. If nothing else, the place would smell clean.

She had recovered her large suitcase from the back of the closet the night before and had found it smoke-stained, the lining brittle and ripped inside. She had spritzed the interior with Shalimar before putting her clothes inside. The carry-on was in decent shape, and the cats—Lola and Neko—were nesting nose to tail inside. They had come running when they heard the enticing sound of a zipper. If only she could pack them in and bring them aboard. If only they were the kind of cats who would tolerate a leash. Of course, she probably wouldn't have *liked* them very much if they were that sort, but it would have been charming to walk through the streets of the 18th arrondissement flanked on each side by a royal silver-blue feline. That would make a fetching book cover for her autobiography, she thought. She would be wearing a polka-dot blouse and white slacks, and perhaps a little hat with just an inch of hair peeking out under the brim. She had not yet titled the autobiography. The final name would reveal itself to her, she thought, when she had finally written it. Most recently she had been considering *The Paris of the Perfect Feeling,* a line from the AIDS memoir *Borrowed Time.* The author had been a Francophile, like Laurie, and had also nursed a dying lover. Of course, with AIDS it had been considerably more dreadful than what she'd had to endure. Yet she'd always believed she would have made an excellent gay man. She was envious of her brother in that way. They'd been mixed up at birth. Oh she, *she* would have had fun: the parties, the men, the forbidden loves. She had settled in San Francisco, after all. Her brother was the one meant to be the cat lady.

She didn't know Paulette well but didn't need to: when Laurie's younger sister Barbara—the so-called pretty one—had been pregnant with the girl, Laurie had told Barbara that her firstborn would belong in the spiritual, cosmological sense to her. Barbara had agreed to it, or she had not really protested, which was enough for Laurie. Barbara was an agreeable person, one of her major character deficits. And sure enough the girl had emerged tiny and thin, even as a baby, with a sharp nose and deep-set eyes that everyone said resembled her aunt's. They called the child striking, which suited Laurie, who thought prettiness was overrated; how much more important it was to be chic and interesting.

Barbara had never fit in with the rest of the family. She was the youngest and most likely an accident. Her parents had already had one daughter—Laurie had come first—and one son. What did they need Barbara for? But when they were older, her true purpose had emerged: she would have children on behalf of the entire family, children who could be dressed and taken abroad but which Laurie and her brother David would not have to raise. Being an aunt seemed preferable to being a mother, much in the way she'd found being a mistress far more desirable than being a wife. The world needed people like her, did it not?

Her last lover's wife, Martine, had certainly understood that. They had had a mutual understanding, a friendship even, right up until Philip's death. She could not recall exactly when they had lost touch or who had dropped the thread. Laurie had a tendency to let time get away. She had tried different techniques to slow its progression, but it only accelerated. She attributed this inattention in part to her greater understanding of time, her instinctive knowledge that it was not linear, anyway. She often felt her past lives folding over the present one and was reminded that she was not going from point A to point B at all. It was a comfort to think of her time with Philip not as the past but a concurrent present happening elsewhere.

She had planned to go to Europe at least once a year but had not even left San Francisco in nearly a decade. She had not had the money, for one thing; that was something else that tended to slip away. If it had not been for the small sum left to her from the sale of her parents' home, this trip with her niece might not have been possible.

She would take Paulette to all the places she had gone with Philip. She had visited him once in Paris after he and Martine had moved back home, when Philip's lung cancer had advanced enough that he needed to be with his family. Philip had known the best restaurants and bars anywhere in the world. Laurie had met him, in fact, when he had been a waiter at Chez Louis in Daly City. It looked unremarkable from the outside, but inside its blue walls you could get a nice Peroni and an excellent chicken Marsala.

Laurie dumped out the overfilled ashtrays and wiped them down with the rag, then put them back at their regular stations on the desk, next to the couch, and at her bedside table. She tucked a stack of mail into a kitchen drawer, and inched over the area rug so that it covered a stain on the carpet. She removed the arm covers from her recliner, revealing a fresh patch of periwinkle fabric underneath. Still, she couldn't account for her nerves. She could have taken a Xanax but she was saving the few she had left for the trip. Perhaps there was too much anticipation, too much expectation of all the old sensations and memories. And she'd forgotten her French, there was that. That was cause for concern.

She was relieved when the front buzzer finally rang. She could barely make out a young woman's voice through the static that was the intercom's primary language.

"Just hold there," she yelled into the box. "I have to come down and fetch you."

When she opened the front door to the building, she found her niece even smaller than she'd remembered; she had expected her to still be growing and was startled to discover she'd stayed the same. She was shivering outside.

"It's windy, I know," she said. "Get in here. San Francisco for you." She went to take the girl's bag. "It's just a walk-up here but I'm only on the second floor." The bag must have weighed fifty pounds. "My, what do you have in here?"

Laurie could only pull the thing up step by step, and even so, she was gripping the stair rail with her left hand. She had big hands and feet, like Barbara, but not the strength that should accompany them.

"Mostly clothes," her niece said. She did not seem to get the hint that Laurie could use help.

"Are you sure it isn't novels? Feels like novels to me. Russian ones," she said. "First editions."

Her arm was trembling by the time they made it to the landing. At least the thing had wheels.

"Let's get you inside," she said. "I've forgotten your hug, haven't I?"

It was not an especially pleasant hug. Laurie was skin and bones and her niece was, too. She needed to hug heartier people. But Paulette smelled awfully good and she told her so.

"A romantic smell," she said. "I approve."

Back in the apartment, Laurie realized how dark it had been inside and she turned on her extra lamps. Even so, the front room looked a bit yellow.

"Well, I need a drink after that," she said. "What're you having? I think I'll have a gin, myself, but I have plenty of alternatives."

"Do you have a Dr. Pepper?"

"No, I'm afraid I don't have much in the soda department. A Dr. Pepper—that's quite specific. I should have asked before. I knew I should have."

"A root beer?"

She would be asking for chocolate milk next, she thought. "Don't you drink?"

"I just got off the plane," she said. "It makes you thirsty."

"This is true," she said. "I'd forgotten. I've got cranberry juice. And water."

"Water's fine," she said, but when she saw Laurie pour it, she added, "Is it only from the tap?"

"San Francisco water is excellent water," she said. "Why don't you sit down?"

Paulette was standing there like a child, both arms at her side, surveying the room with a look that could have been disdain. Or fright. Laurie felt as though she'd just adopted a little orphan, perhaps an orphan with that strange disease where young children look like the elderly.

"Right over there," Laurie said, pointing to the cleanest chair. "Lola! Neko! Come see Paulette!" She poured herself two fingers of gin. She wanted lime but didn't feel like cutting one. "You have cats at home, don't you?"

"Dogs," she said. "A Chow and a Chihuahua."

"Oh yes. I think I knew that. Did I know that?"

She brought her the water and sat down on the edge of the couch nearest her.

She hated toasting when the other person was not sharing a drink with her. It affected the entire atmosphere, the mood. It had always been a pet peeve. When Philip had been too sick to drink she would pour him his juice in a highball glass and only then had it been all right. But this occasion certainly called for a toast, water be damned.

"A votre santé," she said, holding her glass up. "To the city of lights. To petit-fours. To Shakespeare and Company. To—" she paused so that her niece could contribute. Paulette looked at her blankly. Laurie nodded at her. "To—"

"The Eiffel Tower?" she said.

"Certainement!" she said. She touched her glass to hers. "You'll drink in Paris, won't you? You *must* drink wine in Paris."

"I drink wine," she said. "Well, wine coolers, mostly in summer. Or Margaritas."

"Your mother always did care for those. In that case, we'll find an aperitif that suits you," she said.

Lola and Neko finally made their cautious way into the living room. Neko worked his way around the perimeter while Lola went to the high spot on the cat tower, scoping the scene. They always worked the space like detectives, assessing the worth of new people. Paulette looked uncomfortable, sitting as erect as though she were in an interview, but Lola still found her lap worth exploring. She jumped a little when Lola landed on her.

"Hi there," she said, but kept both of her hands up by her shoulders. "Hi, Lo-la."

Lola meowed loudly, demanding that she be stroked.

"She's the articulate one," Laurie said.

Her anxiety began to abate as she neared the end of her first glass. She appraised her niece, who was wearing a velour tracksuit, of the variety grown women had suddenly taken to wearing in public. It was plum-colored with a crest silk-screened across the chest. Most baffling to Laurie was the lettering that read *Juicy Couture,* and she could hardly imagine what, by definition, could be said to be couture about a tracksuit. Surely those were just her airplane clothes, and she would not be wearing emblazoned velour in France. If it weren't for the lines around Paulette's mouth and the deep vertical line between her brows, she could have been a tween. It was an odd generation, Laurie thought, where children became teenagers so quickly, and teenagers seemed to never grow into adults. Only someone like her sister Barbara could have forged ahead with pro-creation after seeing a film like *Rosemary's Baby.* Laurie was glad that she herself had not contributed another member to this generation, although there was a time in her early twenties when she'd been engaged; a boy from college had asked her and she had said yes, only because her mother had convinced her she may never be asked again. Her brother David had saved her with a scathing description of her fiancé-to-be that made her suddenly see him for the provincial sales clerk he was. But her mother was right. No one else had ever asked.

"So that's all clothes?" Laurie said, nodding to the suitcase. She got up to fix herself another. "What all did you bring?"

"Comfortable stuff, mostly. And sweaters. I'm always cold. But no tennis shoes. I know those are tacky in Europe. Mom told me that."

Barbara had never been to Europe but at least she had that much sense. "Well, part of the fun will be shopping while we're there, of course." Laurie rounded the corner into the kitchen. She made the drink stiffer this time. She did not want to have to refill it so many times in front of her niece.

"What are you most looking forward to?" she asked when she returned. She wished Paulette would just sit back in the chair a little. She reached over for her Pall Malls. Barbara smoked as much as she did. Surely her niece wouldn't mind. She felt so much improved now, with the drink and cigarette in hand.

"The Eiffel Tower?" Paulette said.

"Yes, that seems to be top of mind, doesn't it? Anything else?"

"The museums, I think. I was going to buy one of those travel books but then I thought since you were planning it, I would just be surprised."

"In that case, we'll go to all the essentials. The real essentials, I mean. And I do want to go to the countryside for at least a day. I'd like to find the spot where I died."

"Where you what?" Paulette tried to gently push Lola away, who only took this as a sign of affection.

"Died," she said. "You know this story. I know I've told you this story."

"I don't think so," she said. "I think I would remember that."

"For the biography you wrote of me. For that school assignment."

"That was Jenny. For her freshman English class."

"Was it? It was over the phone. Your voices sound alike, I suppose. I don't remember, I guess? I thought it was you, not your sister. That's my memory for you. Time. And age."

"I have a good memory," she said. "I always have. I'm always correcting Mom."

"Yes, our mother was that way, too. Always correcting father."

"I can tell you what I was wearing on any given day," Paulette said.

"Oh, is that so?" Perhaps those outfits had been more memorable than her present one, Laurie thought.

"I used to write it down each day in a notebook, so there'd be no repeats. But then I got so used to it it just came naturally and I could do it in my head."

Repeats, god forbid. "I hope you saved those notebooks for posterity," Laurie said. She was suddenly sure she had not had quite enough to drink. "You know, French women tend to only have a few outfits," she said. "But each of high quality."

"Oh I prefer quantity," she said. "If I like something, I buy it in different colors."

"Can I get you something else?" she said. "A juice? Or have you changed your mind about a drink?"

"I'm kind of hungry, actually."

"Hungry?" She looked at the clock, which was perpetually twelve minutes slow. It was nearly 9 p.m. "I suppose we could order delivery from down the street. I've got nuts . . . and pretzels, I'm afraid."

"I really should eat dinner. They didn't feed us on the plane."

"What do you like? There's an adequate Thai place a couple of blocks away. Vietnamese. A pizza place that's all right, but we'd have to order at least a medium to get delivery."

"What kind of pizza?"

"I don't know, pizza. The thin kind. Chewy crust."

"Like Domino's?"

She looked at her. Maybe she was joking. Maybe her sense of humor was dry—undetectably dry—even more so than David's. She laughed. Paulette did not react.

"Quite like Domino's, I think," she said.

She reached for her glass ashtray and held it on her knee while she made the call. Her niece was sneezing now that Neko had reluctantly joined Lola, and she was not so subtly pushing both cats away. They circled her like sharks.

Hadn't Barbara taught her daughter anything? She had always thought of her sister as unimaginative and a little unadventurous relative to the rest of the family, but she was hardly *this* dull. She tried to remember what Paulette had been like when she was younger, but all she could conjure was the image of a girl in braces with headphones strapped to her ears. Thinking back, perhaps those bright conversations had been with her younger niece, Jenny.

After the phone call, she poured a third drink and decided to give it another go. She'd ask Paulette about her job.

"Same one," Paulette said.

"And what is that, exactly? It's for the college, where your mother works?" She had lost track of what Barbara did—there had been various promotions—but it had something to do with systems. An analyst of some kind. Not the kind of thing she could ever imagine Barbara doing.

"Registration office."

"That's been steady, then."

"Eleven years."

"There are advantages to being long-term," Laurie said. "If they know you, they tolerate you, even when you're not your best self. You're like family. It's hard for them to say good-bye."

"But sometimes I wish they would," she said. "So I'd be forced to do something else."

Here at last was an observation Laurie could understand. She remembered that feeling from her early days at the law office. She had spent all day, every day, wondering what else she could be doing besides answering phones and greeting guests. Later, there had been a chance for her to become a paralegal, but that would have meant *committing*. Now she'd spent most of her life at the office and the partners were elderly men who still gave dictation and thankfully did not know what modern assistants could do.

"But work isn't everything, is it?" Laurie said. "That's something your mother never understood. The rest of us have always known that. Barbara was always so industrious. Perhaps because she had to work harder than David or me in school, you know. And she was always such a saver. David and I never knew what exactly she was saving for. Me, I've always gone in for a job that's not all that stimulating. I don't want to use it all up at work. I want to save my energy for other things."

She tilted her head back and blew the smoke straight up. She watched her niece, who was looking around the room again. Perhaps it was not self-evident, by these surroundings, what those other things might be.

"Like travel," she said. "Or reading. You can understand that. You've always loved to read."

Her niece finally sat back a bit on the couch, but she looked more deflated than comfortable.

"That's my sister again," she said.

"Oh no, really? That's your crazy aunt for you."

She distinctly recalled having a lively late-night conversation with one of them who had been reading *The Fountainhead*. She had told a story about the time she went to the Ayn Rand Institute for a lecture, and Paulette—or Jenny—had joked that Laurie actually looked a bit like Ayn Rand.

"You've never read *The Fountainhead?*"

Paulette shook her head.

Perhaps it was Jenny who had always taken an interest in her but she had forgotten this, seeing as how Paulette was the firstborn, the one she considered hers.

"We were talking about the field, weren't we? The field where I died. That's how we got on all this. I discovered this in hypnosis and I think I can find the place. See, what I told your sister and only thought I'd told you, was that in my most recent past life I was a French boy who lived in the countryside on a farm. My father was a lavender farmer. I had an unfortunate limp from polio but had gotten along just fine. Except in the Second World War we were bombed and when the sirens went on everyone ran to the shelter and I couldn't run as fast, you see? My father would have carried me but he wasn't at home and my older sister wasn't strong enough. The last thing I remember is running across the field dragging my left leg and turning around to see the planes." Her cigarette was almost out, so she lit another one, end to end. "That was the last of me. But you see I think that's where my obsession with all things French comes from. I died too soon. My French life was totally unresolved, as it were. It's only natural that I'd have this longing for it. All of those deep longings come from somewhere like that, don't you think?"

"Are those sirens?" Paulette asked.

"Oh, disregard," Laurie said. "Those are constant around here. I should have moved years ago, but rent control, you see." She raised her voice. "At any rate, I have an image of the farmhouse in my mind. Assuming it's still there, of course. I thought we'd rent a car and drive out of the city and see if we could find it. I know that's a little silly. I won't be terribly disappointed if it isn't there. I'm not a very good driver, of course, since I never drive here. Oh, don't give me that look. It won't be like at the family reunion."

The buzzer rang. She left her cigarette burning and pushed herself up. When she rose, she was a bit wobblier than she expected to be. "You can always drive out there if you insist," Laurie said to her now. "They do drive on the right side of the road so I won't imagine you'd have any trouble."

Laurie started down the stairs before realizing she had forgotten her money. She came back in looking for her purse. She thought her niece might object, might offer to pay for the pizza herself, considering that she was nearly thirty and not the thirteen-year-old she seemed to be so successfully impersonating, but she did not.

It wasn't such a big box but even so it threw her off balance going up the stairs. She had to carry it in her weak left hand and the box was hot. It stank of fennel from too much sausage.

Inside, her niece stared at the pizza as though evaluating its similarity to her fast-food preferences. Laurie decided she would make an effort, too. It wouldn't hurt to have something in her stomach, little bits of crust floating like buoys in the sea of gin. She sat down and made a show of a few bites before her gut registered its protest.

Her niece ate a piece and half, and the other six slices would go to waste; Laurie would have to put the box out in the morning before they left. She would try to remember that.

"What time to do we need to get up?" Paulette said, eyeing Laurie's glass.

"It's still early," she said. "I don't sleep much. But I should look, I suppose. You did bring your passport, didn't you?"

"Of course," she said. "It's brand-new. I got it for the trip."

"I used to carry mine on my person at all times," she said. "I got it in college, just to have, you know. As a promise to myself. You never know when you might just up and leave. No warning, no planning. You can't just disappear without it."

"Have you ever done that? Just boarded a plane?"

"Well, no." She set down her glass, scanning the room for the tickets. She had put them on the desk by the front door but she didn't see them now. "But still. It makes it different, no matter where you happen to be. Knowing that you have that freedom to leave."

She knew she had set the tickets out. She had put everything safely in her worn leather folio that she'd had for decades and that still smelled like every trip she'd ever been on. But it didn't seem to be on the desk. There was her old heavy Swingline, her Parker pens, her blotter calendar, which had been left at May 1997. A stack of bills neatly opened but unpaid. Library books that were several years past due.

"Excuse me," she said, beginning to look through the drawers. In the top were letters from her brother, typed and printed on the old dot-matrix printer he managed to keep running. Even though he only referred to her in person as sister, dear sister, or my dear Laurie, he always used her full name—Loretta—on the address block. She thought of her mother when she saw it spelled out that way and had long preferred Laurie to separate herself.

"You don't have the tickets, do you?" she said to Paulette.

"No, of course not," she said.

"I mean I know you didn't bring them but I wondered if I might have handed them over earlier—for safekeeping? And forgotten? We've had that talk already about my memory."

"Are you all right?"

"Of course I'm all right, I just want to check the time on the tickets, that's all. You were the one who asked when we needed to leave. A good question, I'll grant you. It would be good to know when we need to wake up. Of course I'll be ready. I don't shower in the morning. Will you need to shower in the morning?"

"Yes," she said. She looked cautiously in the direction of the bathroom.

"Young people usually do shower in the morning," she said. "I hope it doesn't take you too long to get ready. While on the trip, I mean. I'm rather impatient in the morning."

Perhaps she'd put them on the nightstand instead. She walked to the back of her apartment. Her bedroom was dark and smelled like cat piss, but all the little slips of paper she could usually find on her vanity or nightstand were missing. This was why she hated tidying up; once she put something away, she would never see it again.

Her old luggage was sitting there, packed and patiently waiting, like a kind old dog. Half the size of her niece's. Oh yes, the luggage. The tickets were there, in the front pocket. She had already moved them that morning from the desk to the packed luggage so that there'd be no chance she'd forget. She looked out for herself like that, early in the day.

"Flight is at 8:20," she called out with tremendous relief. There was an open bottle of scotch on the dresser. She had been in a gin mood all evening but she could get a bit of that without her niece watching.

She heard her niece coughing from the front room. "Can I get you some water?" she called out, wiping her mouth with the back of her hand and screwing the cap back on the bottle.

"Could you just put that out?" Paulette said. Laurie had left her cigarette burning in the living room.

"I'm sorry," she said. "Sometimes I get two or three going at once. A shame I don't know how to juggle," she said. "Although you must be used to it with your mother."

"I make her smoke outside."

"Oh. And she allows herself to be made, does she? That sounds like your mother."

She sat in the recliner this time, her preferred spot in the room, and farther away from her niece. "I was saying something before. About the farmhouse. I've always thought we might meet the present owners and they would invite us in for some bread and some local wine, and we could tell them about the fateful end of Paul-Henri or perhaps they would have already known about it, perhaps even the history had been passed down and they could confirm the story. And we could tell them how you got your name. You have kept that quite a secret, I must commend you. Your mother has never said a word to me about it."

"A word about what?"

"Ah yes, very good. Like the best secret keepers."

"You might have me mixed up with Jenny again. I don't know the secret."

"No, there's no mistaking this one. It's your name. Even I can keep that one straight."

"What about it?"

Maybe this was parched-dry humor again. But she looked serious. "About your name. How I named you? Our special secret."

"Named me what?"

"*Paulette.* What gives? You do know what your mother named you, don't you?"

"Yeah, of course. But I named myself Paulette."

"Oh no, dear. You most certainly did not. This, I remember. You were here to visit when you were six. I had not seen you since you were two and I found you so grown up already I couldn't believe it. And that name, that terrible name your mother gave you. It was so ordinary. So I'd suggested to you we might change it—we were out having a banana split together—and you were very agreeable. Eager, even. And I suggested Paulette because I wanted you to have a proper French name, and of course, having been Paul-Henri in my past life it seemed especially fitting. And you promised you would never tell your mother who had suggested such a thing because I knew your father would just have a field day. Agreeable as she can be, I knew she would find this taking things a bit far. Straight away when you got home to Phoenix you began insisting everyone call you Paulette. Stop shaking your head now, really."

Laurie got up to stand. She was feeling a bit warm. It was stuffy in the apartment and she should open a window. Neko leapt up and ran right in front of her as she was about to reach for the latch and she stumbled a bit before catching herself on the frame. She steadied herself for a moment before pulling the window up. "How could I forget a thing like that?" she said. The cool air felt like a salve against her face.

"I remember," her niece said. "I chose Paulette on my own. I had always wanted a new name."

"It's just been so long and you were so young that you don't recall." She reached into her pocket for another cigarette. She could blow the smoke out the window this time. "Early memories always get fogged and lost."

She shook her head again.

Laurie wondered if the girl would be any more tolerable if she were sharing a drink with her. She certainly was stubborn.

"If that's the case, then how did you choose Paulette? Why that name that just so happens to be French and just so happens to be a derivative of Paul? Howsoever did you choose it?

"My mom took me to see *Grease 2* the first week that it came out. I wanted to be a Pink Lady. There was already a Stephanie in my class, so I chose Paulette."

"My god. You're joking." She had not had the misfortune of watching

Grease 2 when it had come out, but she knew enough to picture the right sort of character.

"I liked her shiny pants," she said. "I told you that I have a good memory."

"But I remember how fiercely you kept the secret. Your mother wondered if you needed to go to a psychiatrist for godsakes. You showed up at school and changed your name and told the teacher you didn't want to belong to your parents. If it were really as banal as shiny pants, why didn't you explain it to them?"

She shrugged. "I thought they'd make me change it back, I guess."

This was the single most insulting piece of revisionist history—and she'd had plenty, from bosses and old lovers and her parents over the years—that she could have dreamed up.

"You're being cruel," she said. She pressed her face against the window screen. It smelled of metal and dust. She turned to find her glass, which was now just ice. She tried to shake a bit of liquid free.

"I think you should probably stop," her niece said.

"Do you? I appreciate the concern, but I'm not all that interested in what you think right at this moment. And I'll have you know this is not a lot. For me."

Paulette mumbled something.

"What was that? I didn't catch it."

"I said I should have listened to Jenny. She tried to warn me."

"Warn you? About what, exactly? And what does she know? She hasn't been to see me. She promised me she would help me write my autobiography when she was older, but she hasn't. It is an old promise, sure, but so is this one. So is this trip. If you can't think for yourself, if it's all what your mother or your sister or god knows who else has to say . . . I've never cared what anybody says. Not one person."

"But I came anyway," she said.

"When I named you that," Laurie said, "it was my *gift* to you."

A name said so much about a mother's aspirations for a daughter, did it not? And she had wanted to give her faint, subterranean dreams beyond the pedestrian life the girl's parents might have presented.

"I think you're right, after all," Laurie said. "It is late. I'll get you some bedding."

She had washed the blankets and sheets just for her niece, so that they wouldn't smell of cat or of smoke, not that she would appreciate it, she realized now. She would only notice the loose ticking at the edge of the blankets or the faded daisy pattern on the sheets.

She set the bedding in a stack at the end of the couch, then Laurie tore Lola and Neko away from Paulette and herded them into her bedroom, where she shut them in with her. She took two ibuprofen and drank a glass of water from her bottle by the bedside table. It had been so long since she'd closed her own bedroom door that it made it feel like a motel room she had passed into for the night. She never had company, let alone another person sleeping over. This was so much lonelier than being alone.

Once in bed, she fell asleep right away but the alcohol kept waking her. She thought she heard voices. She thought she'd missed her flight. She had been a heavy sleeper until her bedside vigils with Philip had changed her. She had taken care of him when Martine moved back to Paris ahead of Philip, to make arrangements for his return home. His lightest cough or moan would wake Laurie and she would stumble to his bed, checking his temperature and adjusting his sheets. She had never nursed a child through the night but she had nursed Philip; she knew the sensation of never resting but always waiting, so that her ears became superhuman in sleep. He needed water, she thought now in her haze, water and perhaps honey for his throat. Did she have honey in the house? If he weren't feeling well, he wouldn't be able to make the flight tomorrow. Martine was expecting him. She wanted to go back to Paris with him but almost wanted to keep him with her more.

It was 6:30 a.m. when she woke. The time startled her awake, and her mind got caught in fast calculations. They should have left already. She must not have set the alarm the night before.

"Paulette!" she called out. "Get ready! We have to leave!"

She called for the cab, then stumbled through a quick routine—mouthwash, a quick wipe of the face, and a comb through her hair. She had her tan traveling slacks and her blouse set out on top of the luggage already. "I can't hear you!" she called out again.

The cats began demanding breakfast. She set out a few days of dry food in her bathroom. Her neighbor would check on them later in the week.

"We'll make it just fine, I think," she said. "They lie to you about the time to be there, of course. Don't you think?"

She pulled her luggage out into the living room. "Paulette?"

She thought at first that her niece must have gone out to meet the cab, or perhaps had decided to get coffee at the shop down the block. But where was the girl's massive luggage? It was gone, too.

Then she saw the note, written on one of the yellow legal pads Laurie had taken from work. It was the handwriting that caught her attention—bubbly and ludicrous, the letters too fat and round to be taken seriously. She had called her mother, it said, and her mother had told her to come home. In the night! Who would do such a thing? What kind of grown woman would need to call her mother? The note was full of evil things, cruelly obvious excuses. Paulette did not know Paris, she could not speak French, she did not want to drive there. She could not care for Laurie. She would not know what do if they were lost. She could not carry her back to the hotel. As though she would need to!

It did not mention all the money Laurie had spent on the ticket, the money that had come from her *dead parents*—and the promise she had kept after seventeen years. It did not even apologize. Laurie wanted to call her sister that very moment, but the cab had arrived downstairs. She had to leave.

When she arrived at the airport, the old rhythm of travel clicked into place. She slid through other passengers, the too old, the too young, those with children, those immobilized and lost. She was resolute on her flight now, unencumbered by the girl. She was startled at how unromantic the airport had become. When she was a girl, she had liked to imagine herself boarding a steamship or the intercontinental, and despite the vulgarity of air travel, she couldn't help but feel the same sense of possibility, looking up at the destinations like Bora Bora and Morocco on the departures wall.

On the cab ride to the airport, she had rehearsed how she would later scold Barbara about how ridiculous her child had turned out to be. How ungrateful they both were. And what bores. Barbara would probably offer to repay her ticket, as though that would make things better. She had always hated taking money from Barbara, who required in exchange that Laurie endure lectures about behaving sensibly. What was it her sister had said, in one those fits of moderation she was famous for? That there was a congenital epidemic, a congenital epidemic of delusion in the family. She would rather suffer her delusions than Barbara's realities.

With the sum Laurie had received from her parents, she hadn't had to take anyone's money lately. But now that reserve was dwindling. She knew this trip to Paris would be her last. It had to count. It had to carry her through to the end.

After the flurry through security, she managed to arrive at the gate just in time to board. She did not feel as wild with anger as she did vindicated now. It was clear to her how right her choices had been, how much better it was all along to be mistress and aunt than wife and mother. There had been a moment—a blip, really—after Philip's death when she had not been so certain. It was Martine who had been with Philip in his final days and hours, which Laurie knew was both a blessing and a curse. She had felt like the gay man she had always imagined herself to be, the unacknowledged lover who is not invited to the funeral. Afterward, she imagined what a comfort their grown sons must have been to Martine. Men whose faces bore so many similarities to Philip's. In that way for Martine, Philip would never really be gone.

But now she was reminded how terrible it must be to be a mother, after all. It wasn't Barbara who was on the plane to Paris, but Laurie. And how much more complete the betrayal would have been if Paulette had been her real daughter and not just her imagined one. When she had given the child the name Paulette, Laurie had dreamed the name would spark a sense of wanderlust and curiosity. She was grateful not to have suffered the crushing defeat of actually having raised the child who strayed so far from her vision and feeling herself wholly accountable. She pitied Barbara. Laurie had always had the good fortune of requiring only herself for company. She would write this final chapter of Paris alone, as she always had.

The interior of the plane with its familiar stale odor was a comfort to her now, a promise. "Bonjour," she said to the flight attendant who was stationed at the top of the aisle. She found her window seat and arranged the blanket and pillow and headphones in a little pile at her feet. She adjusted the headrest on the back of her seat, leaned back, and settled in for the duration.

HOUNDS

THE MAN HAD NO FACE. OR MORE PRECISELY, HE HAD A FLAP
of skin stretched over the maw of his head, a way station between the
busted gourd his face had been and the crude child's rendering of a face
it may, after dozens of surgeries, someday be. Jess forced herself to look
at the smooth divots where the eyes should have been, as though the
horror of it could reveal something fundamental about herself.

The man's story was told on PowerPoint slides in triptych: beginning,
middle, and still inchoate end. The guest seated at the foot of the conference table didn't turn away or change expression, but Jess watched the
color leach from his face. Surgeons assumed everyone regarded human
bodies the way a butcher eyes a pig, and Jess often had to remind the
doctors what *graphic* meant.

They sat with bottles of cold water sweating onto the table, windows
overlooking a dull parking lot, while the surgeon coolly forwarded
through slides. The surgical program Jess coordinated had become
known around the country for complex reconstructions for service mem-

bers. Their guest was a young staff sergeant himself, just off active duty, who now worked for a billionaire interested in veterans' causes. "He never served himself," the staff sergeant told them, "due to a bum knee."

The surgeon explained how a full face transplant from a donor could provide superior results, how the entire infrastructure of the face—bone, muscles, arteries, and all—would be sawed off the donor's head then screwed on and stitched up, in one clean piece.

"Where would the donors come from?" the staff sergeant asked.

"Private foundations," the surgeon said, "interested individuals. Some funding from the hospital, given the innovative nature."

Jess dropped her pen on the floor. This was the signal they'd developed to tell the presenter when he or she got off course, since the doctors were tired of Jess kicking their shins under the table.

"Sergeant, did you mean the transplant donors?" Jess asked. The only thing surgeons thought about more than blood was money. Donors and donors.

The young man smiled and nodded.

"Of course," the surgeon said. They'd need to be on life support, he explained, still connected to a blood source. "A dead brain and a living face," Jess had heard him say, but was thankful he had the sense not to use the unartful language now. He explained how they could create hyperreal masks that could be placed over the donor's face for an open casket.

"For the family's sake," he said.

"You sure I can't get you a coffee?" Jess asked the staff sergeant. He was still pale. He must have seen worse during deployment, she thought, but perhaps it was exactly that, not shock but fresh trauma that made him blanch.

Jess understood. Sometimes it was too much, sometimes she would stare at the presentation but let her mind slip away and think—of all things—of her sorority days, girls in boxer shorts crammed butt to butt on a sagging couch, their legs stretched out on the coffee table, tan and firm. How they would play lazy-ass rockettes, drunk kicking from the couch. She had not thought of herself as a sorority girl, but her freshman year roommate had been afraid to pledge alone, and Jess had found she fit. They called her the majorette because she knew how to kick off a party—to let out a howl, to drag girls onto the dance floor; she brought the anxious ones out of themselves, she unleashed the wild. The same quality made her good now, with the military men. She was athletic, a little loud, blonde and attractive, but with a deep voice and slumped posture that suggested a masculine comfort in her own skin.

Jess would try to layer the woman she was now, in a black suit slightly too tight in the shoulders and short in the legs, over that sorority girl, but they did not quite align, creating fuzz around the edges. In college, people had sometimes told her she should be a cop, picturing one of the too pretty, smart-assed cops found only on television. It was her broad shoulders and slim hips, she'd decided, that allowed people to imagine her with a gun in hand. It was odd how whole personalities—capabilities, even— were assumed from such details.

She might have been a cop, too, but her mother had died of stomach cancer the summer after college, and Jess had spent so many months in the hospital, getting to know the nurses, the cafeteria workers, the cleaning crew, that a hospital had begun to feel like a place where she could belong.

"I might like a coffee after all," the sergeant said.

At the end of the conference room, they'd set up a carafe of coffee and a platter of miniature bagels. With her back to the group, Jess could get her phone out. It had been buzzing in her lap the entire meeting. She had a message from her assistant: the van driver was out. Jess would need to retrieve Corporal Tucker from the airport herself. He would think she'd engineered it that way.

Jess brought back coffee for herself and their guest. The staff sergeant explained that he'd report back to his boss, that he was impressed with what he'd seen. Jess wondered if they'd gone too far. And yet to be effective, they had to.

"Don't forget your teddy bear," Jess said to the staff sergeant. A housewife in Cupertino had made the program custom teddy bears stitched from surplus fatigues: they had button eyes, stitched U-shaped noses, and red ribbons tied around their necks. Different bears for each branch of the service.

She handed him an army bear. This was how they often ended meetings. They showed people pictures of men with no faces, then sent them home with a teddy bear.

The webcam lagged, but Jess could see Captain on his cot in the corner, where the doggie day care staff at Wagville had sequestered him with the older dogs or the ones too skittish to be out in the yard. Corporal Tucker's flight was delayed thirty minutes, so Jess had extra time at the gate. She'd gotten hooked on logging in, the little hit of pleasure of seeing Captain. Still there.

The month before, she'd had to give the beagle three antibiotic shots a day, plunged into a little tent she would make with her fingers on the scruff of his neck, and he was finally well enough to return to day care. Ninety shots. It was easy at first, but after a few days, he'd whip his mouth around the moment he felt her fingers on the back of his neck. Sometimes he jerked right as she was plunging the liquid in, and she'd have to poke him all over again or it would be too late and the antibiotic would have already landed in his fur. It was hard to stay calm, those times, to not shake him with frustration. He could not understand she had to hurt him to keep him alive. She would calm him, get him half-sleepy, and do it with stealth and speed. When that didn't work, she pinned him down with all her body weight while he resisted. After, he would bite at his soft treat, his rotten teeth snapping, as though fighting the reward even while accepting it.

Captain was dying, but Captain had been dying for so many years without having actually died, that it no longer seemed fair to Jess to refer to this late stage of his living as dying. It was his temperament, the vet said, that accounted for his resiliency, the vet's way of saying that Captain was dumb. Jess had family dogs growing up, ones who thought they were people and for whom old age was a great indignity, leaving them depressed and ready to go. But Captain, who could barely walk or see, who wore diapers and had seizures, seemed to have no notion of these limitations.

Jess stood as the passengers began to exit the plane. The skycaps and airport crew knew the program and let them wait at the gate, in what always felt to Jess like a romantic gesture.

She still called Marine Corporal Nicholas Tucker just Corporal after all these years, even though many other corporals had come through the program since. When he exited the plane he was expecting to spot the driver, so he walked right by Jess, his tall legs spindly, like a boy who hadn't filled out yet. Jess watched him. He kept following the other passengers until he got stuck behind a woman trying to reanimate her toddler's stroller. He dropped his duffel and leaned down to help her, snapping the whole thing up in one flourish, the work of a man who has done time with baby gear. For a moment the woman startled when she saw his face. Then he smiled and she smiled back.

It pierced Jess. She came from people who knew grit, who got on by fighting through. The Corporal was a marine. And yet he sprinkled his grace cheaply with those smiles, like leaflets falling straight from God.

"Corporal," Jess said behind him.

He turned at the sound of her voice. But he was no longer smiling.

"Where's Raul?" he asked.

"Jury duty," she said. "I'm the driver today. Will that do?"

"Do I have any choice?" he said.

Twenty surgeries in and someone from their team always picked him up at the airport like it was the first time. But the Corporal was not there for a surgery that weekend, only an interview for a national TV broadcast and another dinner where he would be the honoree. Over the years, he had become something of a celebrity, had been on CNN, in *Time,* enough that the news of his divorce—the divorce of an ordinary corporal and his wife—was a story that had made its way from Texas to Jess's office without him even having to tell her.

His marriage story had been different. He wasn't married before the war but proposed to his girlfriend after an improvised explosive device had shot him out of his amphibious vehicle, and after he had been left with burns covering a third of his body—two missing fingers, no ear, nose or lips—and after he had come down the airport escalator and dropped to one knee right in public, at the very moment his girlfriend saw his injured face for the first time. People thought it was brave of her to say yes. But what would any woman have said? Who would have been able to form the word *no?*

Jess reached for his garment bag, but he blocked her hand, carrying both his duffel and the bag, one over each shoulder. At the car, he opened her door even though she was the one driving.

She tried to make small talk as they pulled away from LAX, asking about his flight and the weather, but it felt wrong regarding him like a stranger.

"How's Addie?" she asked.

"She wants a puppy," he said. "She's on hunger strike until I cave."

"A girl after my own heart," she said.

They were at a stoplight and she had the impulse to put her hand on his knee. She put it on the gear shift instead.

"And how's my friend Captain?" he said. When Captain had been well enough, she used to bring him to the office, and he'd become a program mascot over the years. With his gray whiskers and stiffened gait, the vets had taken to calling him Captain Yoda.

"Hanging in there, he is," she said.

At the TV studio, a make-up artist with an apron full of brushes leaned over the Corporal's face. Jess couldn't hear their conversation from across the room, where she was speaking with the producer, but he was making the girl laugh, and she kept freezing her brush in midair, like she was telling him to stop. There was a red patch that extended from his nose to his chin, giving him a raw look even after all the surgeries he had had. When the makeup artist was finished, though, the skin was unnaturally matte and even, and he looked less like a war veteran than a Hollywood character actor who'd made his career on a fucked-up face.

The first time Jess and the Corporal had been naked together, he'd run his finger along a thick worm of a scar on her shoulder. "Where did you get this?" he'd asked.

War, she'd almost wanted to joke. She didn't point out the strangeness in his asking *her* to recount the history of scars. But then again, she knew the story of his body, the story had become a public thing. Her body, with its moles and dimples and scars, was still hers.

Sometimes she lied when people asked about that scar. She told her sorority sisters that it'd come from a soccer cleat, and she'd been lucky it hadn't been her face.

"I used to take long showers," she'd told him, running her hand along his chest where the skin was smooth from his burns, "and we only had one bathroom in the house. It made my mother crazy. We had sliding glass doors, the rippled kind you couldn't see through. One morning she was banging on the door for me to get out. And *bam*." She whispered the *bam,* opening her hand in a burst across his chest, "and the glass all fell in one sheet. Sliced right into my shoulder."

Jess had actually laughed when it happened, out of sheer surprise. She was wet and naked, standing in a pool of glass. Her mother had screamed, then started crying, and Jess had to step carefully out, dry herself off and ask her mother to sit still on the carpeted toilet lid. She had managed to dress herself—sticking a menstrual pad on her shoulder—and they had driven to the hospital with her little brother in the back. Her mother had told her to lie at the emergency room, to say her brother had been playing baseball out back and the ball had come through her bedroom window.

"Baseball at seven in the morning? It was an accident, Mom. I know you didn't mean to."

"But you have to lie," her mother said.

"Why is it my fault in the lie?" her brother said. "What if I get in trouble?"

"Please shut up," her mother said.

In the wound, Jess could see her own bone and tendon. It was hard not to look, to take this one chance to see what was inside her. In the ER, they injected painkiller right into the cut—that had hurt—but then Jess had watched the doctor stitch it neatly with a thick thread. She was fascinated by the complacency of her skin, how readily it had opened, and then would agree to shut.

Her mother, on the other hand, had been told to recline in the neighboring bed and the nurse had to deliver an orange juice to get her blood sugar up.

"Did it cure you of long showers?" the Corporal had asked.

"No," she said. "It actually didn't. My mother used to say I was incurable. In general." Then, "I suppose I wouldn't last long in the service."

"There are some who never learn," he said. "Who'll take a beat down all day before they change. That's a good way to die."

The TV producer was an older woman beset by various strings—lanyards around her neck, a headpiece trailing black cords, fluorescent bungees on her wrists jangling with keys—such that Jess had the urge to unburden the woman and show her to a chair. The producer was speaking to someone else on the headset while explaining to Jess that they were starting to plan for the next Veterans Day segments.

"Your team always delivers," she said. "Do you have something we haven't seen yet?"

Before Jess could answer, she lifted her finger, pointed to the earpiece. She paced for a minute, and Jess noticed she was wearing fuzzy house slippers on the set. "No aioli," Jess heard her say. "No a-o-leee."

She came back and raised her eyebrow, the cue for Jess to speak.

"We're doing a full face transplant later this year," Jess said. "One of the first of its kind."

"My god," the producer said, the *god* hushed and low, in recognition of the horror of it, but her eyes glinted *Oh my God!*—a producer's dream.

Jess explained how the new face would be a hybrid of the donor and the recipient, resembling both. She repeated the surgeon's explanation: they had put the Corporal back together like a Rubik's Cube, turn by turn, but this would be like laying down a clean sheet on a bed and tucking in the corners.

"We'd have to be careful about how much we ask of the patient," Jess said. "He may want privacy."

"Mm-hmm," the producer said to Jess or to someone in her headset.

She sounded pleased, perhaps picturing the telegenic possibilities of the recipient meeting the deceased donor's family. The surgical program was fueled by images, like Operation Smile in the third world: cleft palate, no cleft palate. Before and after. What could be more satisfying, what could provide a greater hit of pleasure?

They all wanted the next fix to be greater than the last. Jess had felt it herself, the disappointment when a new patient arrived with less dramatic injuries. They had already treated the worst disfigurements, and now just routinely changing lives with a foot or an elbow surgery did not seem enough.

Jess wanted more. She had closed her eyes at night and pictured—almost against her own will—a man with no face entering her, and it had given her a nauseating thrill.

On the set, the Corporal's interview started. He and the correspondent were angled toward each other, so close their knees nearly knocked. The woman looked prettier but older in person than she did on TV.

"People stare," he was telling her. "Of course they do. I don't look like I did at twenty-five—but who does?" He laughed, and she laughed with him.

"But before, they *wouldn't* stare. Even kids would look away. Now they just ask what happened to my face. Because now it *is* a face. I don't know how to say this exactly," he said, "but it didn't seem fair, before, for my wife to have to look at me. Because it was really hard to look at. It wasn't something you could just get used to. I may not be pretty now," he smiled again, "but you can get used to it. It's not a shock over and over again."

The woman leaned in to him. The Corporal's throat burns had left his voice raspy and high so that he couldn't raise it, which had the effect of drawing people closer.

"I read recently that your marriage has ended," the woman said, "and I was so sorry to hear it. Your wife was a marine as well?"

They'd agreed in advance that there would be no questions about his marriage. The producer felt Jess tense, raised her arm to keep her from moving toward them.

"In Fallujah," he said. "She had it worse than I did."

"And you now have custody of your daughter?"

"I do," he said.

Jess saw the woman's eyes gleam with the combination of compassion and infatuation single fatherhood (and in a disfigured veteran, no less) elicited in most women. She looked ready to lean forward right into his arms before she regained her journalist's composure.

"What's next for Corporal Tucker?" she asked. "There are some people who'd like to draft you into politics. Your gift for oration has been called presidential."

"It's flattering," he told her. "But I think my era of public service has come to an end."

"Where did you learn to give speeches like that?" she said. "Where does that gift come from?"

"Conviction," he said.

Captain had come along after the breakup of the one long relationship Jess had managed after college. She'd inherited an Irish temper from her mother and was impatient with men after a point. They were slobs, or they thought she was a slob, which she was when she wanted to be. Coupledom, she thought, was its own solitude, until you had three or four kids to liven it up. Single, she could work 24-7, could surround herself with other people, stay in perpetual motion.

The guy, Vince, had been short but cocky, wore his roman nose like he wore his leather jacket. He was fun. He wanted to be a commercial pilot—was *going* to be a commercial pilot, if you asked him—but had been stuck for years hauling cargo on prop planes, spending untold hours in wood-paneled depots. He had too many traffic tickets and repossessions. He could fly, though. He could charm a plane. But no one was ever going to trust him with passengers. He had a tow-headed six-year-old named Gracie, who wore a size 4T but already knew the capital of every country in Africa, and it was the girl who made Jess think about marrying Vince. She couldn't imagine breaking up with Gracie. She thought of her getting older, forgetting that Jess had ever been in the picture.

But that was exactly what had happened in the end. And then her friend who worked in the neuroscience research building had called and asked if she'd adopt a dog.

"What kind of dog?"

"A beagle," her friend said. "Like Snoopy."

Jess knew the medical school did research with rats or mice or zebra fish, with their transparent embryos and ability to regenerate. The researchers used code words for animal research like translational or bench-to-bedside, without encouraging people to think about what that meant. But Jess hadn't known about the dogs. They couldn't exactly advertise the adoption, her friend explained. The labs had enough protestors as it was.

"So does it have Parkinson's or something?" Jess had asked. Her friend's lab studied neurodegenerative diseases.

"It was a toxicity study," she said. "So the good news is, the drug's not toxic."

Captain, as it turned out, was not like Snoopy. He'd been bred as a lab animal and knew no other life; he wasn't housetrained and was not, in Jess's estimation, very bright. His vocal chords had been cut, but he silently howled all the time: at his own image in the mirror, at the shows on television, at the neighbors from Jess's postage-stamp patio.

But he was a happy dog, and Jess projected onto him a knowingness, a sense of joy that came not from his dogness, his tongue flapping in the wind—but from knowledge that he had escaped almost certain euthanasia. When she was with him, she felt that she, too, had escaped something and was grateful to find the relationship with Vince in her rearview mirror. Her life, it later felt, had been impossibly sad before Captain had come along. After a bad day, she would stroke his head almost too hard, the eyelids pulling back from his eyes. Then she would put her head down by Captain's bed and take in his corpse breath, which, as the smell she had come to associate with him, filled her with a weird pleasure.

"I don't want to be honored," the Corporal said as she drove from the TV studio to the hospital hotel where he would get dressed for the evening event.

"It's a tough gig, I know," she said. "Getting all these awards."

"I'm serious. I can't do it."

They'd had versions of this conversation before. He had met A-list actors, the president, Prince Harry. He had spent more of his life being honored than he did in the service, and in hyperbolic moods, he'd compared himself to Kim Kardashian, the infamy of the grotesque. All he did was get blown up. The second he started to believe it was actually about him, he said, this would have to end.

"It's a few minutes," she said. "You'll get up there, and you'll do that thing you do with your hands." Because he couldn't raise his voice, he compensated by gesticulating like a pastor. Jess had named the motions: the karate chop, the elevator finger, the calipers, the hand to God.

"The clapping," he said. "The relentless clapping at these things. Do you know how much I've grown to hate that sound?"

They had reached the hospital hotel, and she leaned over his body to open his door.

"Even the best show pony gets retired eventually," he said.

But when the surgeries had rendered a face as good as it was going to get, burns got stiff again and required touch-ups to keep the flexibility in the features. So a guy might come back year after year, until the surgical fatigue was too much, when one more time was one time too many.

"You're ruining me," he said.

Jess did not know if the *you* meant the program or Jess or both or if there was even a distinction for the Corporal anymore.

Jess waited at the front desk at Wagville, which was filled with dog food disguised as people food—sushi rolls, cinnamon buns, ribs—and got the report on Captain's day while a handler went to get him.

"He slept most of the day," the girl said, "after he got settled in."

Handlers brought the other dogs out on leashes, sniffing, leaping, nearly knocking their owners over. A young man in khakis and a lime-green polo held Captain in his arms instead.

"He can walk," Jess said, and clipped the leash onto Captain's harness, and the tug from Jess gave Captain a burst of energy. The white tip of his tail stood at alert. "Come on," she told him. "Let's take a walk before we get into the car."

The walk was a slow investigation of the perimeter of the Wagville parking lot, sniff after deliberate sniff. She had read about beagles when she'd first adopted Captain, how the big ears were bred to capture scents and keep them close to the nose. Captain's ears were extra-large. When he sniffed like this, she often thought of his first time on grass. The lab where he had been raised required daily exercise, but there were only indoor runs. When she'd taken him home, he had stayed in his open crate for a full fifteen minutes as though awaiting further instructions.

"Why do they use beagles?" she'd asked her friend at the time.

"For the same reasons they make good pets."

She'd been told not to force him out, that his hound's nose would eventually lead him, and it had. He'd been light footed on the grass, like he wasn't sure its softness could be trusted.

Now, when they got home from Wagville, she gave him three pills—a steroid, a thyroid pill, and another antibiotic—each one tucked in a piece of extra sharp cheddar cheese to mask the scent. She'd become religious about his pills. He'd needed all the injections because he'd developed antibiotic resistance, what the vet called a MRSA-like infection raging in his blood. It had been her fault, Jess thought, from those times she hadn't completed his course of antibiotics because he'd gotten cramps or diarrhea.

She unwrapped one of the little bars of soap she saved from hotels and took a short shower to wash the day off. She wanted the smell of the new soap on her skin. She caked on extra makeup, thick and slightly dark foundation that would photograph well on the step and repeat. She picked out a short, tight white dress, with thick straps of fabric that smoothed every bump and transformed her into one seamless curve. It was the sexiest dress she owned; looking at herself in the bathroom mirror, she felt like an ex-wife who had left her husband but still wanted to be wanted by him.

She hadn't meant to sleep with the other men after the Corporal and wasn't sure she could be honest even with herself about why she had. The first had been Javier, one of the single men, the guy most popular with all the other guys, who tipped a lot at the bars and drank too much, whose athlete's frame had gone soft and fat. They had been alone together plenty of times, the last two to leave a party, Jess just another one of the men. And then after a football game where the guys had been honored on the field, they'd had too much—they'd started at the tailgate—and she and Javier were sitting on bar stools at a place down the street from the stadium, when he'd turned to her, suddenly serious. "God, you look good," he said, in a voice she'd never heard from him before. She should have turned away, but kept her eyes on his instead, and he slid his knee between hers and spread her legs apart, just a few inches, right there at the bar. And she felt that burning that came on in an instant. And there was a small voice, sublimated by the beer and the burning, that had protested. But she had gone too far. Her body was in charge. So he had fucked her, sloppily, in the back of the program's van.

Javier and Corporal Tucker were both from Fort Irwin. There was no way the Corporal would have told anyone about him and Jess. But Javier was a talker, and even as she'd asked him the next day to keep it confidential for professional reasons, she could see him gloating to the Corporal, trusting he'd be the one friend who would keep it quiet. And she had felt the Corporal take this in and give Javier a congratulatory slap on the back, still smiling, while everything he'd had with Jess unspooled behind his eyes.

Sex with the others had been sad: the men were wounded in ways the Corporal was not. She would want to look at them, to watch their faces when they were inside her, but they would turn her over, or the sex would just be her face in their groins, as that was all they could muster.

She had been lonely—that was one true thing—and they had been even lonelier and she had wanted to fill that loneliness with herself in a way that was narcissistic and ennobled, like she should be applauded for being someone who would want them. But she suspected that she had done it to blot the Corporal out, to mask her feelings by pretending this was a fetish, to make herself irredeemable in his eyes.

She recognized what had happened with the Corporal because it had happened before during her senior year in college, with a friend she'd hung out with for years. He was a guitar player, sweet and low-key, with a kind of understated retro style too sophisticated for his age. She had never noticed attraction between them, just a daily comfort she'd grown to like, until one day she went to her car and he was standing there, leaning against it. He asked her if she wanted to go somewhere. He took her to a rock formation just outside of town called erratic rock—which all the college kids called erotic rock—and it became clear he'd been watching her all those years. She was flattered. She was used to athletes, men who could conquer her own masculinity with their sheer bulk, their ability to press her down. With him, she'd gone on proper dates, the kind where he held the door and deferred to her when she ordered and looked upon her with meaning. Not in the way of a teenager pretending but with the confidence of a man. And she had not needed the bulk, then, to make her feel like a woman. There was a way he would touch the small of her back, lean her against the car. He had been sexually attentive, too, and it had frightened her. Soon, the worshipful quality had become too much. It would have been just the story of a sad boy if not for her sorority sister who had been pining for him, love that Jess had mistaken for a mere crush. And when the girl found out, Jess slept with all of the boys' friends, which had hurt the boy worse, but which Jess had meant as an apology to the girl, a way of saying, see, it meant nothing, I do this all the time: *you can still love him.*

When she arrived to pick the Corporal up, he wasn't out on the curb and didn't answer his phone. Jess asked the front desk manager to let her into his room.

The dingy antechamber that classified the space as a "suite" gave off the distinct smell of dormitory, even though the rooms were regularly cleaned. There was something about the scents of individual people commingling—scents that wouldn't be objectionable on their own, Jess thought—that created something loamy and sour, in the way even vibrant colors, when combined, turned universally brown.

"Corporal," she whispered. Then, "Tuck."

She opened the bedroom door to find it dark, a tangled mass on the bed. She stopped and listened. She could hear him there. Breathing.

"What are you doing?" she asked, turning on the overhead fluorescent. Under the obscene light, the room smelled more profoundly of sleep. He groaned and covered his head with the hotel quilt. It was patterned with birds-of-paradise and hibiscus, as though this were a Best Western in Hawaii and coming to the medical center was a budget vacation.

She went to the closet and found his dress blues still in the garment bag.

"Sit up," she said.

He groaned again but sat up, eyes closed. He was wearing only boxers—plain white skivvies—and she could see the burned flesh of his chest, so familiar she'd come to see the striae as decorative, like a tattoo.

"Don't make me do this," he said quietly. He opened his eyes.

"I have to," she said, and handed him an undershirt.

She managed to get him standing, his pants on, then held out his jacket for him, one arm at a time, and slowly buttoned it up to the neck. With his missing thumb and finger, he still struggled with tiny buttons. She could feel the hot breath of his mouth on her forehead. It was the closest she had been to him in months. She unwrapped his medals from the cloth where he kept them folded and pinned them onto his left breast.

"Let's just stay here," he said, understanding that the chance to be with him again was the only thing that might earn him a reprieve. The kind of trick women pulled all the time, Jess thought. He was right. She wanted to crawl into the smelly bed, watch the old television together.

She went to the bathroom sink and ran a comb through water to tamp down one of his errant hairs.

"What are you wearing?" he said when she came out, like he'd finally seen her. His mouth was open in what looked like disapproval.

"It holds everything in," she said, looking down at herself. "It's called a bandage dress."

"That's fitting," he said. "We look like it's Halloween. Like I'm the wound and you're the dressing."

There was clapping. Clapping and craning, people awkwardly seated in rounds of ten, moving their forks and knives quietly over plates of salmon while trying to face the speakers. She always left these things exhausted and hungry, with a crick in her neck. This event was like the others: the stage draped in blue cloth and military flags; the lights low, the design a strange hybrid of wedding and funeral; and the theme, yet again, of Heroes, which no one thought required creative adaptation. Heroes: they were standing up for them or rocking out for them or playing Texas hold'em for them.

The Corporal did what the Corporal did best: he remembered names and addressed everyone by them. People wanted photographs, hand-shakes, and he would clasp their hands in both of his. They wanted a piece of him. Jess watched each person walk away from the encounter believing he or she was special, just as she had every time she'd been alone with him. But Jess knew that touching something beautiful to get some of that beauty for yourself only rendered the object less pure, and made you that much uglier for having been the one to taint it.

When the time came for the Corporal to come to the podium, the entire room was already on its feet. He held his hand up and was silent for a long moment, building the drama in the way that seemed instinctual. But when he spoke he said, "The heroes in my life are the people who put me back together. Tonight, instead of hearing from me, I want you to hear from one of my favorite men, Dr. Roy Kapur." He motioned for the plastic surgeon to come on stage, and after he had shaken his hand, he left him there alone.

The Corporal was done. Next year, the man without a face would have features again and would stand on the podium instead, and even though he could not be the Corporal, he did not need to be. His face would tell the story for him. He would scarcely need to speak.

The Corporal wanted a drink, but there was no alcohol back at the hospital's hotel and he didn't want to be at a bar, surrounded by other people. Jess drove to her apartment without asking, because he would not admit wanting to go there—and because he might, if forced to acknowledge it, actually refuse.

Captain came to greet him, even though it took effort for him to get up, his hind legs catching on the lip of his dog bed. His face met a couple of walls on his way to the door, but he could still smell, still knew it was the Corporal. The white tip of his tail shot back and forth like a flag of happy surrender.

"You seem even older, old man," the Corporal said, leaning over to pet him behind the ears. "If that's possible."

Seeing them there, she wondered if it was Captain he had actually come to say his good-byes to, in the way Jess had held on not to Vince but to little Gracie.

She went to the kitchen to pour them both vodka tonics. She found a dried out lime and rolled it under her palm to revive it enough to squeeze a few drops into their drinks. She had never been good at playing hostess. In the living room, the Corporal had taken off his blues jacket and sat in his undershirt, with Captain resting at his feet. The Corporal had teased her about her apartment before: the place had a temporary look even though she'd been there eight years, with a worn Chenille covered couch and scratched oak side tables she'd gotten free from the public library. It could have benefited from houseplants, but she didn't have a good track record. Decorating would be admitting something, she thought.

They sat silently, Jess wondering why she didn't keep better vodka in the house, until she finally had enough drink in her to ask him what had happened with his wife.

"You want to know something I was thinking about today, during that interview?" he said. "That proposal story, how I came down the escalator in the airport and dropped on one knee right there? It's not true. I was still in BAM-C and the first time she saw me was in my hospital room. So I couldn't exactly drop since I was already in bed. I still asked her in about fifteen seconds, so I guess it's not that different. But someone started telling it that way in the media and I tried to correct it a few times but it just kept going. I guess it made a better visual, me coming down, her looking up at me with my wrecked face. But what I actually did was, I covered the bottom of my face with a blanket and told her to look me in the eyes."

He held up his empty glass, still filled with ice. He had never been a drinker, not like many of the other servicemen, the ones Jess could barely match drink for drink. He had gone to Iraq for just ten weeks. He had a vague memory of having been on fire, of rolling himself on dry ground, and the shock of coolness when the fire had been put out. He had only given his face, he'd repeated in speech after speech, when others in his unit had given their lives, but what drove Jess to madness after all these years was that he seemed to mean it, and how could anyone mean that?

She poured them both another, stronger this time. Jess drank half of hers before she'd even left the kitchen, feeling it work its way into her shoulder blades, her knees, creating the kind of supple but strong exoskeleton that alcohol provided.

Jess had met the wife only once, which was unusual; the spouses usually traveled with the patients. She remembered she had sensual features, round eyes and thick lips, but made an expression like she had forgotten how to use that kind of face. She had a way of holding her features stoically, like a person with bony cheeks and thin lips would do.

"I shouldn't have proposed like that," he said. "It wasn't fair to her, I get that now."

If Jess had been his wife, his good nature would have broken her. No one, she thought, should have that much goodness. It was unnatural. And Jess knew at some level that she had wanted to blemish him, that she had slept with him to make him less perfect, to fix the bell curve of human sainthood in everyone else's favor.

He took two long drinks before speaking again. "Anyway, do you want me to tell you it's not your fault?" He tried to raise his voice but it cracked. "Or do you want it to be?"

"I don't want that," she said and hated how feeble she sounded.

He got up and walked over to the faux-walnut wall unit where Jess had stacked old books and DVDs and CDs on shelves she now noticed were covered in six months' worth of dust. At his eye level stood a row of framed photos: Jess with a group of Alpha Phis sticking out their Go Blue! lollipop-stained tongues; Jess and her brother at his law school graduation, the know-it-all kid grown into a know-it-all lawyer; and a much younger Captain with aviator goggles on, dressed up as Snoopy for his first Halloween.

"She had a child with another man, for starters," he said. His back was turned to her. "I knew my war. But I didn't know her war."

He picked up a framed photo that one of the nurses had given Jess for the holidays. Jess stood on the football field in the center of a row of wounded men. It wasn't the same time she had slept with Javier, but the Corporal wouldn't know that. When she looked at her own photos, the glossy-lipped friends at a bar, faces washed out with flash, she would picture *Dateline*, the tight shots of couples on tropical vacation, couples where one of the two had ended up dead; how the producers would zoom in on their smiles over and over again, begging the viewer to project prescience or villainy onto those mouths. And she would look at her own face that way.

"Not everyone gets off on this," he said, putting the frame back on the shelf. "For some people, it's just sad and that's all there is."

She was about to argue—though against what point, she wasn't sure—when she felt Captain twitch at her feet, his body tense up.

"Oh shit," she said, leaning over. He was seizing.

She dropped to the floor to hold him still. Without his bed, he was jerking, had nothing to prop his head against.

"What's happening?" the Corporal said.

"Can you get his bed over here?" she said. "Quick."

He brought it over and she lifted him up. Captain panicked in the air, feeling nothing beneath him, twisting violently left and right in search of a surface. She laid him in the bed and positioned his head so that it rested on the edge. His neck craned back, like he was in a deep howl. His eyes bulged, the balls shifting left and right.

"This has happened before?" the Corporal said.

"For a while," she said. "Off and on."

"What are we supposed to do?" he said. She'd never seen him look panicked before.

"Come here," she said. "Sit on this side. Just soothe him."

They sat on either side of Captain's bed, Jess stroking his head and the Corporal running his hand down the dog's back.

"What's wrong with him?"

"I don't know," she said. "Nothing. Everything? He was a medical research dog."

His hand stopped. "He was what?"

"He was a rescue from one of the labs at work. Who knows what they did to him."

She told him the story, then, how there had been ten beagles—five girls and five boys, the girls named for Disney princesses, the boys for villains. That was how Captain had gotten his name—Captain Hook. "Can you believe they named them?" she said.

"And you never mentioned this?"

She watched Captain, who was still seizing, but she felt his eyes on her. "I got sick of people feeling sorry for him," she said.

"So that's how it is," he said.

"How what is? Stop looking at me like that."

"How long will this last?" he said. "There's nothing you can do for him?"

"Depends," she said. "Sometimes a minute, sometimes an hour."

"An hour? Jess, please."

And it did last, not violently but quietly, like a small electrical charge was rickshawing through the dog's old nerves. It lasted so long the Corporal got up to make them more drinks, and they sat on the floor in silence, stroking the dog with the tenderness they had once shown each other.

"You have to put him down," the Corporal said.

"I know," she said. "I know that."

Twice, when she had been walking Captain in the evening, different neighbors had asked her if she didn't just want to put him down. The neighbors were old themselves—seniors who lived in the affordable housing units on either side of her apartment building. Should someone put you down? she had wanted to say, but offered some cheery platitudes about what a trooper he was.

"You have to," he said. "Promise me."

A few times, Captain had stopped walking and rocked backward on his hind legs—the briefest warning sign—and keeled over right there on the sidewalk, so rigid it looked fake. She had scooped him up before anyone could see and rushed him back to the apartment. She had thought, this is it this time, and steeled herself, whispered permission in his ear, and then he had jerked upright and began panting with thirst, and all was forgotten. How was she supposed to know when to let him go?

"Jess," the Corporal said, "look at me." He tried to raise his voice but it was snuffed out.

"I promise," she said, but even she did not know if that was a lie.

MIRACLE GIRL
GROWS UP

MIRIAM HAD NOTICED A THEME EMERGING AMONG THE MEN
she met. If it were a composition for an English class, she could have
called it *Child Actors and Self-Actualization.*

She was sure it was no coincidence. She attracted these men to herself,
even when her friends set her up on dates. And when the men saw Miriam, her short stature and almost elfin hands, they must have delighted
to find someone as underdeveloped as they were.

The last man had been sweet, actually. He had taken her to a Middle
Eastern restaurant, and she appreciated the effort he'd made to select
something out of the ordinary. It only seemed to raise the stakes for the
date, though, and the dancers in beaded, midriff-baring outfits kept
whirling dangerously close to the table.

"This is neat," he said several times, but he was holding his breath the
entire performance.

He had researched the menu beforehand. "I've heard the shawarma is
lovely," he said. He kept using the word *lovely*—next to describe the

pomegranate wine they'd ordered, and then the garnishes on the mezza plate that came before the meal. It irritated her, managing to sound pretentious and eager all at once, and he applied it without license, even to things that were verging on unpalatable.

He was a gentle looking man, round and ruddy, like he had gout.

All evening, she could feel him leading up to something, a festering secret that was best to reveal early. She tried to let him speak, hoping he'd be out with it that much sooner.

When the revelation finally came, it turned out to be another variation on her theme.

For years, he had been the voice of Winnie the Pooh.

"Not the original voice, of course," he said. "I'm not *that* old." He smiled but shrugged, too, an odd mix of pride and shame. She wasn't sure how to respond. Clearly, this was the sort of thing that usually garnered a reaction. It was the punch line of his life.

"It's nothing to be ashamed of," he said. "Most of my income comes from royalties. And the voiceover classes I teach. It pays the bills."

He kept patting his hands on the napkin in his lap, a slightly effeminate gesture.

Anything she could say would be the wrong thing, she thought. She took a sip of the lovely wine—it was bitter but beginning to grow on her as the alcohol kicked in.

He had ordered far too much food. Lucullan pools of hummus and mutabbal glistened, and the dolmas lay untouched, fat little cocoons she imagined would open, birthing another course of appetizers. The fat on the kabobs had started to harden, and she had to avert her eyes. She didn't know why excess made people feel something was an occasion. She had just the opposite impulse, preferring discrete, pretty little bites, everything controlled in the center of a tidy plate. The Japanese had it right when it came to food.

She distracted herself by drinking more wine. With its unusual taste, she imagined it was a medicinal potion, something that would fortify her. Anytime she tasted something tinny, the medicines came back, as potent as ever. There were big gaps in her early years where the memories had sagged with weight until they collapsed entirely. But her tongue remembered it all. Even textures remained; when she had mashed potatoes that were too starchy and stiff, she would be transported back to the hospital bed.

"I just don't want to be the Winnie the Pooh guy you went out on a date with," he said.

But you *are* that guy, she thought. That is precisely what you are. And he was right to worry. People in L.A. had a habit of reducing things to cocktail stories about the party at Pauly Shore's house or the day David Duchovony brought leather pants into the dry cleaners. Now, with reality TV, it was even worse—there were that many more minor figures to encounter in the streets. Miriam was privately obsessed with reality television. When she watched it, she allowed herself the full range of human outrage and weepy sentiment. No slight was too small for tears. But she also liked to watch the ways everyday people were being ruined. It comforted her. She was a survivor, but she was also a victim of sudden obscurity, the kind usually reserved for child actors and reality stars.

Here he was, telling her how the money just kept coming, and yet he was feeling sorry for himself. Sometimes she shared in this kind of self-pity; but just as easily, it could turn to spite.

I'm a fucking miracle child, she thought, watching him stuff a little fist of lamb into his mouth. She sometimes thought this during dates but did not say it, even though she knew it would make kindred spirits of these men. They would have been drawn in, then just as quickly repelled. As she was repelled by them. She wanted someone whole. Someone whose childhood connected seamlessly to his adulthood, things turning out exactly as they were meant to be. She wanted a man to tell her how he had wanted to be a veterinarian since he was a little boy, and then tell her how he loved the work as much as he thought he would, even the hard parts, even when he had to put an animal down.

Instead, she said to him, "I just *love* Winnie the Pooh."

He smiled but looked disappointed.

"It's not exactly Pooh I like," she continued. "It's Piglet."

It was true. She had loved Piglet so. Just saying the word filled her with surprising feeling. It stung. She hadn't thought of her plush Piglet in years, the soft pink ears she had liked to stroke between her thumb and forefinger, like a talisman. Piglet had become such a friend, and she didn't know what had become of him. She wanted him now, could imagine wrapping her still small hands around the striped body.

The man was chuckling. "What?" she said.

"It makes sense," he said, looking at her, then at himself. "I'm portly, and you're petite. It's fitting for Pooh and Piglet."

"I'm not petite," she said. "I'm stunted." She was 4'10"—not *that* short—but her sister Jill was 5'4", and Miriam was sure she was meant to be taller. Her heart-shaped face and doe eyes only made the effect more dramatic; she was thirty-two now and still waiting to look like a woman.

"That's a good one." He laughed. He did not seem to notice that she wasn't smiling. "The guy who did Piglet's voice was a real creep. Strange. Too much work done," he said, pulling back the skin toward his ears. "Like Phil Spector."

The next day, she recounted it all to Jill, who liked to call her after each date. Miriam told Jill he wasn't as bad as Atari guy.

"Atari guy had money," Jill said. "You should have given him another chance."

"Money wasn't the issue."

Atari guy had been in a series of Atari ads in junior high, which had given him the lifelong frustration of an acting dream. Atari guy told everyone he met about the ads, throwing it in like a kitschy fun fact about himself, but he didn't fool anyone. He loved it when people called him Atari guy.

"Plus, you said he was good looking."

"In an obvious way, I guess."

"What kind of way are you looking for?"

"Never mind. Anyway, looks were not the problem."

Miriam was sitting in what she called her "adult" chair, the first one she'd bought brand-new, with a coordinating ottoman. It was deep and cozy, but her feet didn't touch the ground. She hated the dangling sensation, so she would push the ottoman all the way against the chair, so that it became a chaise. She always sat this way when she talked to her sister, and buttressed herself with a Manhattan. She didn't drink much, but she allowed herself this indulgence to ease the ways her sister would inevitably slight her, a reward for tolerating it all. Her sister, on her end, also allowed herself a glass of wine, because the phone call was considered a treat, the one reprieve from her motherly world, and she liked to make a little party of it.

Miriam told Jill about the restaurant he had taken her to, about the hookahs and the dancers with oiled bellies. The only part she'd really liked had been the gritty and sweet coffee, which was served in a pristine cup. The serving was small, but it shot through her right away, cutting a path through the meat and pitas and going straight to her blood. It had made her sweat.

It was during the coffee that the Pooh had come around to asking Miriam what she did for a living. She always found that expression strange and would think, I live for a living. That had been her greatest accomplishment.

She was an accountant. Her life was like a headline from the *Onion:* "Miracle Girl Grows Up, Becomes Accountant." She was quick to point out that she was a *forensic* accountant. People never knew what that meant, and it sounded vaguely exotic, conjuring images of crime scene shows. She let them think that. If she were in a ridiculous mood, she would remark that it had been accountants who finally caught Al Capone.

"Did he try to kiss you?" Jill asked, like they were still in junior high.

"Not unless you call a twitch a try," she said. "He kind of jerked his body toward me, then thought better of it."

"Still," her sister said, "to have someone take you out to an interesting place. Must be nice."

Her sister could not put a conversation to rest unless she had maneuvered at least one *must be nice* into it, despite Miriam's insistence that she was not leading the glamorous Hollywood life Jill persisted in imagining.

Sometimes, near the end of the conversation, if she'd finished off her Manhattan and was feeling particularly macabre, Miriam would imagine that her teratoma was on the other end of the line instead of her sister. That was how she thought of it. *Her* teratoma, a secret part of herself that had been ruthlessly sliced away at birth. Her mother had destroyed all the photos of it, or so she'd been told, but she knew it had been monstrous. Her face had been melting off into a second face that lay alongside her like an enormous puddle of flesh. Once, when Miriam was in college and her mother was drunk, she'd admitted to Miriam that her father had been afraid to touch her until the thing had been removed. The teratoma was a tumor, but Miriam persisted in imagining it as a parasitic twin. It was made up of the human body. A chaos of her. Though it turned her stomach to think of it, she imagined cutting it open like a steam bun and finding the mess of hair, bone, and teeth it held. Perhaps a little hand, although she'd been told that was rare. She imagined the teeth moving within the cluster of hair in the cavity, talking back to her on the phone. She had stopped just short of naming it.

She heard her niece and nephew squealing in the background, the sounds rising and falling, like they were riding a roller coaster. Her sister was threatening them with various forms of deprivation, apparently all of which they'd endure for the opportunity to scream.

"Then you're going to get spanked!" The threat was muffled. Jill must have been holding her hand over the mouthpiece. The squeals gradually deflated into limp whoops. "Is that what you want?"

Recently, Miriam's boss had assigned her to a project at a children's hospital. It wasn't the same hospital where Miriam had been treated but the one across town. I thought you'd find it interesting, her boss said, smiling as though he were doing her a favor. Her boss was a squat man who liked to drink Tecate on the weekends and host BBQs. He was affable and harmless, but she had heard from other staff that he had been a political prisoner in his youth. She had wanted to ask him about it but never had. When it came to personal matters, there was only half-hearted honesty between them, enough to keep up the ruse that they cared. He knew about her past but not really.

Maybe that was why the Pooh had laid it all out on the first date, she thought—to avoid misunderstandings. To put it all past him and give the date a chance.

To her surprise, she had been thinking about the Pooh. He had e-mailed her after their date with an article about a forensic accountant who solved a big case. Normally she would have been immune to that kind of gesture. But it had seemed sweet.

Miriam hadn't been inside a children's hospital in over ten years, since she had gotten busy in college and stopped volunteering as a tour guide. She tried to prepare for the visit, as though such a thing were possible. She felt nerves usually reserved for a job interview, but there was a sicker dread, too, like the job interview would end in death for candidates who weren't selected. Yes, it was more like a court date, she thought. And fittingly for a court date, her attempt to dress in a way that would be taken seriously had gone awry. In her black skirt-suit and tie-front blouse, she had ended up looking like a stewardess. A stewardess from the days when you could smoke on the plane.

She could have said no to her boss, she was sure of it. But there was a part of her that was curious. There was no way to know how she would react in the hospital. It was best to turn on her critical brain, to walk fast, to proceed directly to the accounting office.

The hospital's main tower was newly constructed, so that it didn't look like a hospital much at all. In the parking circle at the entryway there was an Olympic-sized infinity fountain, the water pouring smoothly off the edges. She didn't think it was a very good fountain for children, until out of the stillness, a single droplet flew up into the air and back down again. And then another, rising and falling with mechanical precision. It was a dancing fountain, merely disguised as an infinity pool. She wondered what kind of idiot had come up with that idea.

The lobby looked more like Candyland than a hospital, pictures of purple puppies and Kool-Aid hued kittens. The hospital where she'd been treated had been much more subdued, with pastel butterflies and seahorses. This hospital practically accosted you.

It didn't smell like a hospital—she could give it that much. But as she moved farther in, past the peppermint and licorice elevators and around the back, the halls became increasingly grim. She crossed a bridge that connected the main hospital to a crumbling tower hidden behind it. There were always things hidden in a hospital—rooms, people, jobs that no one gave any thought to.

It reminded her of one of her inpatient stays when she was thirteen, how she'd roomed with a boy who liked to tell creepy tales of off-limits floors. He'd told her about the morgue in the basement and the adjacent hall of medical oddities. He claimed that an orderly had let him in, and he'd been able to see tumors the size of baseballs, detached limbs, jars of premature babies without heads.

The morgue made sense. Children died in the hospital, and they'd have to put their bodies somewhere, she had thought. But she'd been skeptical about the oddities.

She had a favorite nurse at the time—one who played mancala with her during the night shift. Miriam never slept as much as she was supposed to in those days. She had developed a fear of dying in her sleep. She was strangely prepared to die, in the way only a young person can be, but she wanted to be surrounded by her family and by the nurses. She wanted to be watched. One night, as she was setting up the mancala board, Miriam asked the nurse about the hall of oddities.

"What?" the nurse had said. "Who told you that? No such thing." But Miriam had been in the hospital enough to know when a nurse was lying. Nurses didn't lie like normal people. They looked you right in the eyes when they did it and smiled in the most reassuring way.

But Miriam had sort of liked the thought of the oddities. She'd been born in Arizona, so she knew her teratoma couldn't be down there. But it seemed like just the sort of thing medical students would want to see. She wondered if someone had saved her own teratoma back home, if she could be reunited with it someday.

The accounting office was appallingly dingy, especially in contrast to the soda-popped lobby. The staff set her up in an out-of-the-way desk, a sort of vestibule of things past. Above her head were shelves stacked with dusty adding machines and ledger books. The staff was nervous around her, although she could tell they were relieved not to have been sent someone more formidable looking. They kept offering to refill the noxious coffee.

The chief financial officer had left the hospital abruptly after decades, leaving a briar patch of books. Miriam kept requesting files, and the harried accountants kept bringing them, until she was practically bricked in to the vestibule. In moments like these, she thought of her koan: *the sheer fact of living.* It had started as an affirmation, but over the years had soured, become just another emblem of tedium.

Later that week, the Pooh called. She was feeling vulnerable and strange after her visit to the hospital, almost itchy, so that when she answered the phone, she couldn't predict how she would act.

He sounded relieved that she'd answered the phone at all. "I really—," he started, "I really had a nice time the other night."

"Oh?" she said. "I didn't so much."

She never said that sort of thing, but perhaps the last week had made her think of her life passing, had made frank brevity a necessity. It wasn't that she didn't have sass, but the sass had been carefully folded up and tucked away in an interior pocket. Because attitude harkened back to a period she jokingly called The Entitlement. She still burned with shame to think of how she had behaved in her young-adult years, before her life had found its current, perfectly blunt shape. It was hard to pinpoint when the years of earnest, survivor's gratitude had given way to absurd expectation, when she had thought the seas would continue to part just ahead of her as she moved through life.

The Pooh was silent for a moment, as though he were deciding if he should consider that a joke.

He chuckled quietly, and said, "Well, then. Let me make it up to you."

"How?" she said.

"I'll make you dinner at my place. No shimmying. No worm-shaped foods."

She shouldn't go to his place, she thought.

"All right," she said.

The Pooh lived in Studio City, up a thorny, badly worn road that seemed incongruous with the charming Tudor-style homes lining it. The neighborhood conferred status without ostentation, a place for serious behind-the-scenes Hollywood players. His squat, midcentury house was obscured by willow trees, and she almost missed the turn. She had to back up, then power her car up the steep driveway without crashing into his living room.

He looked pleased to see her, but he didn't awkwardly lunge forward for a hug. He just took the bottle of wine she had brought, cradled it appraisingly, then offered an enthusiastic, "Great."

That was a relief. In the restaurant, he had struck her as the kind of man who would be eager to demonstrate his knowledge of wines. She did not like those sort of men. Once, she'd gone to a party with one of her girlfriends who'd been on a date. The man brought a bottle of wine, which seemed like a polite gesture until they arrived and he demanded a decanter, then seemed thoroughly put out when the hostess could not provide one. Never mind that it was a young, easy drinking red that did not need decanting. Miriam had found the man so unforgiveable that she had held the incident against her friend ever since.

The Pooh's house was unintentionally hip. It looked like *Sunset* magazine from 1955—the bulbous lamp over the kitchen sink and the stacked thermador oven people would pay good money for now. The place had an open layout, a small living room with built-in bookshelves and a slanted, beamed ceiling. The furniture was old, too, all pieces that had come around again. He had a squat Danish dining table and well-worn Eames chair in the corner of the living room. The Pooh must have been even older than she'd realized. Something about that was oddly comforting.

"I try to grow all native plants," he said, looking at her. He must have thought she was looking past the furniture, to the view from sliding glass doors that took up the entire back wall. Instead of a cement patio, there were wild plants that grew all the way up the doors. The fact that it wasn't too manicured was another reassurance.

For dinner, he had prepared a zucchini lasagna, with paper-thin layers of the vegetable substituted for the noodles. It was unexpectedly delicious and light, and she thought back to the pools of grease left on their plates at the Armenian restaurant.

"I'm sorry," she said suddenly, putting her fork down and wiping her mouth with the cloth napkin. "What did you do with the guy I met on our first date?"

He looked as though he might choke. Or burp.

"I might have had some bad coaching." He laughed, looking down in his lap. "I should apologize for that."

"I'm just grateful to see that your place isn't full of Winnie the Pooh memorabilia."

"Oh God," he said. "Is that what you were expecting?" He shook his head, then took a drink of his wine. "I shouldn't have mentioned that. I just wanted to get it over with."

"It's all right," she said. "I just tend to meet people who are stuck in the past. In their glory days."

I am one of those people, she wanted to say. She wanted to tell him everything, starting from the very beginning, from the womb, in fact, and bringing him up to the present day. She had not told someone every-thing—or even anything—in years. It was part of the reason she tolerated her weekly conversations with her sister. Because if nothing else, her sis-ter knew. But even her sister could only see it from her own vantage point, the lucky sibling who couldn't help but feel that she was actually the unlucky one.

This impulse to tell was unexpected. She felt flush, the heat building up the sides of her neck and behind her ears. She focused on the food and let it pass. There would be other times for telling.

After dinner, they sat on his couch and finished off the wine. She kept looking at the bookshelves across the room, trying to make out the titles. A good number were art books, but there were history books and novels, too. All sorts, really. It was so hard not to judge. She knew that's what she was doing, squinting to see what she could find. But wasn't judgment a great saver of time? Why wait and see? Why not assess as soon as possible and save the trouble?

Miriam did not generally believe in second chances. Jill was always pleading with her to give a guy another try, to see if he would grow on her over time, which conjured images of unruly extra appendages springing forth. It was true that Miriam appreciated other acquired tastes—dark beer, espresso, strong cheese—but it was harder to tolerate a man who was bitter, even rotten at the outset.

Later that week, she was eager to tell Jill how she'd granted the Pooh a second date.

"Wait," she said. "What? Why *him?* He didn't seem especially worthy of a second date."

"Oh come on," she said. "I thought you'd be pleased."

"Well yes, but isn't this the guy who kept saying *lovely?*"

"He was nervous. No such modifier abuse this time."

"So he was different." Jill said this rather smugly.

"Quite," she said. "Only, I'm not sure it matters, anyway. It didn't end especially well."

Her sister grunted. "Then why are you telling me all this? I was getting hopeful."

"So was I," she said.

"What happened?"

"I behaved badly," she said.

He had asked more about Miriam's work; perhaps not having a regular job had made the minutiae of office life interesting. He wanted anecdotes. Reluctantly, she told him about her current assignment at the children's hospital, about the vestibule, and the decades of paperwork. About how she suspected fraud. So far, she'd found little evidence, but she had become rather determined about it. She had been going through all the donor-restricted funds to determine if monies had been spent contrary to intent. But it was hard to see what she was looking at, there was so much bad recordkeeping all around. Insufficient documentation, poor tracking systems, but so far, nothing willful.

The Pooh had listened to all this intently. If he'd been faking interest, he was convincing. And then he had made some tossed off remark—she didn't remember the first part of the sentence, exactly, since it was the last word that had hooked her and snapped her back to reality, like a clown enjoying the stage a moment too long. He said something about being at the hospital and seeing all those sick kids, and jeez, wasn't it *terrible*.

"Yes," she had muttered. "Terrible."

And then she had abruptly stood, and thanked him for the zucchini thing, and said that she had to go. He had been turned toward her on the couch, one leg up on the cushion tucked under him, his arm resting on the back. He frowned, right between the eyebrows like a little boy, but she could see that his body did not want to move; each part looked pained as he plucked it from comfort—his arm, then his torso, then the leg down on the ground, and finally the whole body heaving forward to stand. By then she was already near the door, and she didn't wait for him to open it for her.

She feebly waved and marched down to her car alone before he could catch up.

He didn't know, she told herself. He *didn't* know. He didn't *know*. She hadn't told him. And everyone except terrible people thought sick kids were terrible. And he had chosen the right word, really. Sad didn't adequately describe the repulsion, the horror. Nursing homes were sad. Sick children were frightening, unnatural.

Jill was talking, but Miriam had not been listening.

"Hello?" Jill said. "Why do you do this?"

"I was thinking," she said.

"No, I mean, why do you do this to yourself?"

"I shouldn't even be alive," Miriam said. "I was meant to die as a baby. Why press my luck?"

This was why she still spoke with her sister each week. Only with a sibling could one snivel such. They always knew the worst. Sometimes only the worst.

"My sentiments exactly," her sister said. "Are you drunk?"

"Maybe."

Miriam had been doing the thing she did not let herself do. On the floor, at the edge of her once fluffy, now matted rug were photo albums, the kind with sticky pages and the thin film that reminded her of Kraft cheese singles. Photos were dangerous. Especially long forsaken photos, which had regained some of their potency, their power to conjure the past.

There were photos of her in various stages of wellness, attending at least a dozen charity events. Some had been silly and small—like the Strike out Cancer! Bowlathon—but most had been red carpet affairs. Because she was stunted, she looked years younger than her actual age, making her seem precocious and preternaturally wise. They kept inviting her back. Plus, her mom had always been willing to drive her. For a small-town woman like her mother, the celebrity allure had been just too great. The stars always told Miriam how she inspired them. How special she was. They asked her what she wanted to do when she grew up. She would say she wanted to be a senator, and they would chuckle and grin and shake her hand and say they couldn't wait to vote for her.

There was a picture of Miriam with Madonna outside of the singer's compound. They had met as co-honorees at an event and had started a letter correspondence. And then, for her fifteenth birthday, Madonna had invited her over for a movie night at her "house." She didn't let Miriam take pictures inside, but they'd posed outside the entry gate, Miriam in her matching doggie pajamas, Madonna in a fancy sweatsuit. Madonna had done the notorious Letterman interview the year before, when she said fuck thirteen times and kept trying to get him to smell her underwear. Most mothers didn't want their girls watching her videos, much less spending time alone at her house. But Miriam had learned the rules were different for kids who'd recovered from cancer. For the movie night, they were supposed to watch *Forrest Gump,* but Madonna could not stop talking about Tupac Shakur. She was like a schoolgirl, replaying everything he'd ever said to her. She kept pausing the movie and trying to imitate his voice to Miriam, saying "hey, Ma*donna.*"

Miriam had also met the president, but it had been disappointing. Miracle kids had come from all over the country and as one of fifty, she had barely gotten a good look at him. For some reason, they'd given all the girls tiaras to wear in the photographs. Most of the girls were bald, scarred, crooked, or in wheelchairs, grinning in their matching oversized shirts.

At school, pity had quickly turned to envy. Miriam was used to being stared at. But this was such a wonderful new feeling, shiny on her skin. At the time, Miriam had begun to believe that she was more special than even the glittery people around her—they told her so. And she credited the teratoma. It always came up in the interviews. The leukemia she'd been diagnosed with at thirteen was aggressive but nothing exceptional. It may or may not have been connected to the teratoma—the doctors couldn't say. But people liked to hear about it, they liked the storyline that she'd been *battling to live since birth!* Even though the first dozen years of her life had been healthy and she had thought of Jill as her secret twin, not the ghastly blob she'd been born with. Jill had been her best friend, in fact, until Miriam and her mother had moved to Los Angeles for Miriam to get the treatment she needed. It was supposed to be temporary, but it turned out to be a convenient excuse for her mother, who did not want to go back to Arizona, where Jill and their father had stayed. You would have thought Miriam had gone off to arts school, the way Jill acted, like Miriam's life was so strange and special. Their parents never lived together again.

Miriam's boss wanted to know how things were going at the hospital. "You've been there a lot," he said.

It was true. She had devoted extra time to the assignment. The first visit had been the hardest, but after that, she made up excuses to go back. Her diligence, if not her stature, intimidated the staff. They would often remark apologetically about the former CFO's senility. Miriam was dimly aware that she took some pleasure in making them scurry.

"The action plan is going to take a while," she said to her boss.

She had gotten a little zealous. The nature of the job suited a zealot; it required the slow untangling of knots, the ability to work them loose over weeks or months, knowing they would come undone eventually.

"What are we looking at here?" he said. "A negligence case? You're not finding any signs of fraud, are you?" He had an impatient tone that she'd only heard a few times in her five years working under him.

"Well, it's a mess," she said. "A complete mess. If there were fraud, it'd be hard to find it. What can I tell you?"

"Don't get carried away," he said. "The woman is retired. It's not like they're going to take her to court. Just work on a loss quantification for the trustees. We're not there to punish anybody."

She wasn't punishing anybody. She was helping the hospital. Wasn't she?

"Guess what?" the Pooh said by way of greeting. Miriam had never liked being greeted that way. In spite of her bad behavior, the Pooh kept calling. She wondered if he displayed this level of determination with all women.

"What?" she said.

"Your assignment at the hospital got me thinking," he said. "So I called

up their volunteer department and asked if they'd like the Pooh characters to come out. I mean, we used to do that sort of thing. But it's been
years. And I was remembering how fun it was. They said yes!"

"You did *what?*" She should hang up, she thought. Or she should tell
him.

"I just called them up. Offered to have the whole gang out."

"Do kids even know who Winnie the Pooh is anymore?" she said.
"Would they even like it?"

"Ouch," he said. It was hard to insult this man. He almost refused to
be insulted. "It's as popular as ever," he said. "Some things last. Elmo.
Winnie the Pooh."

She was quiet.

"Plus, I'm not working that much at the voice-over school. I should do
something else with my time. And you're working there, so I thought,
you know, I thought it made sense."

He was trying to bond with her, to give them a shared activity, not
knowing how impossible that was in this case.

"It would be nice to give back," he said.

"Don't say that," she said harshly. She tried to restrain her voice, but
couldn't. "I hate that expression."

And if anyone was giving back, *she* was. Giving back in a way that her
glitzy appearances had never really allowed. She was in the hidden part
of the hospital this time, finding the hidden things.

"Okay then," he said. "It would be nice to make a kid smile. How about
that? Plus, you can meet Eeyore. And Piglet."

"I thought you said that guy was a creep."

"Not that kind of creep. He always has three girlfriends at once. He
cuts people off in traffic. But he's got a soft spot for kids."

For *sick* kids, she thought. The whole fucking world had a soft spot for
sick kids, and once you'd felt it, you expected everybody to congratulate
you for the rest of your life.

Miriam waited in the hospital lobby for the Pooh but couldn't get a moment's peace. People were so damn helpful in that place, offering up glasses of water, making sure she'd already been helped. She must have looked like a grieving parent, someone lost and forlorn. Even a pet therapy dog approached her. It looked like a retriever, but she wasn't sure. She didn't know much about dogs. He sat right in front of her and gave a plaintive stare, like he could smell the sick kid in her. He licked her knee with his pink tongue. The natural instinct to comfort the aggrieved had been fostered in these dogs, and they wandered around the hospital's walls, sniffing out clusters of hurt like other dogs found drugs or explosive devices.

"I'm fine," she said to the handler, looking away from her and out the front windows. "Really. I'm just waiting for someone."

But the dog did not want to leave. The handler had to tug hard on the leash to redirect him toward a kid in a wheelchair who was approaching.

It should have occurred to her that they would be costumed, but when she saw them coming, fully decked out like theme park cast members, she was taken aback. She had been so worried about how she would manage the day that she hadn't given them much thought. But here the trio came in man-sized suits. The proportions were not right, of course. Piglet was almost as big as Pooh, plus Eeyore wasn't on all fours. The Pooh waved at her.

"Hi," he said, in his normal voice, but it was muffled by the head piece. "Can you hold my pot of honey for a second?"

He handed her the honey, which was stuffed, and took off his Pooh head. He was already sweaty, his bangs stuck to his forehead and his cheeks red.

"Do you ever stop to think, and forget to start again?" he said in his Pooh voice. He sounded like Pooh, she had to hand him that. He kissed her on the cheek. "This is Jason," he pointed to Eeyore. "And this is Kenneth." Seeing this full-size Piglet, she was not hit by the waves of sentimentality a plush animal would have brought on. She wondered how creepy he looked underneath the costume.

"I'm Miriam," she said.

"Tigger is on his way," the Pooh said, "but he's running late." A kid walked by, and he quickly put his head back on. She handed him the honey.

When Tigger arrived, a volunteer coordinator led them through the wards. They couldn't really speak through their costume heads, so they just waved.

The first stop was the orthopaedic wing—kids with heads stuck in halo traction like badly outfitted astronauts or others using miniature walkers, complete with tennis balls. And she had thought it would be the easy floor.

The Pooh was so wide he kept bumping into medical poles. He could barely squeeze into the patient rooms. They volunteer coordinator told each patient how they had come on an adventure all the way from the glen just to visit them. They took pictures with an instant camera, tacking the photos to whiteboards next to the patient beds. The nurses kept telling Tigger that he was overexciting the kids and to please stop jumping. But that only made the kids laugh harder.

They went to the heart wing and to the endocrinology wing. One nurse said she hadn't seen the kids that excited since the Dodgers had visited earlier in the year.

Things were so different, Miriam kept telling herself. There were electronic charts instead of paper, and the kids had tablets and could listen to music and watch movies on demand. She focused on anything she could find that was not the same.

Then they crammed into the elevator with a boy in a wheelchair. He was wailing. They had tried to wait for the next elevator, but the woman with the boy had impatiently waved them in. The sound didn't seem to emanate from the boy's throat or mouth but from his viscera itself, as though his organs were directly transmitting their pain. His tongue kept slipping out of his mouth, distorting the sound. He was banging his head between the head pads on the chair. A woman was trying to control the chair, but it was motorized and the boy kept reaching for the joystick that controlled it. His other hand was held up at his face, like a claw. The woman must have been used to the sound; she didn't try to console or quiet him, standing silently against the back of the elevator.

The Pooh, who was in the back by Miriam, lifted his arm in a cramped wave to the boy, but the boy's eyes were scanning something invisible to all of them. He did not seem to know they were there.

Miriam smiled sweetly at the woman, but the boy provoked a feeling of heartlessness in her. Miriam had learned to do this long ago. It was the only way she could look at those children, really, like they were lepers or third world beggars tugging on her shirt for change.

Everyone did this, she thought, this shutting off, but it was different for her. She was pinching off access to herself, to the teratoma, to the hall of medical oddities, the grotesquerie that had been cut away and hidden in subterranean floors, transmitting their own songs of protest.

They exited the elevator on the cancer floor, leaving the boy in the wheel-chair behind. They'd arrived at the most cheerful of all the floors. It was too much, she thought, splashed with rainbow colors, completely over-compensating. She thought she could manage it. After all, she had been an ambassador for her hospital for years after she'd gone into remission. She had done all this.

She lagged behind, pretending to study a donor wall shaped like a pinwheel. She was surprised to find that she recognized some of the names from her work in the accounting office. She wondered how many were parents of patients, or the patients themselves, all grown up, miracle kids who went on to do something more miraculous than accounting.

Down the hall, the Pooh had encountered a patient. The girl he was leaning over looked like she wanted to laugh but could only manage a weak smile. She looked like she'd have to take a nap just from the effort.

Miriam ducked into a playroom across from the donor wall. Thankfully, it was empty. She could smell glue and disinfectant. On an "art wall" they'd hung valentines with 3-D hearts affixed to their fronts. They were brave hearts, big and bright red and pulsing right off of their construction paper bodies. Some of the valentines were for nurses, and there were drawings of white-smocked women with old-fashioned caps on top. All the nurses were drawn that way, even though the nurses in the hospital wore scrubs with prints of teddy bears and sunflowers. Maybe the kids wanted nurses garbed for the wars that were under way within these walls. Ceremonial white that could be bleached free of stains, and the bright red cross to remind everyone what was really at stake.

Miriam wanted to lie down. She looked down at the linoleum, glossy and streaked with shoe scuffs. She sat down in a miniature plastic chair, her knees all the way to her chest.

On the table, there were practice baby dolls with little thermometers and stethoscopes. There were doll-sized wheelchairs, too. They called it therapeutic play. When she was sick, she had been too old for the dolls and had been sent to the teen lounge for movies, for escapist time instead. But now, she'd heard that they had video games where kids could shoot cancer cells as they navigated through the body as though it were a black and fuchsia battle zone. What were the consequences of thinking of one's own body that way? What were the consequences of thinking of one's own body at all? Thinking about all the stuff inside, liver and spleen and kidneys all smashed together, the heart that beat magically. It wasn't healthy to reflect on. It was like thinking about outer space for too long. Too hard to accept as fact, really. And capable of skewing all perspective.

When she was sixteen, she had believed that *she* beat cancer, that her aptitude and attitude won the battle. That seemed so foolish to her now.

She picked up one of the dolls—its sock had come off, and someone had marked its chin with crayon. This is what it must be like for victims of physical violence, she thought: it becomes part of the language of their bodies, and they find a way to keep bringing it back. It's wired in, or whatever machine-language doctors were using to describe people these days. So that looking at this doll, she felt repulsion but sentiment, too, thick and oozing all over. She was in remission the way others are in recovery.

The Pooh found her. He squeezed himself into the room and closed the door behind him.

"I can't breathe," he said, popping off his head. He was dripping in sweat, and she could see he had been crying, but he had an exhilarated look on his face, like he'd just parachuted out of a plane.

"Man," he said. "I forgot what this is like. That kid in the elevator." He placed his plush head down on the counter. "The coordinator gave me a bottle of water." He held his paws up. "Can you open it for me?"

She got up and took the bottle. She hadn't noticed her hands were shaking until she started to unscrew it. She hoped he couldn't tell.

"I just needed a minute," he said.

She knew all too well the effects sick children have on the healthy. How being there was draining but cleansing, how dying made the living feel more alive. People had taken that thrill from Miriam, again and again, and she had let them.

"What're you doing in here?" he said.

The thing about the Pooh was that he was actually Pooh-like, big and cozy and guileless. He was not like the others she'd dated, the men for whom the present was wholly inadequate.

She wanted to hug him, hot and sticky as he was, but there was no way to get her arms around the belly.

He put his paw on her shoulder.

"I have something I ought to tell you," she said.

He took her hand and regarded her with an expression both hopeful and worried. She thought her hand in his paws looked like an illustration out of a children's book.

I am sick, she could start. But that would be a cruel way to begin. Sick like Atari guy. I have survivor's syndrome. She had told people the facts, but facts were not her story. And the story itself was not the truth. She did not know how she would enter it, if it would begin with the bruise on her thigh the first day of eighth grade, or if she would go back to the womb.

"What?" he said. "What is it?"

"You look ridiculous in that costume," she said. "But cute. Very cute."

She could ask him what the word *cancer* felt like in his mouth, did it make his teeth feel chalky? And she could explain that even though it felt funny in her mouth, it felt another way, too. Even as the word induced nausea whenever she heard it, it was glittery and bright, and she would see it in her mind's eye like a Vegas sign, like her own name in lights. A show starring her and the chaos of her. And he would nod his head and pretend to understand. Because he was the Pooh. She could tell him to shut up, to sit there like a dumb, hungry bear and listen.

GO FORTH

HIS WIFE BEVERLY WAS ON THE MAILING LIST FOR EVERY conceivable kind of cause, cleft palates and felled trees. He sat at the kitchen table, watching her sift through the appeals that had collected over the last months, as though they were letters from old friends. When he managed to intercept the mail, he threw them all away.

"It says here," she said, tapping the yellow envelope with her nail, "that soldiers who would have died in all the previous wars because of their injuries are now living. Because of surgical advances."

"And that's a good thing?" he said. He had finished his coffee, and straightened the daisy placemat that hid the worn veneer and little divots in the table. It was their oldest piece of furniture, purchased for their first apartment, and they still found themselves sitting there like old dogs in a favored spot.

"Well," she said, considering this. "I don't think that's for me to say." She got up to refill his cup. "It's a fact. So we have to do more to support them now."

There was no point in arguing with her. He saw the flourish with which she signed her name on $25 checks, like she were passing legislation into law.

For nearly a year, he had forgone all coffee in solidarity with his wife. On dialysis, she'd been permitted just twenty-four ounces of liquid a day, and it seemed wrong to drink it—to drink anything, in fact—in front of her.

The coffee was good that morning. By some talent he could not begin to contemplate, no matter how often she made it, the brew was different each time. When he'd remarked on this, years ago, she had told him he could make the coffee, that she was confident it would be *precisely* the same each day, and that that sounded like a thrilling way to live.

He was off guard then—at the old table with his good cup of coffee, on a day whose weather seemed promising—when hidden amid the fundraising appeals, she produced another kind of letter. "Look at this," she said. He could tell from the artificial brightness in her voice she'd staged this casual discovery. The letter inside announced the kidney reunion was in Chicago, in five weeks' time.

"Who is being reunited?" he said. "We've never met any of these people."

"It's an expression," she said. "Would you rather they call it a union? That sounds like a marriage."

"Or is it the kidneys," he said, "that are meant to be reunited with their former hosts?"

Formers owners, he would have said, but that wasn't how doctors spoke of organs. He had merely been a sixty-five-year host to his kidney—a kidney that now, like some foreign student on exchange, had been shipped off, only never to return. And someone else's kidney—Beverly called it Blanche, because all they knew was that it had come from Tennessee—now resided in his wife. Their friends joked that if Beverly started sweetening her tea, he would know why. It reminded him of how certain people, uncomfortable with sex, would name their sexual parts, as though making things precious would strip them of their power.

"There'll be a group photo," she said, handing him the invitation. "And they've approached *People* magazine." His wife loved the medical extremes of *People*—conjoined twins, progeria, shared psychosis—and now, as two links in a sixty-person kidney transplant chain, they apparently qualified for those ranks. He could imagine the schmaltzy paying-it-forward headline, a sidebar with the altruistic donor who had set the chain in motion.

"Do you think my kidney will remember me?" he said.

Beverly took off her reading glasses and stared at him. "Sheldon. Don't you want to meet them?" she said. "I do. I need to meet them. I need to thank them in person."

Oh, his wife. If only she were the kind of woman who roughed up the still moments of his Sundays with ill-timed requests for eggs or ladies shaving cream or canned tuna. If only she had asked for small things all of the time, in the way so many wives did, and kept her reserves dangerously depleted. But she had used the word *need* so judiciously in the last thirty-six years.

Now, five weeks later, he and Beverly were lined up in numerical boarding order at the airport gate. They did not have assigned seats.

"What is the meaning of this?" he asked her. "Why did you choose this airline?"

"It's more efficient," she said. "They've done studies. The planes run on schedule this way."

"You should have been Japanese," he said.

"I'll take that as a compliment," she said, nudging him as the line began to move.

Inside the plane, it did not seem more efficient—there were passengers in window seats and aisle seats sandwiching middle seats no one wanted to claim. In the back, too close to the lavatory, they found a row where they could both sit together. Beverly took the middle so that he could have the aisle. There were crumbs in his seat and a foil wrapper shined in the back pocket in front of him. He had watched the last set of passengers deplane when they arrived. Didn't there used to be a turnaround period when the planes were cleaned between flights? That was what accounted for the so-called efficiency, in his view—not some novel method of boarding but cutting corners. It was unsavory enough to be trapped in a shell with a hundred other people, breathing the same air for hours, without the residue of the last passengers coming to mind.

The world had become so garish, Sheldon thought. It wasn't that he'd been a prude, exactly, but the world had been slyer in his youth. Women's clothing had been suggestive, people spoke in euphemism, and formality was maintained in public spaces. Now people changed genders and exchanged vital organs and celebrated everything.

Ben, one of his close friends from work, was a homosexual, and for most of their lives, it was unacknowledged at the office and at dinners when men brought their wives. Ben had a longtime partner, but no one had met him. And Sheldon had liked to imagine Ben's life like he would imagine India or Morocco—places of dirt and vibrant color both—a kind of beauty and ugliness he could not inhabit. But now Ben and his partner came to parties in their Bermuda shorts and Sperry Top-Sider loafers, their sets of hairy legs crossed on the couch: the India Sheldon had imagined turned out to closely resemble Minneapolis. He'd been disappointed by it all in the same way he had been on the sole cruise his wife had arranged for them in Mexico. Sometimes he thought he suffered from too much imagination.

Once, he had asked Ben, "Don't you miss it at times, being illicit?" Sheldon was sure there was a kind of gay man who would have admitted he did.

"Like you'd miss getting kicked in the nuts," Ben had said.

Beverly reached below the seat in front of her to pull out her tote, where she had tucked in one of Sheldon's thin gray scarves. She had spritzed it with a home scent of lavender and verbena.

"Here," she said. "Wrap this around your neck."

With his nose nuzzled into the scarf, he wouldn't smell the cabin of the plane, an odor so distasteful to him he was forever trying and failing to describe it to other people (as though they had not experienced it themselves). It wasn't that Beverly didn't smell it, but flying didn't make her nauseated, so it was no more offensive than the chemical tang of new-car smell. Before dialysis had kept her grounded, Beverly had flown frequently to see their daughters. Flying wasn't comfortable, but whatever pains her body felt, her imagination stirred—in the way it did in bookstores and home décor stores—with possible worlds.

"I've got radio programs on my phone," she told Sheldon, "if you'd like to listen." If she'd said podcasts, she would have had to explain the distinction, and he would have thought it was something new and therefore objectionable, when it was really just something from his own youth delivered in a different way.

"I'll put one on for you," she said. "It's about history." She had brought real headphones instead of ear buds for his ears, and she gently placed them on him and put the program on. When the attendant came by, she ordered him a gin and tonic. The scented scarf and gin and deep voices of the podcast would soothe him into a kind of pre-slumber, away from his thoughts of germs and declining civilization. She had raised two children and knew how to calm a baby.

"Have you considered that our links could be anyone?" his wife had asked him the night before as they'd packed their bags. "Any age. Male or female. Any race. All sorts of religions or careers."

She was rolling her clothes into snug little cocoons because she had read somewhere that was a better way to pack; another so-called innovation, when he knew she didn't have the patience to properly fold.

"I know that," he said.

"But have you *considered* it?"

"What does that mean?" he said.

"Really pictured it. Imagined the people in the flesh. So that you won't be surprised."

"What are you suggesting?" he said.

She was squeezing the air out of a space saver bag their daughters had bought them, as though they traveled with enough frequency and brought home so many world market treasures that they could not afford to pack air.

"I know this is hard for you," she said.

"I'm fine," he said.

He had not told her about his silly nightmare, in which a new kidney had grown back in the harvested one's place. At first, it had been a good dream—the relief of regeneration—until the doctors made use of this medical miracle. They removed that kidney and another grew back, and another, until he was single-handedly crossing patient after patient off the transplant list.

"Okay," she said. "Let's say I have the kidney of a black man."

"That may be so," he said. "How am I supposed to feel about that?"

"*I* feel it's wonderful," she said. She zipped up the left side of her case; she was finished already, and he had only gotten started.

"How is feeling it's wonderful any better than feeling uncomfortable?" he said. "You *want* it to be a black man, in particular?"

"I want it to be someone different from me," she said.

"You'll be disappointed if it's an older white woman?"

"A little," she said.

"I don't think I understand that," he said, which was the kindest thing he could think to say.

"I didn't expect you would," she said.

The novel Beverly was reading on the plane was a historical fantasy about a girl, sold as a slave to the king of another kingdom, who uses her charms to become queen. Beverly loved stories of reversal of fortune. As a girl, she read books about orphans and their fates and imagined her real parents would claim her one day, not because her own parents were unkind or poor but just unexceptional. But even as she went on to live her own unexceptional life, marrying Sheldon, raising two sturdy, bright girls, the feeling never entirely left her, as though the second act were just about to begin. In the early years of marriage, she had pinned these hopes on Sheldon, convinced his tinkering in the garage would lead to a notable invention. And then she had felt horrible resenting him for being a perfectly good mechanical engineer and provider to his family, his obsessive-compulsive tendencies not a harbinger of hidden genius. She did the same thing with her daughters, too, who had managed to inherit their father's methodical mind and her own intellectual curiosity: Thisbe was an environmental attorney and Laurel a vice president of marketing for a software company and a mother of two herself. They had exceeded all parental hopes and dreams, her girls, but it didn't seem they would do something where Beverly, as their mother, would end up a footnote in history. Her problem, she sometimes thought, was that she suffered from too much imagination. What she had not told Sheldon—or anyone, really—was that the kidney chain was the footnote she had been waiting for. It felt foolish, admitting this; illness was hardly an achievement. Her body had failed her slowly, through no fault of her own. She had no more reason for pride than for shame. And yet. She had printed the story from the *Washington Post* about the historic chain and now kept it in the folder where she had Thisbe's and Laurel's locks of baby hair.

The radio episode his wife put on was from one of the world war programs she often played for him at home. He relished the inexhaustibility of the subject. Sheldon had been six of seven children, and they had little in the way of toys and amusements, but they would fashion guns out of old mop handles and march out to the forest behind their house, where the wet, mossy ridges served as trenches.

It was only Hubert, the youngest, who ever had things of his own, because when he was born the doctor had warned their parents that this would be their last child. Their father had spent thirteen years hedging his bets by having one child after another, and then with Hubert, it had occurred to him and their mother that they might try to enjoy a child before their parenting had come to an end.

At the dining table, Sheldon was second shift, eating after the older kids handed over their used plates and silverware, and he got the bathwater when it was cold and gray. His father had been terrified of germs, but family germs did not count.

When their father would come to call the children in for supper and found them playing war games in the forest, he always told them, "The flu killed more than the war. That's the real enemy."

He had said it so many times that when one of them sneezed, someone else would say, "*You're* the real enemy."

"What would you have us play, father?" Elton, the eldest, had once asked. "Sanatorium? Are we all supposed to act at lying on cots and dying of flu?"

Sheldon had laughed and their father grabbed him by the ear. "There wasn't a funny thing about it," he said.

The Chicago restaurant their daughter Thisbe had recommended was called Forage & Fauna and looked like one Beverly had seen in a food and wine magazine. Beverly had always found a consumptive, irreducible joy in magazines, but during dialysis they had become talismans. The pages never failed to restore the world order, filling her with both longing and satisfaction: a yearning, on the one hand, for places she would not visit, and yet a comfort in knowing that no place would be as perfect in the flesh as the lit and cropped version, that the thing she longed to possess could only be possessed with her eyes on the page. And now here she was, having walked straight into the pages, like one of those blurry young people they shot in the photographs, in motion when the restaurant around them stood still.

She texted Thisbe to let her know that they'd arrived. Thisbe, who had traveled to eighteen countries, humored her mother's enthusiasm for small excursions. She had even bought her a sky-blue passport holder when they had taken the disastrous cruise to Mexico for Sheldon's sixtieth birthday. Up until that point, he'd managed to go their entire married life without fully acknowledging his claustrophobia.

Please make dad go to a musical, Thisbe texted back. *Or better yet, a Sam Shepherd play.*

Beverly had heard of Sam Shepherd but couldn't recall what plays he'd written. Thisbe was making a joke, only Beverly couldn't be sure what kind of joke. She was about to put Sam Shepherd into Google—she kept up with her daughters through research—when she felt Sheldon watching her.

He had been tense in the cab (this isn't what I'd call the middle of the country, he said) and tense in the hotel registration lobby (can you please not do that—engage people prematurely?) when she'd asked a pretty young woman if she were there for the kidney chain reunion. The woman had blinked, uncomprehending, before explaining she was there for a film festival. Beverly had been about to enlighten her about the reunion before Sheldon had hissed in her ear.

While he enjoyed his alcohol, she drank her water. He teased her at the way she still ordered it—water!, with gusto—but the fact of being able to drink unlimited amounts cool, clear water had not lost its pleasure. Before, she would suck on peppermints and frozen grapes—temporary salves against the thirst—but they had been feeble replacements. Now, when she opened her mail appeals about water wells and hunger and thirst in the developing world, she felt a greater responsibility to help.

With Sheldon on his second drink, Beverly could see the beaches of his little island of self were beginning to erode, that he was holding himself less tightly against the rest of the room. In the absence of any diagnostic certainty, she had come to just think of it as *the problem of Sheldon,* a problem that had drawn perimeters around her life just as severely as kidney failure had. As a young woman, she had met Sheldon's father and should have looked—in the way men sometimes did at a woman's mother—for signs of future corpulence, the ways his own traits might swell and distort over time. He was concave, with one collapsed lung, which gave the impression of a man imploded. The house was scrubbed but too worn down to ever look clean, and they lived like poor mountain people, without adornment. She'd sensed a stockpile of cash somewhere in a back shed, because he didn't believe in bankers any more than doctors.

When he was uncomfortable, Sheldon's father had a way of looking confused and disdainful all at once, and she had seen that face in Sheldon's when the transplant coordinator had explained to him the concept of the kidney chain. Sheldon had repeated her own words back to her, as though they might develop greater coherence in his own mouth. "Because we're incompatible, my kidney would go to another person," he said. "And in exchange my wife would receive someone else's kidney. A stranger." The coordinator and Beverly had nodded in tandem. The coordinator explained that they had software to make these matches and that his recipient would have another willing but incompatible cousin or parent or coworker and then that person's kidney would go to yet another stranger and so on, passing it down the chain.

"Like an infection," he had said.

Exactly when, Sheldon thought, had banquettes become passé? Fine dining used to come with expensive chairs, wide and well upholstered. This restaurant was little more than a medieval dining hall, communal tables flanked by hard wooden benches, naked light bulbs dangling, as though they couldn't afford proper shades.

The menu was a slim sheet of cardstock. **Pork cheek**, nettle chimichurri, pea tendril, lacto fermented hot sauce. **Barramundi**, salmoriglio, kohlrabi, oro blanco. The list format suggested nothing about the composition of the dish, in the way some languages omitted vowels in their printed form, knowing the reader was well versed enough to supply the missing sounds.

Beverly brought out her reading glasses and ran her finger along the lines, as though that might improve their decipherability. She'd be tempted to ask the server about the ingredients, he knew, but she understood he hated it when she asked a server to explain things; no matter how obscure, it always made him feel like a rube.

"What do you recommend?" Beverly asked the server when he came around, and then she selected only those recommendations. "Does something have chicken?" she said, pointing to Sheldon. "For him?"

Then she turned to him and began speaking, but he could only make out every third word. "What?" Sheldon asked, leaning halfway across the table. "I'm sure *everything* here is good," she said.

It was so like Beverly to say that. What could possibly have made her sure of this? But he could see it was the adventure of it, of not knowing what they would eat that made her smile. Their lives had been confined to ever smaller circles as her kidney failure had progressed, their time defined by dialysis, their activity by the vagaries of her stamina, her thirst.

But the truth was that he had felt safest and happiest in the smallest of those circles, when nothing more was required of him than to take care of his wife. There had been little thought of going out, of trying new things.

It was too loud to talk in the restaurant, so he watched her. It was odd to him, having been married for thirty-six years, how she did not look the same to him, day to day. There were moments he found her face disagreeable, the eyes too deeply set, and the top lip too thin. As a young man, he had thought this meant he had been falling out of love, only to find her beautiful again the next week. Now, there was a sheen on her cheeks that made her look youthful, and the crepiness around her eyes that she hated looked sweet and soft.

"Do you feel invaded, in a way?" Sheldon had asked her once, a few months after the transplant surgery.

"Dear," she had said, putting her hand on his shoulder, in the way she did when she had to educate him on subtleties. "That's a question only a man would ask. Women give birth to children. Foreign invasion is part of the job description."

He had never thought of it that way, even when his wife had been pregnant. The next time they had made love, he had found her revelation distracting. Now, with the soft look on her face during dinner, he was afraid she would want to make love at the hotel and he was feeling too anxious about the next day.

But when they returned to the room she had indigestion from the food and spent a good hour in the bathroom. He felt a hint of vindication—experiments were not without cost—but sad. "Are you all right?" he asked, lingering outside the door.

Alone in the hotel room, he finally did what his wife had asked: he considered who Beverly's donor would be and who his own recipient would be, and pictured how he would interact with them, what he would reveal in his face. If it were a black man, as his wife had suggested, it would heighten the strangeness, for the same reason it heightened the miraculous. It created visual drama, a reminder of how extraordinary the entire experiment was. What he was afraid Beverly was suggesting was that it heightened his sense of uncleanliness, if that was the word, the queasiness the exchange evoked in him. As though black germs were worse than white germs. That had nothing to do with it. Did it? Once, he had been seated on a plane next to a dark-skinned man—Pakistani, maybe—whose body odor was so intense he thought he might be sick. It was true that the man's very foreignness brought disease to Sheldon's mind. Perhaps he *was* xenophobic. Or racist. Or both. But then, he also viewed every toddler with suspicion, their splayed hands like biological weapons ready to transmit disease. The only person whose germs did not count were Beverly's, since, after many years of marriage, it was hard not to see her as an extension of his self. That was one of the paradoxes of marriage. After all these years, he understood that his wife's inner workings were essentially unknowable to him. And yet her body, having lived in tandem with his own, he believed to be a part of him. The two really did become one. So his kidney, had it gone to Beverly, would not have been entirely lost; it would still have been there, residing beside him.

At the registration table, there were lanyards with plastic tags that announced their name, city of origin, and number in the chain, with a large green D for donor or orange R for recipient. Sheldon was D 35; Beverly was R 34.

The number thrilled her. "I'm R 34," she said without hesitation to the next person who approached the table. Like she was a robot.

The hotel was one of the monoliths from the 1980s, with a main atrium several stories high. In its dated way, it evoked science fiction, and Beverly felt it sufficiently grand. So many things, like sixth-grade graduations, were needlessly ceremonious these days (a complaint of Sheldon's that she had come to appreciate). But with the transplant there had only been the long wait to see if the kidney would be accepted or rejected, waiting for her energy to return, which she had expected to arrive like a wave and not like the slow, imperceptible drip it had been. There had never been a moment for a toast; a moment when someone said, go forth.

Soon, she had met D 13, a young private stationed at Fort Bragg; R 44, a professor of economics from the University of Michigan; D 25, a war correspondent from Philadelphia; and then R 8, who, with her faint brows and smoker's lines, bore an uncomfortable resemblance to her son-in-law's mother. Beverly had so looked forward to meeting her daughter Laurel's future in-laws. Her son-in-law James was an exceptional young man, scientific and solid, a perfect foil to her energetic daughter; the more she knew him, the more his sly humor, his exacting taste emerged. She imagined the parents who must have produced such a young man and pictured new built-in friends, perhaps even a couple with whom they might travel. But the father was a never-do-well, disabled (by what, no one said), bred German Shepherds and rode a skateboard around town; the mother was a humorless school receptionist. Sheldon had not understood Beverly's disappointment; they lived in Sacramento, he pointed out, and they would scarcely have to see them. "But can you believe they produced James?" she had asked. "Can you believe we produced Laurel?" Sheldon offered. "Perhaps we'd be considered a disappointment as well."

By the breakfast buffet, the kidney chain attendees exchanged handshakes and rousing good mornings, the kind heard in church when the parishioners turned to say *peace be with you; and also with you.* Sheldon took his coffee and an anemic looking muffin to an isolated corner. In church, he always wanted to sit in the back where he could reflect, but Beverly was more interested in the social than the contemplative. The people *are* the church, she said; otherwise, you can stay at home and read your Bible.

A few months before they had told anyone that Beverly would need dialysis, a new pastor had given a sermon on the kidney. His sermons were often prescient that way, a quality Sheldon found mildly annoying. What he liked about the pastor, once he had gotten over his youth—he looked the part of the choir boy, complete with teenaged acne—was that he was a scholar and not afraid to give a subject the historical treatment. Sheldon learned from the sermon that kidneys were mentioned more than thirty times in the Bible and that the ancients, positing a reason for the presence of two organs, believed that one functioned to give good advice and the other, bad. They were among the organs God would examine to judge the individual's life. Sheldon had never pictured judgment day as a kind of grand autopsy.

"Let's hope they take out the bad one," Beverly had giggled in his ear.

He had thought of the joke the day of the actual surgery, when he had woken up foggy and dehydrated. By the time they were prepping, his veins had been so collapsed the nurse had had trouble putting his IV in. The hospital had placed him and Beverly in the same preoperative room with matching blue shower caps. She kept laughing at the sight of him, and Sheldon asked the anesthesiologist if he had given her drugs already. She talked incessantly—trying, he understood—to distract him. He kept looking for a place to focus his eyes, but there was no safe spot. He could see black scuff marks on the mauve wall, a red sharps box, presumably filled with dirty needles, and a crooked fire extinguisher with laminated instructions nearby that were smeared with something yellow. Beverly knew he hated going to the doctor and had probably assumed this reluctance was out of a stubborn self-reliance. The truth was too embarrassing. How to explain how an everyday thing like a cotton ball—a little piece of spun sunlight—could evoke such horror when pressed against the crook of his arm? He didn't become faint, exactly, in a medical setting, but he couldn't find the strength to form a fist. Like a single prick of the skin could deflate him, as though he were made of air.

Reclining there, trying not to look at the IV or move his hand that held it, he kept going back to a story his father liked to tell about how Germans had been caught posing as doctors in a medical camp, intentionally infecting the American patients with influenza. He would trot the story out any time a doctor's visit were mentioned, as though the Germans might be lurking still. And then Hubert, the favorite, had almost died at twelve from appendicitis. If his mother hadn't gone to the next door neighbor in the night and asked him to take them to town in his truck, the family might have lost him. His father hadn't visited Hubert in the hospital; he never even acknowledged that Hubert had nearly died, and it had not been from influenza.

The altruistic donor was heavyset and wore black stretch pants and a tunic embroidered with wooden beads. The podium came up to her shoulders. A photographer stood just to the right, taking her photo from several angles.

Beverly took umbrage with the fact that the medical community called this single donor—the one who had initiated the chain with no intended recipient—the altruistic donor, as though altruism had not been involved for all the others. In the woman's remarks, Beverly listened for the story of an aunt or a best friend who had died from kidney disease, some latent self-interest that had inspired the donor, but it never came. She had always wanted to work for a nonprofit doing international aid, the woman said, but an internship in college had led to a successful career in film production. "Then I turned for-ty," she said, dragging out the word for dramatic effect. "And all my friends were doing marathons and I thought, um, no. Running shorts still give me gym class flashbacks. I shudder to think."

Everyone laughed at the altruistic donor. She had saved all their lives and now was being funny, too. Without the altruistic donor, there could be no chain, there would only be a little swap—two incompatible couples exchanging kidneys. Beverly wanted to be the one at the podium, the one who had set the dominoes in motion.

It was true, what scripture said: it was better to give than receive. She had never, even in the worst of her illness, wished her mantle on anyone else—better her than Sheldon or her daughters; she, Beverly, could handle it. But now she was suddenly jealous of Sheldon, sitting erect and dumb beside her, unaware of the gift he had been given. For the first time, she wished their situations had been reversed, that she'd been allowed to be the donor. In church, she had never cared for sermons about grace: forgiveness, righteousness, and prudence, those she could do. But grace was forced upon you, you didn't earn it, you didn't deserve it; it was your job to receive it, whether you wanted to or not. It was the hardest part of being a Christian, their pastor had often said, and now she wanted to grab Sheldon by the shoulders and shake him, to ask him if he understood how hard it was to receive.

Everyone started clapping, and Beverly clapped too, and then they stood, pushing back their chairs, and the clapping seemed to shake the notion out of her. She wondered where she'd been, where she had gone to just then. She was hungry, she decided. Her stomach was upset from the night before and she was only hungry.

The woman before Sheldon had golden eyes; there was the rest of a face, to be sure, but it was hard to observe it under the force of those eyes. A curl of dark hair stippled with gray had come loose and hung over one eye, obscuring it, and it was the only other thing he noticed. Her name was Amrita, and he found her too young to bear a kidney as old and worn as his own. He feared she would begin to feel tired just seeing the source of the organ. After all, he had been right at the cutoff. A few months older, and his kidney would not have qualified. His daughters Thisbe and Laurel had both offered more than once to donate their own kidneys instead, but he wouldn't hear of it.

Amrita took his hand in both of hers. The palms had a polished quality, like river rocks.

She motioned for them to sit, and he followed her. "Is that your wife, there?" she said, nodding with her head.

He had forgotten Beverly. He turned to see his wife speaking with a woman who bore a strong resemblance to her.

"That's my brother," Amrita said, pointing out a striking young man in a camel sports coat.

They were from New Jersey but worked in the city. She had twins, a boy and a girl, and produced a photograph of them. They were darker than their mother, but had the same golden eyes, and wore what looked like Easter garments. "Do you have children?" she asked, and he managed to find himself again.

He had pictures. Of course he did. He pulled out his wallet instead of his phone. She murmured with approval when he told her what his daughters did; it was something he never would have expected, but these days people judged a man by what his daughters did for a living. "Entirely my wife's doing," he assured her.

She had a surprisingly deep voice. He thought she might be a social worker or a therapist.

"This is strange, isn't it?" she said.

"So very," he said, feeling flush with gratitude that she had said it.

"Like arranged marriage," she said.

He wanted to ask her if she had an arranged marriage—she was Indian, he was fairly certain—but was afraid to say the wrong thing. He had often offended people, without intent, and this woman had to live with his kidney; he could not afford to have her associate it with anything unpleasant.

"I don't want to frighten you with gratitude," she said. "I am sometimes on the receiving end with my patients," she said. "And I know how over-whelming that can feel. But still," she said. "I must say it. I must tell you how grateful I am."

He shook his head. "Your patients?" he said.

"I'm a physician," she said.

"What sort?"

"Infectious disease," she said. "You're smiling. What is it?"

Josie was from Jonesborough, Tennessee, the oldest town in the state, home to the Chester Inn built in 1797, where no less than three presidents had stayed. Her eldest daughter worked for the National Storytelling Festival, her son was a forest ranger, and her youngest worked at the Cumn-Go, but that was only temporary on account of her still getting her education. As for herself, she used to work at the Sewing Bee on weekends, mostly catering to the quilters, before her husband's diabetes—type 1, no fault of his own—had gotten so bad she couldn't go in. He had put in his twenty years already in the force, so now they could both retire early.

All of this Beverly learned in the first thirty seconds of meeting Josie. She was ten years younger than Beverly but had sunspots across her cheeks and jowls that aged her. Like Beverly, she had short hair, dyed a champagne blonde that barely covered the gray, and wore wire-rimmed glasses. The shirt she was wearing looked like a poster project—all glitter and appliqué. Over the yoke was a tremendous dragonfly, positioned so that it was flying straight for Josie's jugular. As though this embellishment weren't enough, the entire background of the shirt was a blue swirl, a pattern somewhere between tie-dye and camouflage. It wasn't that Beverly hadn't seen this kind of shirt before; she saw them on older women all the time, but had never felt so confronted by one.

Josie was still talking and when she stopped, Beverly realized to her alarm it was because she'd asked a question.

"This is really something," Beverly said.

Josie and her husband Rick had bought themselves a thirty-five-foot 2009 Itasca Suncruiser (they had considered the Keystone, but had splurged for the Itasca in the end) with just 25,000 miles on it with a jackknife sofa and stainless steel appliances. They'd be gone for at least six months and though she wasn't sure what her youngest would do if she had to make her own meals, she thought it might be best for her to learn to manage.

"Where are y'all going to go?" she asked Beverly.

"We don't have an RV," she said.

"I used to read all these books when I was kid," Josie said. "Like my eldest, Jennifer. You could not get my nose out of a book. And I always thought I would go places and now I've barely made it out of Tennessee. But Jen went to college up north and went on a European tour and seeing her do all that made me feel silly for not doing it. Now with Rick and his new kidney, I guess I'm fresh out of excuses."

Beverly searched the room for Sheldon. She had been keeping him in sight as she had made her way over to Josie but had lost him.

"You should really see it," Josie said. "It's a beaut."

"Mm-hmm," Beverly muttered.

"It's right here in the parking lot," she said. "Go get your husband. That who you looking for?"

"Pardon?"

"People love it." Josie was standing now, grabbing Beverly by the arm. "Go get your husband, and I'll go get mine with the keys. I won't take no for an answer."

Was this like a time-share opportunity? Beverly thought. Josie could have been a paid representative of Itasca recreational vehicles.

Beverly hoped she and Sheldon might retreat to their room for a few minutes, but by the time she found him by the coffee bar, Josie was right behind her.

"How is Blanche?" he said, grinning in an irritating way.

"Blanche is a Josie," she said. "Here they come."

Sheldon put his hand out, but when Josie reached to take it, he pulled her to him and embraced her, crushing the dragonfly against his chest, while her husband Rick and Beverly looked on. Then he hugged Rick, too, and Rick patted him so hard on the back Beverly thought he would burp.

It was hot in the parking lot and even hotter with the four of them in the Suncruiser, which did not dampen Josie's enthusiasm for its features: the flat-screen TV, the queen-sized bed, the shower that looked like a cryogenic chamber.

Beverly watched Sheldon wipe his brow—whether from the heat or from his claustrophobia, she wasn't sure.

Josie directed them to sit on the main cabin couch while she and Rick sat in the front seats, like they were about to turn the RV on. "Just the two of you, anywhere in the country. I tell you," Josie said, looking out the windshield as though she could see a landscape there. She and Rick swiveled to face them.

"Josie likes to keep a journal of every grocery store chain or convenience store we've never heard of before. Those little things. It's a big country."

"Press that button," Josie said to Sheldon, pointing to the side of the couch. "Just press it."

The couch purred and began to tip back.

"Keep going. You two can go all the way back like that," she said. "An extra bed for our guests."

Now they were on their backs, facing the underside of Josie's oak cabinetry, their legs resting awkwardly, like they were injured and forced to keep their feet elevated above their hearts. Beverly strained her neck to sit up properly.

"Can you make us upright again, please?" Beverly asked Sheldon.

"You two the cruising types, instead?" Rick asked.

Were those the two types into which people of their age were divided? Beverly thought.

"Sheldon. Can you make us upright again?"

"It's stuck," he said.

"Let me help with that," Rick said, but his help proved unhelpful. "It does this sometimes," he said. He knelt down on Sheldon's side.

"We bought it used and we think the former owners had kids in here," Josie said. "For the first few months we found hidden sticky spots."

When the couch proved intractable, Beverly and Sheldon had no choice but to wiggle themselves over the bump and off the sides, where they stood looking back at it, not unlike the way they had looked at the cruise ship when they'd disembarked, as though it had unexpectedly harmed them.

"We went on a cruise once," Sheldon said.

"We are *not* the cruising types," Beverly admitted. Sheldon looked at her.

Up until then, she had only told people Sheldon was not the cruising type. In truth, she had not enjoyed the cruise any more than he had, a fact she had not shared with her daughters. She had displayed a woven basket on the living room wall, as a world traveler might do, but she had been bloated and queasy the entire time and found the ports dirtier and more hectic than she imagined. There were beggars and trash and the smell of rot, and the cheapness of so many painted wooden magnets and toys made her want to scream. She was afraid she was not as adventurous as she imagined.

Beverly's phone buzzed in her handbag. It was Laurel.

Mom, photos? I want to see the donor. Has Dad passed out yet?

Beverly had forgotten that she was with her donor. If Beverly could get a word in, she was obligated to thank Josie. But the gratitude had left her just then. Standing in the stagnant air of the Suncrusier, twenty more years of life—which had always seemed impossibly short—now seemed long, too difficult to fill. There had been the children and grandchildren, and Beverly's illness, and any imperative to do something with herself had been easily deferred. The problem of Sheldon had become interchangeable with the problem of Beverly, because she had never really had to know what kind of woman she would be unencumbered by Sheldon, and she was no longer sure she wanted to know.

"I'm thirsty," Beverly said, and Josie and Rick and Sheldon all stepped into action to move her back into the hotel, because once you'd had kidney failure, the word thirst became encoded with a deeper, unquenchable need.

"Excuse me," Beverly said to the only woman in the purple Donate Life T-shirt she could find in the hotel. "I haven't seen *People* magazine. They were supposed to be here."

"I know," the girl said, looking at her phone. "We were upstaged by the Pope."

"The Pope."

"An unexpected medical procedure."

"He's only one person," Beverly said, and the woman laughed and touched Beverly's shoulder, like that had been a good joke.

"Who else is here?" Beverly said.

"The photographer is excellent," the woman said. "You're going to love the photos. And they'll be up on the Donate Life website."

"The website?" she repeated back, wanting her tone to be strident, even shrill. "The website?" But it had come out so matter-of-fact. Why was her voice so incapable of displeasure?

She pulled her compact out of her purse and pressed powder on her cheeks. Then she snapped the compact shut in a disapproving way.

Now they were to line up, just as they had at the airport gate, by letter and number. Rick was R 32, Josie D 33, Beverly R 34, Sheldon D 35, Amrita R 36, and her brother D 37. Sheldon introduced Beverly to Amrita and the brother, whose name was Neil, in the moments before the picture was taken. Beverly wanted to ask them questions, but they were beautiful in a way that made her feel chastened.

The last time she had seen the blissed-out look on Sheldon's face was at Laurel's undergraduate commencement, when she had been summa cum laude.

"You've always had a weakness for a good-looking face," she whispered to him, looking over at Amrita.

"Nonsense," he said. "I married you for your legs."

Then the photographer swept across them in one great panorama, like they were a wonder of the world too wide for the lens. Beverly had wanted a commencement and this was it. But to commence, as she had heard at every child graduation she'd ever endured, was not to end but to begin.

Beverly did not know what she would do with this feeling, this imperative to commence, but already she feared that the execution of it would be small. She would go to one of those paint and drink studios, where everyone in the class had too much Sauvignon Blanc while attempting to produce the exact same painting with the same techniques. She would come home with a blue pond set against purpled mountains and a little house in the distance with one lit window. And she would hang her canvas up in the den and think that hers had been better than most. Perhaps she had missed her calling.

When the group photo arrived in the mail, it would be Sheldon who took it to the framer to get a custom frame and put it up in the hallway. Beverly would catch him stopping at it. She thought he was imagining his ennobled kidney off fighting disease in its upgraded owner. Living vicariously through an organ. But for weeks after, when they were sitting at the kitchen table, Sheldon would say "Good old Josie," and wonder where the RV was headed off to now.

TEETH APART

KOFI ANNAN WALKS INTO THE BAR. IT SOUNDS LIKE THE SET-up to a bad joke, but it is an ordinary evening here in Davos. Outside, meeting goers are swaddled in jackets thick as mattresses, and Laura has forgone her perilous walk around the town just before dusk. The treachery of the ice seems like part of the joke to her, as though this place was chosen not for its remoteness or neutrality but for its ability to fell world leaders, to add the human element of sprained ankles and sore asses.

If this were a joke, Kofi would be flanked by Madeleine Albright and Angelina Jolie, ordering pints. But Laura doesn't know bar jokes; she only knows jokes about yogis and linguists, the latter variety told by her ex-husband Arthur and ending with Noam Chomsky delivering punch lines like *wait a minute, you're* telling *it all wrong.*

Kofi Annan wears a gray suit, followed by men on either side who thrum with the menacing energy of mechanical wings. Kofi has a certain presence that Laura would expect in a well-bred man, but his face doesn't reflect the strain of such a compromised life. Only his eyes are partly cloudy—whether from age or diplomacy, it's hard to say.

All week, Laura has been secretly hoping to run into him, in a giddy and almost guilty way, as though he is an old lover. He is an old love, at least. Tomorrow is the last day of the trip, and Laura had started to think she wouldn't find him. Seeing him walk in, she realizes how badly she wants to be judged, in the way only God or an old lover can so scathingly deliver.

But perhaps that sudden desire for abuse is the scotch talking, bringing her back to old ways. She has decided to make Davos a space outside of space, and allow herself to drink, to smoke, to eat fat little sausages. As though Davos were Las Vegas. Because physically, she is a woman of discipline. She was born in Montana to extreme people, and in the absence of a hard-labor life, she has found other ways to work her body. She wonders if extremism isn't built in to her genetic programming. She isn't wild about DNA, about all the biological determinism of recent years. Although she's sure there's some truth to it. There is some truth to just about everything.

The scotch is not of her own choosing. Her second husband, Peter, was supposed to meet her an hour ago but was delayed at a session. It was too cold to go back outside, so she opted to play field observer, getting a good look at these World Economic Forum people from the perch of a barstool. She wasn't there a minute when a man slid a glass in front of her and took the neighboring corner seat.

"Toast to the end of the world?" he said.

She couldn't *not* toast to that, especially coming from a man who looked like he could have engineered the whole thing, the elegantly aging sort, bold enough not to ask a lady what she's drinking.

"It's the end of somebody's world all right," she said, lifting her glass to him. She couldn't remember the last time she'd had scotch; she expected it to hit her throat like a fist but it crawled in smooth, just thin, teasing fingers. That is the difference, her husband would say, that quality makes.

Funny to drink with a real Davos man at his own funeral, she thinks. She has chosen to come in 2009, of all years, only when the World Economic Forum has reached new levels of irrelevance, when the news reports that the Davos man is dead, depressed, or having a midlife crisis. He's taking Prozac or buying a Porsche.

She remembers other worlds ending—being eight and waking to an unusually silent morning in July in Montana, convinced the rapture had come. Her father must have taken the dogs out for a run. Paralyzed in her cool sheets, she was convinced God had left her behind. She started to plan how she would stay alive as the lone girl on a ranch for delinquent boys.

She remembers a hotel rooftop in 1999 with old college friends, knowing the world was not going to end but loving the recklessness of the moment, the wind pushing them back from the edge. She remembers September 11, not knowing what kind of end that would prove to be. You wait for the world to end, and then it does. And ends and ends again.

This time, here in Davos, it's a whimper and not a bang.

She has been getting a lot of attention from men the last few days. For starters, there aren't many female attendees at the forum's annual meeting, and apparently, the wives have stayed at home. She can picture it: *Women of Davos,* the world's most sedate twelve-month calendar.

At some point in her early forties, Laura became handsome. She had been attractive in her youth but almost plain. Not the sort of woman men send drinks to at the bar. But age has done something to her; it is as though this face has been waiting for the flesh to thin so it could reveal itself. At least she can appreciate the attention in a way she wouldn't have as a younger woman.

When Kofi begins to walk toward a back room, the man who ordered the scotch gets up. She could have eulogized with him for a while, but he excuses himself and goes to Kofi, who cups both of the man's hands with his own when they shake. She has never been left for a diplomat before.

Laura has been working more on a certain mindfulness, reading a lot of Shinzen Young and practicing exiting the body by focusing on sight, on the objective visual field. But in this place, it has been particularly hard to stay with what's in front of her. Shinzen says that the visual field is uniquely loaded with memory triggers that take you right into fear or fantasy. She is trying to just *see* Kofi, for instance, but instead she is thinking of a story from the newspaper about Kofi being honored at Brooke Astor's home. Astor was one hundred at the time, and turned to her friend Henry Kissinger sitting beside her at dinner and asked, "Who is that black fellow sitting across from me?" When Kissinger told her it was Kofi Annan, she asked, "Is he distinguished?"

A doyenne of her age and power must have seemed a withered white oracle, a woman alive only to transmit supernatural power. The questions must have sat in front of Kofi, like a transcript from the book of life on his day of reckoning: *Who is this black man across from me? Is he distinguished?*

For the first few days of the Davos trip, Laura distracted herself with museums and walks through town. She read books, although none about economics. She'd intentionally packed fluff.

Her husband Peter is the invitee, and she is the guest. She is the wife of the invitee. Unbelievable, in a way. Her husband, who is as loyal, athletic, and bright as a dog. A man who has smiled his way through life. He meets her dumb, unconscious needs she has never been able to acknowledge. He has made her terribly happy.

Why does she feel this sudden need to justify Peter when she never has before? Being here is too much like facing an invisible inquisitor, a place where you come for answers but are the subject of the questions instead. You save up a lifetime of thoughts and when you're in front of the big man himself, it is all too big to chip away at—and any word limits a conversation you do not want limited. You want it to remain vast and full of the possible, the world solved like a mathematical proof. And you want to be forgiven.

She grew up in a place where people talked to God. Her parents were in charge of spiritual development on a boys' ranch—her father serving as chaplain, her mother as cook and social secretary. The family lived on the grounds in a small brown house provided by the church. Because her father's work was a calling, they seemed to think they could pay him almost nothing. Or perhaps they'd just surmised that he wasn't the sort of man who'd complain. And they were right. It was like a mining town. As long as you stayed and kept working, everything was fine, but you could never have the means to leave.

When she was young, she had thought of her home as a dangerous place. She understood that her parents had to sacrifice everything—even their own daughter's safety—to do God's work. It was like a Bible story to her, the kind of thing God asked righteous people to do all the time.

The summer she turned eleven, the boys began to frighten her in a new way. It wasn't what any one boy said or did, it was a feeling of their omnipresence, a creepy watchfulness that before had been only reserved for God. Then she thought: What kind of parents would do this, would raise their children among delinquent boys, in a place with almost no other playmates? The imaginary friends who had occupied so much of her time abruptly abandoned her, and now all she could see were the rundown buildings, the miles of fences, and the dirty rows of teeth on boy after boy.

But by the time she was eighteen and old enough to leave, the boys— with their starved, empty looks—no longer seemed like the dangerous ones at all.

Laura is almost drunk. She decides to retire to the restaurant section of the lodge, set up with tufted booths and proper tablecloths. It's still early, and the server seats her in a warm corner at the back and brings her a basket of soft bread. There's a view from her side of the booth of the little street, the buildings with their shutters and dormers and hand carved eaves and the chalets nestled up against the mountainside. It is a setting more fitting for an international meeting on chocolate or cheese or wooden dolls. The sun is setting and the town looks too idyllic to last, as though it will fade away along with the light. If she were a little girl, this would be a fairy-tale future, a scenic European town and a man who runs the world, a modern day prince, handsome and deferential to his wife. The thought makes her laugh.

It's unlike Peter to leave her waiting. He was surprised when she agreed to accompany him on this trip, of all trips. In their six-year marriage, she hasn't often traveled with him, since it disrupts the rhythm of her yoga practice. But she has opted for disruption now. Lately, she has felt untested, living as a tourist on a smooth sailing ship; she wants to crawl down into the squealing grime of the engine room, to be among the raw elements and the crude man-made extractions and to see if it makes her slow, still dance on the deck seem more or less absurd.

When Peter finally arrives, his face is flush from the cold. Laura likes seeing him in this weather, in a camel coat and striped scarf. He has a strong jaw and deep-set eyes that she would have found too obviously handsome when she was younger. She wanted her men to be unusual looking. Now she wonders if she didn't think herself worthy of a handsome man.

He comes to her side of the booth and kisses her on the check with his cold lips, apologizing for keeping her waiting.

He has never seen her drunk. When they met, she was already an ascetic. She wonders if he'll notice, if words will even come out right. She's been sitting there silently for some time, chewing on a crust of bread.

"What happened?" she says when she finally finds her words. "Is

Queen Rania here after all?" Her husband is disappointed that the beautiful women have not come this year.

"You might not have seen me for the rest of the week." He winks. He is a winker. "You know," he said. "Davos is *no* place to have an affair."

"They should import some women just for the occasion," she says. "It couldn't hurt attendance."

"Although it might affect concentration."

"This is sounding too much like a conversation from the fifties," she says.

"Haven't you heard? The fifties are back. Super hot."

This kind of banter is important to him, much in the way debates were to her first husband. She had once believed those debates were central to her arousal, that she was the sort of woman for whom politics was foreplay.

When she first became serious about her practice, she had blamed yoga for her disinterest in sex with Arthur, believing that yoga had created a body free from the dynamics that sex required. That there wasn't enough power structure left. She remembers having rationalized it quite nicely. But it was that she and Arthur had never connected bodily during sex. They had been acting out something happening in their minds, like their bodies were marionettes strung up by their assertions.

"How was your day?" Peter says.

"You're looking at it," she says. "But I did see Kofi Annan. He's here somewhere in a back room."

"Just him? No Bill Gates sighting?" All week Peter has been joking that he'll end up at the urinal next to Gates.

When he laughs she can see his wrinkles. He has magnificent wrinkles, especially around his eyes, and thick, graying hair. She never tires of looking at him and it makes her feel like a girl.

"What is it?" he says.

"I keep thinking funny things," she says.

"You *look* a little funny."

She's starving. She has spent so many hours drinking and nibbling at bar nuts—another indulgence—that she hasn't noticed her hunger taking complete dominion.

"I want a steak," she declares. "With horseradish."

Maybe tomorrow she will give in more, even sneak into a forum panel. What harm could it do?

"I don't think I heard you right," he says.

She doesn't claim to be a vegetarian because she doesn't find declaring things like that to be useful, but it is true that she rarely eats meat. It has been a couple of years since she's even had a piece of fish.

"And steak frites," she says.

"Is this your final supper?" His forehead frowns, but he's starting to smile. "Is there something you're not telling me?"

Later, when the steak arrives, she has a moment of pause. She's not sure she can stomach it after all. It looks large and odd, like a shoe on the plate, its little garnish of green parsley only making the mass stranger in relief.

But then some old instinct kicks in and she feels hungry again.

"This is really a sight," he says, watching her.

"So what did you learn today?" she asks.

"The failures of America are spreading like a disease," he says. "Oh, and what is old is suddenly new again." He grins.

"Is it?"

"Several experts agree. Also, in the future, we won't have to speak. The written word is seven times faster than the spoken. So for efficiency's sake, we won't talk."

"We could be accomplishing *seven* times more during this dinner?"

Ordering the steak was ill-conceived; she'd forgotten the texture of it, dull and tough like a baseball in her mouth. Maybe this entire trip was poorly thought out. It feels foolish in a way, her trying these old things on like clothes at the back of her closet that no longer fit.

He puts down his fork and wipes his mouth.

"Actually, today was a little scary," he says. "A lot of science fiction. All about biomechanatronics and neuroeconomics."

"Neuroeconomics?" she says. "Sounds like an ad man's wet dream."

That's a word her ex would have loved to unpack; if Arthur were here in Davos, he would be casting an invisible linguist's net wherever he went, then holing up in his hotel room, laying out his captured words on the bed like stolen treats. Sometimes she wishes she didn't have his ears, but that is how it is with marriage. They were together for fourteen years, and it is as though he has permanently occupied parts of her brain. It is not that she thinks *of* him—because she rarely does—but she thinks *like* him. To this day, she still has to defend her own assessments against his.

She knew when she fell in love with Peter that she may very well have been looking for the anti-Arthur. And she knew she had found him when she and Peter visited the Temple of Dendur at the Metropolitan Museum of Art. She had been there years before during graduate school with Arthur, who had spent the entire afternoon talking geopolitics, artifice, simulacrum. All Peter had said, so many years later, was *wow*. He seemed to derive physical power from the space, as if he'd captured some ancient force. And while Laura understood the artifice, she, too, felt the awe, the sanctum frozen in time, surrounded by the indoor pool, the glass wall with a view of Central Park. In grade school, she'd had a glittery gold keychain that read *God is Awesome*. She had understood even then that it did not mean God is cool but that God is worthy of awe, and she would look at the glitter and try to imagine the vastness.

Sometimes she goes to a little replica Temple of Dendur in her mind during her meditation; it is like a trapdoor that leads to feelings of vastness and human smallness both. It is a way to see all of God's three faces at once, and they are not meant to be seen that way; you are meant to turn around the three-headed monster, accepting all but only gazing upon one at a time.

She has thought of Peter as Mr. Wow ever since, a private nickname she has not even shared with him. She watches him gently beckon the waiter with his hand in a gesture of pure confidence, the ease that comes with unexamined authority.

"Let me ask you this," Peter says. "There was an entire debate about whether dopamine is the currency of the brain. I mean, what does that *mean?*"

"I don't know. But if there's a currency, there's a market. How about a futures market? You should get in on that early."

He lets her tease him this way. To Peter, economics means exotic products, vast exchanges of bundled nothingness. To her, it conjures images of people finding ways to keep their hearts beating.

Out of the corner of her eye, Laura notices a man approaching the table; she assumes it is someone from the day's panels stopping to say hello to Peter. She is watching Peter's face to get a read on whether this is someone he looks forward to seeing, gauging how effusive and wifely she should be. But Peter is watching her instead, waiting for her reaction.

She looks up and sees a ghost. Even with the beard, she recognizes Dr. Campos immediately but cannot respond yet. It is as though her brain is still sifting through old images of him, waiting to verify his identity.

"I'm old and fat," he says. "I wasn't sure if you'd recognize me." He *is* older and has a belly threatening his shirt buttons. But he still looks charming.

"Of course I *know* you," she says, and stands to embrace him. He smells of cigar smoke and sweat. He must be how old? Nearly seventy. He was in his forties when she was a student in Managua.

"But you, Dr. Harmon," he says, pulling away and grabbing her by the shoulders, "are better looking. That does not seem fair at all." It has been so long since someone has called her doctor; she was a sociology professor for such a brief while.

On her feet, she feels her drunkenness more fully. She is struck by a wave of sentiment that must be amplified by the scotch. It has been so long since she's thought of Managua, the hot green of the place, swampy air sour with diesel. She was lonely at the time and constantly sick, but it is hard not to romanticize it now, especially in this cold place.

"What brings you here?" he says. Then he raises his hand. "No. I'm going to venture a guess." He closes his eyes. His accent is fainter than she recalls, probably from time spent abroad. "The department of labor," he says. "No, too cliché. An NGO of some kind. Amnesty International?"

She tries to protest, but he keeps on going.

"This is my husband," she interrupts. Peter looks relieved and extends his hand. "This is Dr. Campos."

"Nestor," he says. "Please."

"Sit down," she tells him. "Join us for a while if you can." She hadn't imagined running into an old acquaintance, but now that she has, it feels as though this is what she's come to Davos for. This place is filled with all her old loves.

Nestor waves at a table across the room, and Peter shifts over to accommodate him on his side of the booth.

"You're going to be ashamed of me," Nestor says. "I'm on a panel about foreign capital in Central America. I am the world's worst ex–labor secretary," he laughs. "A life of action is a life of compromise, eh? But what are *you* doing here among the fat cats in the snow? You are not fat," he says. "Are you on a crusade?"

"Actually, my husband is the attendee. I'm just tagging along."

She can see Nestor's surprise, but he quickly says, "Ah. So *you* are the fat cat." He seems to find the phrase funny, and the way he says it, it sounds like phaatcaat. "And you are married to the fat cat."

"I'm afraid so," she says. When someone talks like that, she is reminded that they are wealthy; sometimes it seems as though wealth is as wasted on her as youth is on the young.

Peter is smiling because he is trained to do so. He can pretend almost any conversation is engaging. But she knows him. He's wondering if Dr. Campos is an old lover. In fact, there was always a flirtation between Laura and Nestor, a sense that they could become lovers at their next encounter. They kept in touch for years, until she had moved or he had moved, and her time in Nicaragua seemed hazy and far.

"This one is much better looking than the first husband," Nestor says.

"Oh?" Peter says. "Keep talking."

"Dr. Campos and I go back to Universidad Centroamericana," she says. "He was a professor there at the time."

It isn't that she has never mentioned her time in Nicaragua to Peter, it's just that it's been a postcard mention, something slid in with all her other travels.

"You know," Nestor says, turning directly to Peter. "I had never met anyone like her. I had not met that many North Americans at all, back then. I thought maybe they were all like Laura. I thought this one would disappear into the jungle somewhere. I used to tease that she was a guerilla. A little gringa guerilla."

"This one?" Peter says. He's looking at her curiously. He is probably imagining that she'd have to unwrap herself from padmasana—lotus pose—first. "Were you studying there?"

She nods, intentionally stuffing a piece of steak into her mouth. It feels strange to be questioned by her own husband, as though they are on a first date.

"I remember," Nestor says. He lifts his finger as though testing the direction of the wind. "I'm an old man now. I have to do this. I have to test the memory again and again." He has always been a man of many words. "It was something to do with the media. The media coverage of the revolution, if I recall. I know that's correct. Although I can't say I remember more than that. I don't recall the thesis, exactly."

"It seems you remember about as much as I do," she says.

"Other Fulbright scholars came after," he says, "but none of them could hold their liquor as well." He pounds the table as he says it, emits a choking kind of laugh. Peter shrinks away a bit.

Her tolerance was legendary then, especially for her petite frame. She had a taste for tequila and ouzo and any other alcohol sure to make anyone an eventual teetotaler. The only intoxicant her body can tolerate now is maté that she brews at home.

Nestor turns to Peter. "Your wife should be on a panel here."

"Oh, I agree," Peter responds, full of foolish husbandly pride, as though any dutiful man would agree that his wife could run the world.

Nestor shakes his head. He waves at a server coming past, and the man stops to take more drink orders. She is already drunk, Nestor seems nearly there, and Peter is far behind. She should stop this.

"So how have you found the discussions so far?" Nestor asks. "The mood of this thing."

He is looking only at her, waiting for her answer.

"I haven't attended any of the sessions," she says.

"The mood is downright chipper," Peter adds. "Considering."

"You're serious?" Nestor says to her. "Why have you come?"

"I'm vacationing," she says.

"In this weather?"

She deserves the dubious look he gives her, she thinks. She could be in the Amazon at the World Social Forum instead, spared of the chewing pain she gets in her feet in cold weather, a permanent hangover from frostbite she had in high school.

There's a part of her that wants to go to the sessions, but she doesn't really need to hear the debates about whether the cure for capitalism is more capitalism. She can re-create the arguments in her own head.

But she wants to feel the apocalyptic air, the collective energy of ants crawling over each other in an anthill collapsing around them. She doesn't want to feel that the day of reckoning has come and she's been left behind again.

"I am confused," Nestor begins. He starts mumbling gripes in Spanish. He does not understand any of this, he says, thinks it is an elaborate joke. Peter is watching him. She is sure he can tell that whatever Nestor is issuing, it isn't a declaration of love. Peter is always uncomfortable when he doesn't understand what's being said. She raises her hand to stop Nestor, but he is already done. "*Como?*" he finally says.

But she is at least a decade past explanations of this sort. She shrugs. His confusion is not really her concern. There is no way to take him from that point, so long ago, to this point, not without his image of her completely degrading along the way. It would be impossible to hold the pieces together. Her experience to get here cannot be summarized. It can be aphorized, at best.

To tell the story, she would have to stop and switch to a different language. Both the language of academia and the language of yoga have led her to the same lonely horizon, where no one except the fully initiated can understand her. So she has become the sort of woman who goes on silent retreats, a woman who can go for weeks in her own mind. She has thrown out the lingua with the linguist.

"You must tell me," Nestor says to Peter. "How did you two meet? How *do* two such people meet?"

Peter doesn't acknowledge the insult; he seems grateful to be spoken to, and in English.

"She was my yoga instructor," he says.

He begins to tell the story about how his girlfriend at the time had convinced him to go. It was not the kind of class Laura usually taught, but she had been subbing for a friend who was out of town.

As she remembers it, it began with a simple movement, a hand placed at the back, right at the bottom of his trapezius. She had done this many times before, and it never failed to make the recipient feel she'd worked some special yogic magic. She could have talked of scapular elevation and depression, but most people didn't care to know. Instead, she would apply a slight pressure at an exact location and release the muscle's hold. She would tell the student about fight or flight, their evolutionary impulse to tense their shoulders. For advanced students, she might explain that they were breathing with their trapezius, and she might gently guide them back, and back again, to the diaphragm.

Peter was no exception, but he had been a particularly bad case. He lived in his upper shoulders, asking them to breathe, lift, and think for him. He marveled at the simple pressure on his back; he said it was like a drain had been cleared, something come loose and flushed. She told him he'd get more oxygen to his brain. He interpreted that to mean he would earn more money.

It was later, though, that she taught him a simple mantra: lips together, teeth apart. This had proved nearly impossible for him at first. He could only manage it for a few seconds at a time. But the simplicity was effective for him. If he could master nothing else, he could return to this. Lips together, teeth apart. He credited the mantra with so much of what came after. Although it was simple, really. He breathed deeper. He clenched less and ached less. He had always had a quick temper when it came to his working life, but his anger was like a combustible that had to be ignited by his flinty teeth; without their tension, it failed to build. He credited the mantra and thus credited her by extension; it was classic transference, and she had tried to tell him so. She remembered herself as an undergraduate mistaking some new kernel of insight as pangs of love for a professor. She'd thought he would outgrow it, would see eventually that she was not his lucky charm.

But here they are. If time proves anything, this is love, after all. Not that it matters to her anymore what it is. She's developed a functionalist streak in her middle age, and this thing with Peter works.

"Oh I know," Peter is going on. "I see your look, Dr. Campos. You should never date your instructor."

"Is he joking?" Nestor finally says.

"Not at all," she says.

"Yo-ga."

"Yes, yoga," she says.

"Oh, she's very sought after," Peter tells him. He always has the need to do this, to legitimize her profession to others. Whereas she's never been entirely comfortable with it being a profession at all. Peter can't help commercializing things. "Quite in demand."

The next round of drinks has arrived, and Peter is working quickly to catch up. Laura knows she should stop drinking. She chews on another piece of bread while staring at the barely touched steak in front of her. The piece of meat makes her think of one of the Buddha's crudest examples of the perception of self: that the butcher perceives a cow until at some point when it is carved up and divided into small enough parts and the perception of meat arises instead. As the perception of self as a thing no longer seems a thing at greater resolution, when separated into parts that normally fall together. It is not that Laura has forgotten her past or forsaken it or even that she no longer believes in a self. There is still a selfiness, she might say, that she perceives. But it is no longer a *personality*. But what the hell can she say to Nestor? You are looking for a cow and all I'm giving you is meat.

Nestor sits and drinks, uncomprehendingly. He begins speaking in Spanish again. She can see a speech coming on. He is one of those men given to long pronouncements, or at least he was when she knew him. He takes another drink, either to arrest himself or grease the pipes.

But this time, Peter raises his hand. "What is he saying?" he asks.

Nestor stops and regards her, as though eager to hear her translation. "He is asking about where we live," she lies. "What it's like there."

For a moment, they are silent. The sounds of the restaurant sweep in, and the clamor of knives and forks is so loud, she wonders how her mind has relegated it so perfectly to background noise.

"I was asking no such thing," Nestor says. "I can see clearly that you've gone to California. You've gone and have not come back." He adds a quick laugh as though it were a joke. He takes a long drink, then puts the glass down too hard. He turns to Peter. "On the contrary, I was telling a story," he says. "Remembering when Laura made all of us in the university get on our knees so she could pour tequila down our throats. She practically threw me down, bruising my kneecaps. Then she had the idea we would dance, all the academics." He stops and looks at her. "You were the worst dancer I'd ever met. I didn't know a woman could dance so badly."

"Hey now," Peter says. "Don't insult my wife."

"Am I the one insulting?"

"It's true," she says. She shakes her head. She had been one of those book smart girls who was scarcely aware she *had* a body.

But Nestor was not, in fact, telling this story in Spanish. Now they have both lied. He was saying she looks sexy, that she *looks* the same, and yet he doesn't recognize her. There was a time she used to justify how an academic became a yogi, tidily explaining she was a teacher either way, that both were studies in expansion and then articulation. Some people—mostly women—would be satisfied with this, nodding *ah, a nurturer.* But Laura herself has never entirely liked this narrative. When her yoga students now question the ultimate value of their practice, she is forced to offer up a lonely contradiction: personal wholeness can't create wholeness in the world, and yet nothing else can. But she is not even sure Shinzen Young believes—as he says he does—that the enlightenment of millions of individuals would heal the world.

Nestor has regrouped, turning his attention to Peter instead. He asks what Peter does. Peter begins to enthuse about alternative asset management. Nestor looks physically pained by the predictability of this answer—although not as pained as her ex Arthur had looked when she told him about Peter. He seemed to believe Peter was chosen as a personal affront to him.

Nestor starts up again in Spanish, but Peter stops him.

"I don't understand," Peter says.

"English won't help that," Nestor says.

He's free to insult *her*, she thinks, but not her husband. Peter is an innocent. She is the one who has changed—Peter has always been on a course and she has merely joined him at a late juncture.

She leans over to Nestor and smiles, like she's about to offer a sweet nothing. It is her turn to speak in Spanish. She puts on a light tone for Peter's benefit, but tells Nestor it was lovely to see him again, and now he needs to leave.

For a moment, he doesn't look at all inclined to listen. She sees him gathering a challenge behind his glazed-over eyes. But then Kofi Annan emerges from the back room he's been dining in, a larger entourage in tow. Kofi, like her own busted up deus ex machina thundering into the room. Nestor turns to watch. The man to the left of Kofi is vigorously rubbing and then patting his back, like he's burping a flatulent baby. The man is red-faced and loud, and Kofi seems to be straining to retain his usual countenance, while avoiding the man's spit. Another man is gently pulling the drunk one away, who takes this as an invitation to grab Kofi around the neck and pull him closer. Even through the rough laughter, it is a violent gesture, the confiding embrace of a mobster about to betray someone.

Nestor looks at Kofi then back at Laura, seeing an opportunity. "I'm afraid I have to leave," he says. He is obviously frustrated by the aborted speech, like a man cut short in a sexual act. He reaches his hand to shake Peter's, and then shakes his head. "The world is not the same," he says. It sounds like a half thought, like a punch line delivered too early or too late.

They forgo dessert. Peter has a glass of port while she tries to compose herself for the walk home. She had forgotten the heaviness of alcohol and meat; she feels she has put on a fat suit and been spun around like a child.

The cold air outside slaps her straight. She takes Peter's arm and lets him lead her over a dirty little embankment; it's dark, but the lights lining the path cast a yellow tint on the snow.

It feels good to be linked to him like this, arm in arm. It feels right. It is hard to explain this kind of right.

They both have their scarves wrapped up around their mouths and noses, so they don't talk on the way home. Peter feels steady and strong, and she's afraid she'll be the one to slip and take him down with her. But all of her practiced grace comes in handy.

The air is good for her; by the time they reach the hotel, some of the body suit has melted away. She's left with a sort of blankness. This was the feeling she used to dive for when she drank, this was what she had once liked.

The massive white hotel bed seems an invitation to further blankness, like she can find annihilation in this cotton vastness. She wants to blot this out, this blank decade of zeros. Davos. This ghost from the past. This demand to explain herself. She is so lost in this space that she barely registers Peter. She normally observes the smallest gesture or shift in his physical language.

He has disappeared into the bathroom for a long stretch. He usually wants to get in bed quickly, especially when he has no leftover work to do. He could spend his whole life in bed, and he has just the sort of life that doesn't permit any kind of lingering.

It is not until he comes out of the bathroom and gets into bed and she is half-asleep that she becomes aware of a tension vibrating off of him.

He is on his back, not turned toward or away from her.

"I didn't know you had a Fulbright," he finally says.

With great effort, she props herself up so she can see his face.

"I'm sure you did," she says.

"No. I would remember."

The scrim has slipped, and he has seen beyond it. It's not that she minds. It something she's put there for his sake, to preserve the kind of continuity people demand of other people's lives. Her past, fanned out flat like a series of cards, would not make the proper sense when turned over.

"I'm sorry," she says.

"It just seems like a strange thing to keep secret," he says. He's frowning ever so slightly between the eyes.

She doesn't know what to say to him without using mystical yogi-speak, which is her truth at the moment. The things she would say are meant to be realized rather than spoken, and hearing them alone sounds tinny and empty, like the sound of a cheap gong. She would tell him: the self ends, and ends, and ends again. And yet.

Wouldn't it be better to be able to speak of these things? But she married a linguist: she has been to the place where everything is spoken and nothing is said.

"It wasn't a secret," she says.

It doesn't matter to her that Nestor regarded her like a stranger, only that Peter now sees separation and feels that separation as a hurt. When what she has tried to communicate to Peter has been what's essential. If he gets any closer into the details, she will fracture and break up, like dots in a pointillist painting. His distance is the right distance.

"I'm sorry," is all she says. "I'll tell you all about it sometime. We can talk about anything you like."

She can see the tension in his jaw; he suddenly looks tired, his face holding on to awareness, to his image of her. She notices then the tension in her own mouth, the way she often discovers herself in the presence of a student, and finds herself offering up to him or her what she most needs.

"Lips together," she whispers.

"Who are you?" he says, disobeying. Then he closes his mouth.

"Teeth apart," she says.

You always have to return to the same things, she has told him. But they mean something different each time. Each cliché gets a new limb, until they are great beasts. But spoken, they are the same old clichés.

THE PROGRAM™

THINGS HAD GONE BADLY, AND BADLY IN WAYS SHE COULDN'T
have imagined, not for herself, not for anyone she knew. The story had
been in the paper—first on the bottom of the front page, then in the back
of the news section, next to an article about a new chimpanzee at the Los
Angeles Zoo. Thankfully, she had not been named. The only people mentioned were a few department heads who hadn't been aware what their
subordinates were doing. She knew. She had participated.

But now she was at The Program™ and had been handed a clipboard
with a pen attached by a flexible spiral, the kind they give you in a doctor's office. She was filling out the heavily Xeroxed introduction forms,
with lines too short for anyone's name or address to fit. Even though she'd
used her tiniest handwriting, she ran out of room and had to squish her
name around the end of the line, so that the *rg* in *Lynn Von Whittenburg*
tumbled off the edge, as though the letters had had too much. She thought
someone might interpret this as poor planning on her part, that she
should have looked ahead to the end of the line, spaced out the letters

with little dots first, making sure she'd have room for her entire name. She was positive they'd make something of it.

She lived at 3341½ West Allesandro Boulevard, so that didn't fit nicely, either. She always felt a little ashamed when she added the ½ to the street address, as though she'd be branded as a person who didn't merit an entire number. She half-considered asking for another set of forms, but the receptionist who'd handed her the clipboard was busy on a phone call, and if she asked for new paper they might think her wasteful, which was perhaps worse than lacking forethought and cramming her info onto the page.

Everything she knew about The Program™ came through a friend who'd been through every kind of self-help regimen—fad diets and new religions, real estate seminars and purification retreats, pyramid schemes and booty boot camp. With this wealth of experience, her friend had determined that The Program™ worked. Unlike other spiritual/empowerment/enrichment programs that were easy enough to come by in Los Angeles, The Program™ had a few distinct advantages. There was no travel to fancy Radisson hotels in other cities, no strange uniforms for neophytes, no belief in God necessary, and no high-profile celebrities. Best of all, The Program™ was cheap. Bargain basement cheap.

While her friend could not divulge any trade secrets of The Program™—lest she sabotage Lynn's success—she did tell her about the founder, Morton Feingold. Morton claimed he was the last Jew living in East L.A., and despite his moniker, he was a fairly young man (he was actually Morton Feingold IV, but elected to omit the suffix, not wanting his mentees to feel he was stuffy). Mr. Feingold's ancestors had lived in East L.A. when it had been filled with temples and kosher markets and before Canter's Deli had moved over to Fairfax, where it'd remained ever since. When the borscht left, orthodoxy followed, and then even reformed types had moved, so that all that was left of the Jewish population were cemeteries. It was beside one of these cemeteries that Mr. Feingold had set up his self-help center. He said he liked knowing the history was nearby, although the only thing noticeably Jewish about him besides his name were the few Yiddish phrases he peppered his inspirational talks with, and even those he used incorrectly.

The introduction forms were lengthy, and they asked Lynn a host of personal questions she hadn't anticipated answering.

Under the Health heading the questions included:

How many times a day do you typically urinate?

How many times a week do you typically defecate?

She wasn't sure. It seemed like the kind of thing she should know about herself, but she'd never bothered tallying.

Farther down, the questions under the Relationship section were even worse:

How many times have you been in love?

It was hard not to doubt things when you had to commit a number to paper. She let the tip of the pen rest in the space, then decided on a small 3. It seemed a safe number; it included those people whom she could still say, with the wisdom of hindsight, whom she had loved. It excluded all her more short-lived obsessions, or people who had merely loved her and who she only thought she'd loved back. There was Lee, a bass player she'd loved with a teenage clarity she'd never experience again; Alan, a fitness enthusiast to whom she'd been instantly and inexplicably devoted to until she realized, far too late, that she didn't particularly *like* him; and there was Craig, whose love had been so regular and steady, she'd once thought of it as continued nourishment, like small, refreshing sips of water. Until the drops had begun to feel like Chinese water torture.

The forms were long, and the sun shone on the left side of her face through the windows of the waiting room. She pinched her button-up shirt and pulled it away from her body, letting her skin breathe.

She hated forms. It was forms that had gotten her into this trouble in the first place. She had already thought about how much to reveal if they asked what had brought her to The Program™. But she hadn't yet settled on the right response: she could just admit to being fired or explain that she was one of the city clerks who had thrown the documents away. More than half a dozen employees had been let go after it'd been discovered the department wasn't processing city services forms but had been delivering them directly into the shredder. It had been a small-scale scandal in the news; investigations were pending, and more terminations were sure to follow.

It had been the kind of job where a person was doomed to swim upstream. There was always more paper in her inbox than out, even if she exhausted herself with eyestrain entering data. It was depressing to work hard and always be behind. There was a threshold she reached where she was so far behind she no longer cared about being behind: once she reached that point she couldn't be tugged back again. For years, she'd been a paper pusher. Then she'd become a paper flicker, barely able to lift her hand to even shuffle the piles covering her desk.

If she were asked, she'd say: She'd gotten communist. She'd gotten DMV.

Because The Program™ was cheap, really cheap, there was no fancy orientation with miniature muffins or cheese Danishes with tiny cups of coffee. But there was a welcome video that utilized green screen technology and placed Mr. Morton Feingold in front of a montage of inspiring settings. There was Morton, with his slight paunch in front of the Eiffel Tower, and Morton placed awkwardly in front of a flowing creek, so that he appeared to be standing in the water.

The receptionist had had a hard time getting the VCR to work. She kept blowing on the tape and punching buttons, whispering, "Damn it. This damn thing." In between curses, she turned around to smile at Lynn. All of this might have been off-putting to someone else (making him or her seriously question the legitimacy of The Program™) but Lynn Von Whittenburg would have been more wary if things had appeared too slick.

Mr. Feingold explained his program was easier than most: it wasn't cost-prohibitive (and here he made a crack about the quality of the video), it didn't require any unnecessarily strict dietary restrictions, and a person's participation wouldn't garner any emergency cult interventions from his or her family and friends (most likely because no one had ever *heard* of The Program™, Lynn thought).

When the video was over, the receptionist handed Lynn a three-fold brochure that read:

Step 1

Accumluation

Was that supposed to read Accum*ula*tion? Lynn thought.

"See you in two weeks," the receptionist smiled.

The first step was simple enough. She wasn't supposed to bathe or wash her hair or even brush her teeth for two weeks. For the full effect, the brochure strongly recommended that the participant not change his or her clothes. There followed a list of suggestions about how to approach your employer for support in your time of growth, and below that, a list of legal actions one could threaten if the employer proved unsympathetic.

Unlike other programs, The Program™ did not lure its participants with a litany of promised results, claiming to improve your sex drive, complexion, wardrobe, credit rating, capacity for love, colon function, or joie de vivre. At the headquarters, Lynn had found herself looking for bullet points or exclamation marks punctuating claims that were so far-reaching that their very incredibleness dared even the most skeptical to investigate further. She'd been puzzled at the end of the videotaped intro-duction. Where were the testimonials?

"Excuse me," she had said to the receptionist when it was over. "But what does it do?"

"Oh," she shrugged, as though it were an unexpected question. "It's different for everybody."

At first, Lynn found that unsettling. But the more she examined it, the more it seemed patently true; for a program to claim otherwise would be foolish. That explained why so many self-help seminars chose broad outcome measures to chart their successes: 80 percent of participants had a life-changing experience, or 90 percent would enroll again, they'd tell you, avoiding specifics.

Since she'd been fired, she'd worked at home stuffing mailers—it was the only job she could get—so she could fully participate in Step 1 by opting not to change her clothes for two weeks.

After several days, the khakis she was wearing stretched out and deep wrinkles formed where her hips creased when she sat down. Her hair was shiny, and she rubbed a little bit of talc into her scalp to soak up some of the grease before she headed out to the grocery store. She found herself looking down in the aisles, exposed by the bright lights. Looking dirty made her feel poor, like people were watching her, seeing what her choices said about her. She fumbled with her credit card at the register, as though she were afraid it would be declined.

"How do you like these?" the clerk asked her, holding up a can of low-fat potato chips. "I've been wanting to try them."

"They're edible," Lynn said, not meeting the girl's eyes.

When Lynn's card had been approved, the clerk ripped off the receipt and handed it to her. "Thanks for shopping with us, Mrs. Von," she said. Computers could never get her name right. And she wasn't a missus, either, but it was just as well. She could be someone else, her doppelganger Mrs. Von. When she had first moved to L.A., she'd been afraid she might not be able to make it in the city. She would stare at vagrants she passed, wondering if she could end up among them. Now here she was, scraggly and yellow, her hair tangled. Looking like this, people could see her for who she really was. Her appearance finally matched her interior state, and there was almost a comfort in that.

It was already easy to get demotivated sitting around all day watching TV and stuffing mailers, but it was far worse without a shower and change of clothes to get her going in the morning.

Time became slippery. No matter how much coffee she drank, she could not make the morning feel like morning, and she began to take miniature naps throughout the day, waking up parched and disoriented. The sluggishness grew alarming and she began to wonder if she hadn't developed mononucleosis. The grime caking her teeth was getting thicker every day. She scraped some of the crud away with her fingernails, but then wondered if that were allowed, if she weren't jeopardizing the full impact of Step 1.

So far, The Program™ hadn't expressly restricted any kind of consumption, so after 6 p.m. she fixed herself gin and tonics heavy with lime. There was a brief window of time where the gin lifted the fog and she felt light and clear-headed and she'd almost forget she was sitting in dirty clothes and underwear, and then the window would shut with as much breezy force as it had opened and she would be deliriously tired and fall asleep in a contorted position on the couch so that when she woke up in the middle of the night everything ached.

This could not be good, she reasoned. She had expected to be purified, scrubbed with a Steelo pad from the inside out, emerging with healthier looking nails and a better attitude.

As a kid, Lynn had attended a Podunk Christian school where they'd had to read *Pilgrim's Progress* every year. Christian, the main character, had traveled with an unbearably heavy satchel on his back that made facing the challenges presented by characters named Greed and Sloth even more difficult to overcome. She'd always found it a little depressing because Christian was never able to lighten his burden, not until he'd crossed over to the other side. She wondered if she would have to die as well, or if a symbolic death wouldn't do instead.

After two weeks, she had accumulated Pigpen-worthy layers of dirt on her body. When she looked in the mirror, greasy strands of her brown hair framed her oily face and she'd sprouted pimples on her chin and forehead. She felt fatter, too, though she'd hardly been eating. Without makeup or jewelry, she could see the irreversible effects of gravity in the crevices around her mouth or in the slight droop of her eyelids. She was thirty-seven, and she acknowledged each passing birthday as little as possible. Sometimes, when she wasn't paying attention, she had caught herself writing down the wrong year; she'd even started writing 19__ more than once. She knew she'd long been in denial about the velocity of her own life. She coped with this speed by refusing to do anything posthaste, to live as lazily as if her life were going to go on in syndication, never to die.

"You're so dirty!" The receptionist smiled approvingly when she returned to The Program™ headquarters at the end of the two weeks.

"Thanks?" Lynn said.

She filled out more forms, assessing her progress over the past two weeks. She felt awful and was keenly aware of how awful she felt, like she'd been on painkillers her entire life and was just now being cut off, experiencing what the world was really like.

At the bottom of the second sheet, one of the photocopied forms was crooked and cut off. *Do you see yourself as a*

It stopped.

"One of these forms is cut off," she told the receptionist when she'd completed the rest.

"What?" the young woman asked, taking the sheets from her. "Oh. That. That's not important." She shrugged.

It's not? Lynn thought. Then why is it on there? The grease caking her body was making her cranky. She wanted to tell the receptionist just how dangerous too much paperwork could be.

"You have now completed the accumulation step," Morton Feingold said on the second video. In the background, there were quick cuts of landfills and smog and polluted streams. "In this step, you experienced the effects of the environment on your physical body. You have felt the way that the *bobkes* and the *shmutz* of the world accumulate like bird feces on a windshield, obscuring your vision. The world is constantly layering itself on your physical and psychic self."

She'd cleaned her bathroom during the last week, and it had remained spotless from lack of use. She wasn't one to linger in the shower, but when she got home that afternoon, she shaved with a fresh razorblade, scrubbed her back with a loofah and her feet with a pumice stone, and lathered her scalp with extra gusto. She let the water run so hot she could hardly stand it, and it left red marks on her back and legs. The steam leaked out of the bathroom and into the hall.

Wrapped up in a robe and a hair towel, she poured herself a ceremonial glass of wine: she took a few sips that made her mouth feel dry and set the glass down. She'd never felt so accomplished from simply showering. She lit a few scented candles she'd bought at the drugstore and basked in the relief of her accomplishment. Her body felt like she'd just returned from an expensive spa where she'd been dipped in mud or scrubbed with microcrystals.

To her surprise, the inertia of the first two weeks lifted. Now she showered every morning, dressed herself as though she were heading out to a job, and sat down and stuffed her envelopes. She would take a long walk to work out the aches in her back, and she'd make herself a decent dinner. She didn't understand how a shower could have relieved her of the sluggishness she'd slipped into like quicksand. She wondered if her bouts of inertia in the past could have been so easily reversed, if only she had known what would have set her in motion.

She had come to think about whole periods of her life in terms of inertia—she wouldn't have called it that before, but now she could see more clearly the way it had been shaping things—compressing them into a dense, useless mass. What was most dangerous was the way it crept up until it had taken over, the way you could gain weight a few ounces at a time, not noticing and then not acting until you woke up one morning and realized you were fat.

Steps 2, 3, and 4 did not, as far as Lynn could tell, bear any meaningful relationship to Step 1, but she completed them with equal attention.

In Step 2, she was asked to keep the doors to her apartment unlocked for a week, which was supposed to make her realize the ways she didn't trust the world and constantly steeled herself against it, materially as well as emotionally. The message was undercut by the four-page liability waiver she had to sign, releasing The Program™ of all responsibility should Step 2 result in her being burgled, assaulted, or otherwise harmed. When she went to bed at night, she couldn't help but think she was asking for it. She liked to fall asleep to the radio but had to turn it off in case she should miss the sounds of an intruder. But the only nocturnal disturbances had come from the gentle creaks of a bed in the apartment upstairs, where some people were carefully having sex in a long, even rhythm. It was almost sad-sounding sex, which made her feel more pathetic about the longing it evoked in her. She trained herself to fall asleep early, and the week passed quickly.

In Step 3, she fasted on fruit for three days, which wasn't designed to jump-start weight loss but to allow her to feel hunger, so that she'd have a new awareness of how much her body required nourishment, how it was not a self-sustaining machine. She felt hungry all right, but it was not an enlightened kind of hunger, like hot white light emanating from her belly. She spent less time thinking about her body than about food, all the fat voluptuous foods like scalloped potatoes and macaroni and cheese.

In Step 4, she was instructed not to smile for three consecutive days, and conversely, to consciously smile for the next three and observe the difference. Just sitting at home she was surprised how difficult it was not to smile at all, even just watching TV. Smiling turned out to be comparatively easy. Morton's brochure explained that Step 4 was designed to make participants aware of the messages they send themselves and how much they influence their well-being. Lynn did not think she'd been successful; even while smiling, she was capable of thinking very negative thoughts.

Morton Feingold was even less inspiring in person than he'd appeared in the VHS tapes to which Lynn had become so accustomed. In the flesh, she could see that he was balding on top and was knock-kneed in a way that wasn't as prominent in the tapes, and his overall appearance suggested Information Technology Help Desk, the kind of guy most women would turn down.

Lynn had successfully completed Part 1, and as part of her transition to Part 2, she was granted, along with a small group of other participants, a semiprivate audience with Mr. Feingold himself.

It was good to see others, if for no other reason than to see that they existed. She liked that this program did not require group confessions or camaraderie to propel a person along: she distrusted environments that used the energy of the mass to motivate an individual. Ultimately, she figured, a person had to go home without the cheering section, and no matter what he or she pledged to do when they returned to everyday life, it was impossible to recapture the adrenaline of those collective moments.

Lynn couldn't tell much by looking at the dozen other participants. They were not a talkative group, and if The Program™ was working, it was not engendering the kind of newfangled love for humankind that made people open to perfect strangers. She did overhear one woman whisper to another that she was feeling much more "plugged-in," but Lynn wasn't entirely sure what that meant and did not think it applied to her.

It was an eclectic group, and a couple of participants appeared to understand only Spanish, because Morton Feingold translated portions of his presentation into a mangled, incomprehensible Spanglish. It was painful to listen to, but he was making such a well-meaning effort to make himself understood, and the Spanish speakers who were seated up front were making an equal effort to understand him as he explained that Part 1 had been about the Self or *Yo*, and Part 2 would focus on the Other, *el Otro*.

In Part 2, The Program™ borrowed heavily from other programs, like 12-Step and The Forum, in that it required the participant to reconcile with practically every person they'd wronged. Morton explained that they should even make a ceremonial mend with dead persons, which made Lynn think of the Day of Atonement before Yom Kippur, perhaps the last morsel of Morton's Jewish faith that had snuck into his program.

"I know you all have some reconciling to do or you wouldn't be here," he said with a laugh.

There was a lot of nodding in the room. Lynn was not, by nature, a nodder. He explained that the folks who were only interested in the other part of The Program™ always dropped out in the beginning. So the guilty ones stayed, Lynn thought. That was the common denominator among them.

The presentation had been uninspiring, but afterward Morton Feingold was surrounded on all sides by people shaking his hand and scribbling down notes on the backs of business cards. Lynn waited in her folding chair, her butt sore from the misplaced ridge on the seat. As the crowd thinned, she approached, waiting her turn and hoping he would not decide to wrap things up right before he'd gotten to her. She felt like a student waiting to ask the teacher if she could make up a test.

"Hi," he finally said, extending his hand. It was hairy, and his handshake was dead and unremarkable. He didn't do the double handshake she'd thought all inspirational types liked.

"You're nervous about Part 2," he said.

She was relieved that he had at least that much intuition. She nodded.

"Most people are," he said, which somewhat diminished the impact of his insight. "Usually it's one person. One individual they can't bring themselves to reconcile with."

"No," she said. "It's not that. It's that there are thousands."

"Ah," he said. "The thousands." He placed his hand on the small of her back. "Let's take a walk around the block."

The headquarters was surrounded by Jewish mausoleums sandwiched between rolling hills with Catholic plots and ornate statues of saints. All the cemeteries had been built adjacent on inexpensive land, which had created a stretch of still space in the dense city. Even though it might have seemed a morbid spot for The Program™ to locate, Lynn was struck by its odd appropriateness as they walked down Whittier Boulevard.

"There's one question I have to ask," he said. "Have you killed someone?"

"No," she said, with more force than she'd intended. She had been caught off guard. "No."

"Well then," he clapped his hands. "It can't be as bad as you think it is."

She figured that was a standard line. "Wait," she said. "What if I had said yes, I had? Then what?"

He shrugged. "No one has ever said yes," he said. "If they did, I'm not sure what I'd say."

Even with the cheap, really cheap prices, she couldn't believe this program was staying in business.

"Let's turn in here," he said, guiding Lynn under a moss-decayed arch that led into a cemetery. Unlike some of the spacious cemeteries without headstones, this one was crowded with elaborate family tombs and stones engraved with Hebrew letters.

"My grandfather is buried here," he said, stepping up onto the curb that separated the grass from the paved road. "Most of my family is," he continued, "but I like to visit my grandfather the most."

"Is that his?" she said, pointing to a large family tomb that read FEIN-GOLD.

"No," he shook his head. "That's another Feingold."

The right Feingold was farther along the road, near the modern mausoleum in the center.

"My grandfather sold tonics called Gold Blood. They were wildly popular for a while. Mostly just alcohol. They were supposed to cure bad temper, hysteria, surfeit," he said. "I imagine they just got people drunk. You could say he was a swindler," he said, pausing in front of the tomb.

This was not the kind of pep talk Lynn had imagined.

"People talk about corruption now," he said, "but they should have seen it then. Cops were criminals and criminals were lawyers and lawyers were gossip columnists and they were all ministers or aviators or restaurateurs who made pastrami sandwiches. L.A. was full of those people. Making it up as they went along."

He leaned in a little closer to her.

"I want to tell you something," he said. "Please don't repeat this." He put his hands in the pockets of his rumpled Dockers and started walking away from the tomb, as though he didn't want his grandfather's spirit to overhear.

"The Program™," he whispered. "It's not really trademarked."

She stopped walking and stared up at him. He grinned, then shrugged his shoulders. "It's not!"

The trademark symbol was on everything, right down to the coffee mugs. "Why?" she said.

"It makes people feel better," he said. "They like seeing that sort of thing."

"But what if someone steals your ideas?" she asked feebly, as though anyone would want to.

"Great," he smiled. He had a decent smile. He wasn't so bad looking when he smiled. "Maybe they'll help some more people."

She confessed that she'd been one of the people who'd thrown away all those documents in the city clerk's office.

"I saw that on the news," he said excitedly. "People don't usually confess to something I've heard about in the news."

Oh God, she thought.

"Wow," he continued. "It was a lot of stuff, right? In the thousands?"

It had been almost 100,000 documents in all, but Lynn didn't correct him. She'd only thrown away a couple thousand herself.

"People were miffed," he laughed. "Our tax dollars at work."

"I *know*," she said.

"Oh, don't look that way," he said, bending down to look her in the face. "It's not so bad. I've heard much worse. Really. It was just *paper*."

That was true. There were other people who'd snapped at bureaucratic jobs and shot their coworkers or called in a bomb threat.

Still, she'd always thought of herself as an essentially moral person, and a competent one, too—not the kind of person whose negligence on the job warranted newspaper coverage. She'd become one of *those* people, the ones she used to hear about on the news and wonder what the hell they were thinking.

Morton finally recommended she write a letter. "Write an open letter to the editors of all the papers in the city. This has come up before. There was a man who wanted to apologize to a woman whose trail had gone cold. He put an advertisement out in *People* because he remembered she used to read it. That was expensive. But it worked."

"Do I have to use my name?" she asked.

He rocked his head from side to side, considering this, like he was playing a game of mental Ping-Pong.

"I don't see why you'd have to," he said. Then he laughed. "I guess I make up the rules, don't I? So no, you don't have to. Plus," he lowered his voice a bit conspiratorially, "it might be dangerous in your case. You don't want any vigilante justice."

She did not like writing, had procrastinated in the past over memoranda and emails, and even felt nervous hesitation when a birthday or condolence card for a coworker had been circulated. She'd let the card linger on her desk, feeling the pressure to write a pithy comment to a person she barely knew. It was worse if she'd gotten the card at the end of the line and everyone else had already used all the canned congratulations she'd memorized. *Hope the years get better as they go faster!*

This open letter was meant to be an apology, but she felt she owed people something in the way of explanation. How to tell it without making excuses or being abstruse or turning it into a political treatise about the inefficiency in government.

Every time I hear a politician talking about trimming the fat, she imagined herself writing, *I think of myself, being sliced off the shank of the world like a succulent piece of bacon.* A real artery killer.

A clog in the wheel, she thought. *Ha ha.*

Even jilted lovers wanted more than a simple "sorry," she thought—a person needed to know: Was it the kink in my hair or the overcooked steak? Was it me at all?

She did not want to be flip, to say that it wasn't human to dwell in a cubicle, that you inevitably devolved into a cave person, content to smack at the ground with a bone, going millennia without a single worthwhile invention.

She knew human progress existed, but she had no idea how it happened. People had gone to the moon. They'd created *computers*. And at work, it had taken the staff development committee three years to put a soda vending machine in her wing of the building.

She had pursued the job in the clerk's office in the first place because of her boyfriend Craig. She had followed him out to Los Angeles. She wondered how many people moved to L.A. not in pursuit of a dream but in pursuit of a person in pursuit of a dream. At first, she'd been content to be an accessory to Craig's goals, and this had been easy because his career went well, and she hadn't had to nurse years of his disappointment.

Most of the people Craig knew were in the film or TV industry, and he'd befriended a group of comedy writers. He was a film editor, and he wasn't a funny guy himself, but Lynn watched the way he earnestly laughed at all their jokes, and he was a good sounding board. They called him Iowa and seemed to believe that if Craig laughed, audiences in the Midwest would, too.

Craig brought Lynn to many of his friends' parties, which were always kitschy and themed, like the annual Guacamole Bowl, where guests competed with elaborate presentations like "Guac like an Egyptian," "Tequila Guacingbird," and the "Guac Ness Monster."

Once, they'd gone to a Halloween party; the host opened the door bearing knives and covered in torn cereal boxes, as a "cereal killer." Lynn had dressed as Raggedy Ann and soon realized that this was all wrong. She had to be sexy—as a prostitute or a bunny or a devil—or she had to be funny. She detected a look of disappointment on Craig's face, as though he were embarrassed to have come with her, even though he was totally unoriginal in his farmer costume. But he was "Iowa" and he was supposed to be the straight man, so it was okay. There didn't seem to be room for Mrs. Straight Man, too.

They all had interesting jobs at studios or media groups they liked to complain about. When they asked her what she did for a living, she'd smile and say she was a bureaucrat.

They'd point at her and start to chuckle, like she'd just told a good one.

"No, really." That was how she thought of herself. She pushed paper. Of course, when Craig attended parties thrown by her coworkers, they never described themselves as such. They didn't talk about work at all, except to report who had gotten drunk at a recent happy hour, and who had lost ten pounds. Those parties were not themed, and although few of the attendees had any idea what Craig actually did, they knew he worked in the business. They'd try to pitch projects to him, telling him how fascinating a drama that took place in the city clerk's office would be.

"They've got cops, lawyers, doctors, firemen. What about the government? Crazy stuff happens in the government."

"There are already too many shows about the government," Lynn would sigh, pulling Craig away.

He liked the attention at first. Once, as they returned to their car after a party, he even took the opportunity to remind Lynn what a cool boyfriend she had.

"You are *not* cool," she said sharply. He worked in the industry, but she did not think that made him hip. But he didn't need to be cool. She didn't want him to be.

With Craig, as with everything else, inertia had taken root; it moved so slowly and subtly that she couldn't catch it while it was happening. One day never felt any more staid than the day before. The gears shifted imperceptibly, until she found herself looking back to the way things *used to be*. When should she have intervened, made an effort to reverse the course of their relationship?

One of their close friends from Iowa had moved out to L.A. soon after they had, hoping to be a screenwriter. They didn't end up seeing him as often as they'd expected, but every time they went to drinks or to dinner, she was able to see herself and Craig through his eyes, and she remembered the way she'd clung to Craig like he was a lifeline back in Iowa. And then this friend had died, after a short battle with an aggressive cancer of the blood. Lynn and Craig had still been getting used to the fact that he was sick, had been steeling themselves for his long treatments. After he was gone, it was almost like they weren't beholden to their former selves. No one knew the old Craig and Lynn and could preserve that picture for them, and it no longer had any life.

With her Part 2 instructions in hand, she Googled Craig and found his phone number within seconds. But it took her four days to finally dial. When she did, she got his voicemail.

"Hi. This is Craig. And Theresa!" a female voice piped in. Giggle, giggle. "We can't pick up the phone right now, because we're doing something we really enjoy! Theresa likes doing it up and down, and I like doing it left to right—real slowly. So leave your name and phone number and when we're done brushing our teeth, we'll call you back." Beep.

Lynn sat on the other end breathing into the phone like some kind of stalker.

The Craig she needed to apologize to no longer existed. This Craig thought he was funny. This Craig was too busy getting laid to answer the phone. How could she have ever dated a man who would leave such a message? And what would she have said to the old Craig, anyway? "Hi, this is Lynn. The bureaucrat. Remember me? Sorry I let things get rote. Or let you let things get rote. It happens, right?"

One of the reasons she decided to work for the city was because the clerical jobs they offered paid more than their private sector counterparts, and the more she earned the more she felt like her life in L.A. had weight, and the more Craig would value having her there with him. But he only seemed disappointed to be living with a woman with a boring job. He didn't want to see himself as the kind of guy who'd be paired with a woman who worked for the government—not unless she were a spy or a crime scene investigator, jobs that she knew, from having worked for the city, were nothing like they looked on TV.

At first, she'd been nervous and eager to please on the job and overwhelmed by all the departments, the confusing corridors and incomprehensible work flow charts that were supposed to show her where she fit in.

But it was a culture suspicious of hard work. If someone nearby heard her fingers tapping the keys too industriously, they'd ask why she was so damned hyper. If she walked too briskly down the hall, she'd be told to watch where she was going.

She hadn't started the rash of document dumping. She hadn't even been an early adopter, but had watched for months as colleagues in the office threw things away, leaving their desks completely uncluttered. One of them even boasted about it, and Lynn kept waiting for the shit to hit the shredder, so to speak. But it didn't.

An audit had estimated that they were backlogged by at least nineteen months. But Lynn didn't see how throwing things away helped.

And then she got it. The document that swung it all. A Rent Stabilization Ordinance Complaint Form, not unlike hundreds of its ilk except that it had been filed by BERNARD LADOSTE and BERNARD did not even live in an apartment. She knew this because Lynn had processed his Request to Remove Trees from the front of his home, his Graffiti Removal Request, ADA Grievance Procedure Form, LAPD Complaint Form, Sign Language Interpreter Request Form, Street Light Service Request Form, City Ethics Commission Complaint Form, Alarm Permit Request Form, Excavation Permit Request Form, Industrial Waste Permit Request Form, DWP Service Application Form, Campaign Finance Form, Claim for Personal Damages Form, and her personal favorite, the Cable Television Comment Form.

BERNARD liked forms. If he'd been Argentinean, he could have been a *despacho,* one of those professional filers whom people hired to wait in lines in government offices for them.

It was BERNARD who clogged the system. It was BERNARD who kept things from working for everyone else.

So she tossed it. She held Bernard's form over the slot atop the locked blue shredder bin, waiting a moment as though it might make one last plea for its life, and then she let it slip through, where she couldn't retrieve it even if she'd wanted to.

She felt momentarily guilty and had to go to the bathroom and run her hands under cool water. But once she returned to her desk and keyed in the information for someone else's request—someone who actually *needed* something—she was pleased to know that she'd been able to process the legitimate request just that much quicker without the encumbrances of BERNARD.

It didn't take long for her to become indiscriminate about who needed something and who didn't, and eventually she threw away several large stacks of forms on the basis that they were so old that the requests had to be obsolete by now.

It was the custodians—not the supervisors—who eventually realized what was happening in the clerk's office.

Dear Editor:

I am writing to you and your readers as one of the clerks who was involved in the recent city of Los Angeles' "Permitgate" ~~as it has been dubbed by the press~~. I began working for the city ten years ago. ~~I had no real aspirations to be a clerk.~~

~~The volume of permits filed in the clerk's office is overwhelming, and many of the requests are perceived to be redundant or gratuitous.~~

~~It was all BERNARD'S fault.~~

I am deeply sorry for violating the public trust.

~~Slow service is better than no service.~~
~~Objects at rest tend to stay at rest.~~

The week after her letter appeared in the *Los Angeles Times,* the paper ran a small selection of reader responses.

> *It is people like you who make people lose faith in the government, and then they stop voting, stop fighting for change. And Democracy collapses.*

> *I don't understand how these cultures are created and then perpetuated. If governments could hire and fire at will like corporations, maybe this wouldn't happen.*

And then there was this:

> *For a gang member to be initiated into a gang, he or she has to perform an act of criminal boldness, to prove he or she has got the mettle. Welcome to the Gang!*

The last letter had to be from Morton, she thought. Who would write that, who besides a self-help guru who was headquartered in East L.A.?

"You know," Morton said to her after she'd returned for the Part 2 Evaluation. "You might have thrown away one of *my* requests."

"Really?" she said.

"I requested additional street lighting on the block," he said. "I don't want any participants getting mugged when they're trying to improve their lives." He laughed.

"Have they?" She brought her hand to her stomach, like she'd felt something move. "Gotten mugged?"

"Not yet." He shrugged. "You could be the first."

The Program™'s graduation ceremony was only slightly more eventful than its orientation. There were M&M's in a blue plastic bowl and generic soda served out of two-liter bottles into Styrofoam cups.

There were seven guests present, all milling around the conference room, spooning chocolate into their mouths.

"Do you think it worked?" one of the women asked her friend, pouring herself a cup of fluorescent orange drink. Lynn eavesdropped.

"Here's what I think," she said. "I don't feel different so much as I feel different about how I feel."

"How do you mean?"

"Well, I think I realized I'm not a certain *kind* of person. I'm just a person. I'm not immutable, you know. I'm good and bad. I'm happy and sad."

"That rhymes," her friend said flatly. She slumped, like gravity worked extra on her body. "You always thought that, though. You told me that years ago."

"I did?" The other woman raised her eyebrows.

"Yep," her friend said, biting a chunk out of the lip of her Styrofoam cup.

"Well, I might have said that before, but now I've *realized* it. Isn't every truth something you already knew? Then you only remember that you knew it?"

"You read that in *Conversations with God.*"

"Did you read that book? You told me you never read it. You liar."

Her friend shrugged. "I'm not a liar. I'm a person who sometimes lies and sometimes tells the truth."

The group sat down on the folding chairs set out for Morton's parting words. He was wearing a necktie for the occasion, brown with a shooting stars motif.

He clapped his hands together once and surveyed the group.

"Well," he said. "You all look very sharp this evening. I hope you're enjoying the refreshments. I won't say much, but I do want to tell you a parting story my grandfather shared with me."

Great, Lynn thought. A story from the alcohol peddler.

"It's a story about the farmer and the rabbi. If you've heard this one, bear with me. The farmer lived in a one-room cottage with all four of his children. The farmer went to his rabbi and told him he just couldn't take it anymore. 'It's one room, for all five of us. I can't stand it. What should I do?' The rabbi said to the farmer, 'You know those cows you have out in the field?' 'Yes,' the farmer said. 'I want you to take all those cows and bring them into the cottage.' The farmer objected, but the rabbi told him just to do it."

Morton had raised his voice, and feedback from the microphone screeched across the room. He jumped back, startled. He continued cautiously, dropping his voice.

"Then the farmer returned to the rabbi and told him he had done as he'd asked. 'What now?' he asked. 'Now I want you to take the goats that are out in the field and bring them into the cottage as well.' Perplexed, the farmer went home and followed the instructions. Weeks later he came back to the rabbi. 'Please help me,' he said. 'This is awful. We're all living in the cottage. This is even worse, rabbi. What should I do next?' The rabbi told him to go home and take all the cows and goats out of the cottage. The farmer did that. And suddenly the crowded cottage seemed spacious, even with the farmer's four children, and the farmer felt very relaxed."

Morton motioned toward his receptionist. "Anna, could you pass out our gifts?"

Anna moved down the front row with a paper bag, placing something in each person's lap. When Lynn got hers, she could see it was a bar of transparent glycerin soap, with flecks of gold inside and a piece of paper set into the middle of the mold. The paper said:

Bye-bye, shmutz

"You're not allowed to save this as a keepsake," Morton said. "I want you all to use this soap. I got the idea from the 12-steppers. Only their soap doesn't say 'bye-bye, shmutz.'" He laughed.

She wondered if she wouldn't miss Morton, at least a little. It didn't seem likely that someone so uninspiring could make her feel better. She sure didn't feel warm in his presence. And yet. She lingered at the end, until the receptionist had put away all the Styrofoam cups and was turning off the lights.

He set low standards. Standards even Lynn felt she had met. "The world has got a lot of give," he would say at the end of each of his green-screen videos, pulling his pants away from his waistline to show the little slack that was there, as though the Dockers could always accommodate another inch.

"Lynn," he finally said, noticing her as he was about to exit the room. "After all this time, you're still in the dark."

Lynn said she had to ask him about the farmer. She moved up the aisle toward him.

"What happens the next time he gets sick of the one-room cottage?" she said. "It's bound to happen again. It always does." She'd been thinking about a similar problem ever since she'd taken the shower at the beginning of The Program™. It had worked so effectively, but she knew she couldn't just not bathe every time she'd been in a rut, just so she could have a purifying shower at the end of it. "He can't just move the cows and the goats back in again and again. It won't work the same." The story had to continue, she thought. It didn't just end in the farmer's one moment of relief.

"Does he have to keep coming up with a new trick?" she added.

She did not want to keep putting herself through regimens of randomness for the rest of her life.

Morton smiled broadly, like he was genuinely surprised and pleased that anyone had listened to his story and given it any thought.

"He just has to remember," he said. "He has to remind himself every day."

But Lynn thought that even if the farmer had tattooed himself with a cow's head on his forearm, so that each time he looked at it, he'd be reminded of the smelly beasts lounging on his rug, it would still lose its potency.

"That's what the soap is for," Morton said.

She frowned. When her relationship with Craig had soured, she had tried to remember the beginnings. And although she could still recall those days, those memories lost their polish with age and no longer evoked any feeling. They were as flat and distant as scenes from a film.

In a women's magazine she'd read that love in relationships is always growing or diminishing, and that every day you have to steer it in one of those directions. At the time, she'd thought that was nonsense. Most of the time, things remained the same, she'd believed. But Morton, a man who looked like he got dressed in the dark, had understood the invisible shifts. Eventually, there would be another job and another man and she would have to learn to feel the ground moving beneath her.

"Do you want an extra bar?" Morton offered.

She knew a lifetime supply of soap wouldn't help. If she looked at it long enough, even the ridiculous **bye-bye, shmutz** bar would begin to look like any other bar.

"No thanks," she said. She tucked the bar of soap into her purse. She couldn't trick herself forever. She would have to learn to fight inertia the same way she indulged in it, in tiny shuffling increments. Morton put his hand on her shoulder and guided her to the door. She turned to look back at the room with its laminate flooring and folding chairs askew in their rows, and she wanted to memorize the particulars, knowing that by the time she was in her car she would already be forgetting.

STRAY

LILY HAD READ ONCE THAT SAN FRANCISCO WAS THE MOST European of American cities, and the observation had stuck in her mind like a burr. But she didn't think of Paris, Rome, or London, any of the congested urban centers of the continent. Instead, she imagined Amsterdam and Copenhagen, candy-colored row houses, florid parks, and wooden toys. It was only when she moved to San Francisco that she realized her image of it had come from the opening sequence of the television show *Full House,* shot on the green lawn of Alamo Square with the painted ladies standing beyond. Her entire idea of the place, and what an adult life should look like, had been based on soppy comedy.

Lily had been living in San Francisco for just three weeks. She hoped it would be a place with softer edges, less brutality. As she navigated through a mass of bodies funneling past Golden Gate Park, she watched for elbows and uprooted stretches of sidewalk and, in her usual way, avoided the eyes of strangers. She looked up just in time to catch a flock of swans, their necks stretched high, flying over the street toward the water. It was the first uncomplicated thing that had happened that month.

But one of the swans flew just a fraction lower than the rest and skimmed the electric tram wire that ran down the center of the street. The bird's body stopped as though it had hit a window and fell hard to the pavement. The other swans continued on. It lay in the middle of the street, where a wave of cars would soon crest over the hill. Lily had never realized how enormous a swan could be; its white mass dominated the black pavement, the size of a child. She just stood there, but a woman in a wool suit and blocky heels ran into the street and put her hands out at the traffic. She wore a silk scarf and an oversized handbag and did not look like the kind of woman who would run into the street to rescue a bird. Two men ran out to help her.

They will break its neck, she thought. They will twist it, in one sharp motion, and its fluttering will be over. But as the woman held back the traffic, the men lifted the swan and carried it out of the street and down toward the park. Its neck hung limp, like an arm at its side. Lily followed at a distance behind them. In the park, they set it at the edge of a fountain and wet its beak. After a few minutes its neck grew stiff again and it raised its head and lifted itself into the fountain.

It'll go back to Strawberry Hill when it's ready, she heard one of the men say. She stayed to watch after the others had scattered off, as new people came by, pointing out the swan and smiling, unaware. It must have looked as fanciful as the bison grazing in their paddock, just another scenic detail, like the windmills and model yachts. But Lily could still see the red stain completely out of place underneath the dense feathers of its white wing.

When she was a girl, she had wanted to be a veterinarian, before she had understood all that the job required. Her parents had not thought her capable of it. They entertained her insistence on putting Band-Aids on stuffed animals and wrapping their heads in gauze, but once, when her aunt had been visiting and Lily was supposed to have been asleep, she overheard a conversation where her aunt had said how sweet she was, and her mother had said it was because she was a simpleton. At the time, Lily hadn't known what the word meant. In their small town in the north-western tip of Idaho, to call something simple was a high form of praise. For years after, she had misunderstood it to be a compliment. In the end, Lily had become a court reporter instead. All it required was that she listen and observe, and there were few opportunities in the modern world that allowed someone to stay so resolutely in the wings.

But now, watching the swan recover in the cool bath of water, she wished she had been the one to run out into the street.

In March, there were the shrimp. Lily lived in a Vietnamese district behind the Nguyens' Market, which sold everything from imitation Barbie dolls to cough drops and dried plums. The street outside was alive with the smell of sea salt and oranges and blood and rotting rice.

At night, she would open her street-facing window and listen to the sound of Vietnamese. The language comforted her; she didn't find it as harsh as Japanese or Chinese. It was nasal and sweet, and she liked to hear the tongues clicking against the tops of people's mouths, making all those *N*s. But the air was cold and the wind would twist her white curtains; she would scoot closer to the radiator, until her knees and hands were burning and her face was still cold.

It was when she went walking at night, under the naked fluorescent bulbs that lit the shops and sidewalk, that Lily felt the bok choy was reaching out to her and the chickens would go spinning off their spits and wreak havoc in the street, and she would begin to get dizzy.

She became fixated on the shrimp tanks. After she rode the BART home from the courthouse at night, she would go to the fish market down the block and watch the shrimp in the water. They looked nothing like shrimp that were served at restaurants, but had large black eyes and countless legs and their bodies were straight, not curled into commas. They were corpse gray instead of pink. And they could swim. She had never pictured shrimp *swimming*, exactly. She'd imagined them lining the ocean floor, ready to be swept up by fishermen.

There were so many shrimp in the tank that only the ones on top could move. The rest sank in an indistinguishable heap of gray matter, while the others pushed off their backs and tried to spring to the top. There's nothing out here, she wanted to tell them. Nothing but oxygen and plastic and pavement.

After a few weeks of watching them, she bought fifty. She communicated to the market keeper's son that she wanted them alive, in a bucket of water. She hadn't planned this. But when she'd thought about just crossing the street and continuing home to her empty apartment where she'd slide into her house slippers and put the teakettle on the stove, she couldn't go alone.

"It's about time she bought something," the boy said to his father. It turned out to be a heavy bucket, and it took some time to clomp it up her two flights of stairs. On the way, her landlord came out of his door and she told him it was rice, although both of them could see the rings of water the bucket had left on the landing.

Once inside, she filled her bathtub with temperate water (too hot? too cold? she couldn't be sure) and gently scooped the shrimp into the tub. They were half-dead already, but most of them made an effort to swim out and separate themselves from the others. She bought fish food at the pet store and sprinkled the flakes across the surface.

When she came home from work the next day, all fifty shrimp were dead. She sat down by the side of the tub and dipped her hand in the cool water. It had been a bad day. In the trial to which she was currently assigned, a man was accused of killing his longtime boyfriend and his boyfriend's new lover. The bodies had been found in the latter's bed, though the forensic reports showed that they hadn't been killed there. Apparently, the accused had murdered them separately and brought them together, propping them in bed beside one another. The boyfriend's lover had been castrated and his removed parts were found lodged inside the other man, in some gruesome reenactment. The autopsy report showed that the castration had occurred *after* the time of death. That detail made Lily feel at least a bit better.

The defendant was representing himself in court; pleading psychological self-defense, emotional abuse, he was hoping for manslaughter. It appeared he wanted to be caught, perhaps hoped to be punished. He seemed to need to tell the court how badly he'd been hurt. It was a difficult case to work because the evidence was graphic, and she couldn't allow herself to lose focus when the defense attorney produced photographic enlargements of the scene. She could tell by the solicitous smiles of the other court reporters at her agency that they hoped she'd gossip about the case. Her lot were quick to pass judgment. But she refused to indulge them. The case just bewildered her. She had believed that gay men were incapable of such behavior. But then her image of gay men, too, had probably been shaped by *Full House*, sexless, corny men in mom jeans raising three cute kids.

She didn't shower for days and let the shrimp remain in the tub, knowing how depressing it would be to drain the water and dump them into garbage bags. But after the stench spread from her bathroom to the living room and finally out the door, so that she could smell it even before she entered her apartment, she was forced to take them out. She put them back in the bucket and drove to the bay, where she poured them in. And although it left her with such a sour feeling that she promised she would not do that sort of thing again, it was only a few weeks later that she began collecting stray animals. A stray might mean any animal—with collar or without, well fed or scrawny—roaming the streets without an owner. She would lean down to pet the animal and ask, "Whose dog is this?" and when no one answered she would pick it up or, if it was too heavy to lift, lure it home with a bit of cheese. For the few animals that had tags she called the owners and left messages. Two of them eventually picked the dogs up. One was grateful for Lily's rescue, while the other had eyed her suspiciously, as if she'd snatched the terrier with some hope of a reward.

She had tried this before in Boise, when she'd lived in a ranch house with a backyard that would have been suitable for a small farm. But her boyfriend at the time hadn't let her collect animals. Every time she'd tried to bring a tabby or a little mutt into their car, he'd protested that the animal probably belonged to somebody, a child who'd be crushed to find the family pet missing. She would promise her boyfriend she'd knock on all the neighborhood doors the next day, but that they should take it home for the night. "Look at it," she'd say, nudging the animal toward him. "It wants to come with us." He would tell Lily to get back in the car.

"It's going to get hurt," she'd say, climbing into her seat. "That's all I can think about." It would take her days to forget about the animal's fate, to stop visualizing the trucks that could come speeding down the street and flatten the poor dog or cat. Of course, she questioned her boyfriend's motives. It was all an excuse: he didn't want pets around the house. But eventually she stopped going after the strays. In an effort to hold on to him, she became the sort of woman who didn't do such things.

Now, collecting animals, Lily thought that there would be no more men, no more clumsy attempts at relationships. Her life would be as sexless as a '90s sitcom. She'd never had much luck with men, anyway. It wasn't that she was unpretty—no, she was pleasant enough to look at—it was that she was neither perky nor purposefully *un*-perky and sardonic; men seemed to want at least one or the other, sometimes both. A woman who was cynical about the world but not cynical about men. A woman who was fun and fun-*ny*. Lily knew she was neither.

It didn't take long before her neighbors started to complain, sniffing out-side her door in the hallway, saying, "I smell cat piss. Do you smell cat piss?"

Lily didn't know what to do with the animals; she couldn't take them to the pound. None of them were kittens or puppies or even adoptable adults. One of the cats had an ashy dry socket where an eyeball should have been, and one of the dogs limped, though only slightly; they all had filthy gums and cloudy eyes and their coats were too thick or too thin. She didn't know exactly how the pets were euthanized, only that it could not be as innocuous as the euphemism *putting them to sleep* suggested. She could not stop picturing little veterinarian gas chambers.

Lily rented a minivan, then waited until the middle of the night and crept downstairs, putting her ear to her landlord's door. Mr. Neskovitz had strictly forbidden pets. She could hear the laugh track from a televi-sion show and thought she heard snoring. She carried each animal down-stairs, keeping them occupied with cheese and other treats so they wouldn't bark as they descended. She padded all the floors and seats of the rental with special car diapers she'd picked up at the pet store. It was a good thing, too, because by the time she'd driven two and a half hours out of the city, the van was foul with excrement. When she'd suddenly hit the brakes, all the dogs had gone sliding off the seats, banging their heads into the seats in front of them, and landing in the feces they'd been care-fully avoiding. She had put the cats in cardboard carriers and they screamed violent meows the entire way there.

She drove until things began to look scenic. When she thought she'd gone far enough, she took a small tangential road out for twenty miles, so that the animals would not be in danger from highway traffic. She found a spot where the long parallel rows of dirt mounds had been over-taken by a stinky weed. She couldn't see a building in any direction. The dogs had an easy time of it, quickly bounding out of the van into the space and running in nonsensical patterns. The cats looked more stunned, as if coming out of anesthesia; they stumbled a bit and walked cautiously around.

When she was fourteen, Lily had encountered the word *simpleton* again, when they were assigned *Of Mice and Men* for English class. The teacher had called Lennie a simpleton, and when they read the first pages, Lily realized she meant he was mentally disabled. He'd been described like a dog, with big dumb paws for hands. She had run home crying after school, but wouldn't tell her parents what was wrong. "Did someone pick on you?" her mother had asked. Lily had always earned good grades in school and compliments from her teachers. She knew she was not retarded, not like Lennie, but as she read on, she felt for him, for his simple dream of living on a farm and stroking the soft fur of animals. It was not unlike her dreams, and she thought perhaps she was a simpleton, after all. Reading it, she had been sure they would get their farm. But it had not turned out to be that kind of story.

It was almost midnight on a Saturday night in November when she saw the girl crying. Lily was having coffee after watching an ensemble romantic comedy in the theater, the kind that filled her with a foolish anticipation of cold weather and hot chocolate and holiday shopping. The child was standing precariously close to the street, the Saturday evening traffic cutting close by. She seemed simply to have materialized—Lily hadn't seen her emerge out of any stores or wander down the street. She was just there, her fists rubbing at her eyes. The girl didn't call out or look around for her mother. She just rubbed her eyes so hard Lily thought she might push them out of their sockets.

When she saw the girl, she thought of the swan, her own hesitancy, and the swift reactions of the other passers-by. She walked over to the child.

"Are you lost?" Lily said, but she did not react, did not remove those burrowing fists from her eyes.

"Where's your mother?" she asked. "Your daddy?" she added self-consciously, thinking it old-fashioned and offensive to ask about the mother first.

Lily tried to pry one of the girl's arms away from her face, but it wouldn't budge; she was unnaturally strong. This was obviously something the child did often, this rubbing—she had practice. A stream of snot dangled halfway down to the girl's tennis shoes. Lily could see scabs lining her forearms.

"I'm trying to help you," Lily said, but the snot and sobs continued. The girl's chest heaved with each chop of air. "If you won't talk to me, I can't help you." Lily believed children should be reasoned with, not persuaded by toys and trickery.

"Please?" she said.

Lily peeked her head into the closest store, a place that sold glass bongs and appropriate accessories—bundles of incense, black light posters, mushroom-shaped candles.

"Did anyone lose a girl?" Lily called out, although the shop was empty. At the back, she could see light creeping out from underneath a curtain that covered a doorway; she could hear muffled voices, too, but she wasn't going to the back of a head shop to investigate. If she saw something illegal, the people might have to kill her. That sort of thing happened to witnesses, and she hoped never to be witness to anything.

When she walked back into the street, she saw that most of the other stores were closing, metal gates screeching across the front windows. The street was emptying out, and the girl continued to stand there, still dangerously close to the traffic. Lily nudged her toward the paraphernalia store. She looked up and down the block once again; there seemed to be no one looking for a lost child. The girl was shivering. Lily was, too. The sky had been swollen and heavy all night, and Lily thought she felt a drop of rain hit her cheek.

She picked the girl up. It was easy enough. The child continued to sob but didn't hit her or cry out. Lily walked down the street, her pace quickening. She glanced behind her, expecting the mother to rush out and seize the child and shower her with hard, worried kisses, glaring at Lily suspiciously. But no one came after them, and she carried the girl, who became quite heavy after a while, all the way home.

Lily knew that police stations in San Francisco did not close at night like they did in rural Idaho, but it was nearly one in the morning, and she thought it improper to carry this little vagabond in at that hour. If no one claimed her until the next morning, the child would have to spend the night at the station. It could traumatize her, Lily thought, and imagined how cold the room would be, with the glaring lights, dirty beige furniture and dueling smells of crime and disinfectant—no place for a child to rest her head.

Back home in her kitchen, she got a better look at her. She had stopped crying, but the jerky sniffling continued. She wore a white sweatshirt, the cuffs and collar soiled; there was a puffy appliqué of grinning sheep on the front. Her brown hair was chopped in an awful bowl cut that made her look like a boy. Lily thought that only a terrible mother would do that to her daughter's hair, but she scolded herself, thinking the girl's parents might be modern people who didn't believe in traditional notions of gender. But still, she thought, the hair didn't look like a cute short cut, no, it looked like her hair had been urgently chopped. Yes, she realized, that was it. She looked like she had had lice. Lily remembered her school nurse with fat hands who had parted the girls' hair to examine their scalps. One of the poor girls in school had an infestation too far gone for simple lice shampoo and comb. She was not allowed at sleepovers and no one visited her house.

This child was too young to be in school, she thought. She looked about four, but Lily wasn't very good at estimating that sort of thing. She didn't have any younger siblings and never did any babysitting as an adolescent. That certainly would have come in handy now, but while her friends had spent their adolescent summers chasing drippy children, Lily had always managed to secure work licking envelopes or emptying trash-cans. No one trusted her with their kids, which was the fault of her own parents, who liked to complain about what a "sensitive" child they'd raised. Or, rather, ended up with—they weren't claiming credit for the way Lily had turned out. It was because of her, they'd say, half-jokingly, that they hadn't tried for any more children.

So she hadn't a clue how old the child was or what should be done to take care of her. She certainly behaved like a toddler but she was tall and her face looked older, thinner. Maybe she was underdeveloped, Lily thought. No one had taught her to talk. She could also feel the padding of a diaper in her pants. Lily had never changed a diaper before.

The girl's mother was a prostitute, Lily decided, or cheap, at least, the kind of woman who sought out groups of male friends and slept with them all, a transient living off the men she serviced. She was blond, a frazzled, permed, burned-to-the-quick blond with brown roots. She wore obscenely tight shimmer sparkle stretch pants that did not flatter her deflated, U-shaped bottom. She wore cheap, unstable shoes that irritated her downstairs neighbors. She wore fuchsia—lipstick, nail polish, and eye shadow, all coordinated.

But Lily scolded herself again. All those things did not make this woman an unfit mother. No, that was nothing. It was the fact that this woman kept no food in the house, no animal crackers or milk, nothing but warm beer in a crate by the television set. She pushed and smacked her daughter, smiled in the presence of strangers, phonily held her daughter's hand in public, but began dragging the child as soon as they were alone. She was the sort who yanked her daughter's arm when she would not sit up or cooperate or walk fast enough; yes, the kind of mother who dislocated her daughter's shoulder. She was the sort of woman who left a toddler alone for hours—or days—and never got out of bed to attend to her cries, the sort of woman who spanked her child's bottom until it was raw when the girl would not go potty on demand. She was a *because I told you so* sort of woman.

Of course Lily meant to report the lost child—as soon as she'd given her a bath, a good meal, a comfortable place to sleep for an evening, after which she'd take her to the nearest police station and hand her over to some strange man who was more accustomed to dealing with criminals than children. But she'd wait until a decent hour, not so early that the officers would still be groggy and unwilling, not so late that they would suspect her of foul play.

But things did not progress as she had planned. To begin with, she didn't know what the child should eat, and the girl was not cooperative when Lily tried to gently pry her mouth open to check for teeth. The girl smashed her lips together with fierce determination, and when Lily was able to forcefully jam one index finger in, the girl bit down, hard. She had teeth. Sharp ones. The girl blinked her enormous brown eyes, and Lily wondered if she saw a glimmer of contempt.

First thing in the morning, she took her to the organic food store. On the way down the stairs, Mr. Neskovitz came out of his apartment and eyed them. He liked children even less than he liked pets and college students and smokers, never mind that he had a talking parakeet and smoked a pack and a half of menthols every day.

"Babysitting," Lily said, ducking her head and scratching the back of her neck with her free arm to avoid looking at Mr. Neskovitz.

Lily was thankful for the limited selection at the cramped and loamy smelling Harvest Market. She was terrible at grocery shopping. At her rural home, her mother had grown many of their vegetables and herbs, and they'd bought fruits in season from their neighbors who ran farms. When they went into town they'd buy sacks of flour and rice and sugar. Leah Sanderson, a wiry woman with manly hands who ran the Holstein

Farm, always delivered their butter and cheese and milk. Things had been easy. But when Lily had moved to Boise to go to court reporting school, she'd had to face the enormous one-stop supermarkets.

Her mother had predicted failure. And on that first grocery store trip, Lily had doubted that she *would* make it. Standing in the bread aisle under the profound brightness of the fluorescent lights, she'd become dizzy. She'd never seen so much bread in her life; it stretched across the entire aisle, from top to bottom. At first she thought she would look at each loaf, read the ingredients, check for freshness—but it didn't take long to be overwhelmed. She stood back against the cookies opposite and stared at the loaves until they no longer looked like bread, or like anything at all, but had become discrete units forming a long rectangular grid. Lily stood there for what felt like an hour before she slumped to the ground, exhausted. One of the stockers, a plump boy whose skin smelled of oranges as he touched Lily's face, called the paramedics. They delivered her to the emergency room where a doctor declared, after a number of tests, that there was nothing "medically" wrong with her. Panic was his best guess.

But now, even in this miniature market, Lily was having trouble deciding on something suitable. Lily had hoped the girl would point, as she always saw children in the grocery store do. In good conscience she couldn't feed her miniature hot dogs or soda pop, though she wasn't going to impose her own vegan standards in case it should stunt the girl's growth. She steered clear of peanut butter and other allergens she'd heard about in the news.

In the end, she settled on organic canned spaghetti and mango-peach applesauce, and as the clerk rang up the yellow baby shampoo and floral-scented diapers Lily had added, she told her she had a beautiful child. Glancing at the child, Lily thought she did not look beautiful, but dirty and disheveled; when she looked back at the checker, though, a girl with freckled skin and sloppy hair tied back in a burgundy scarf, she saw a glimmer in her eyes. "I've been trying for one of my own," the checker said.

Lily gave a small smile. "Of course," she said, picking up her canvas grocery bag and taking the child home.

But the girl would not eat her spaghetti, not by herself nor with Lily's assistance, not at any of the various temperatures at which she prepared it, nor with any of the trickery she could devise. She felt panicked. She didn't know how long a toddler could go without a meal. She considered force feeding, but Lily had already had one finger bitten and she thought such measures might constitute abuse. "Abuse," she scolded herself, "is what you're rescuing this child from."

They sat at a standoff, Lily holding a fork of spaghetti in her limp wrist, the girl sitting on two phonebooks in the perpendicular chair, her lips held ruthlessly tight. Snot began to run from the girl's nose, but she ignored the mucus and kept her hands tucked beneath her legs.

Bathing the girl wasn't much better; she didn't physically resist, but didn't cooperate either, and it left Lily with the creepy sensation that she was doing something against the child's will. She allowed her to untie her shoes and slip her small feet out, to lift her arms and tug her soiled sweat-shirt and sweatpants off. While she knew the girl couldn't take a bath by herself, she wasn't accustomed to taking off other people's clothes, and it seemed an invasion of privacy. Earlier, changing her diaper, she had made sure not to look at the child's body any more than necessary. She removed the diaper now, still unsoiled, and gently lifted the girl by her armpits and placed her in the water that she'd prepared to a gentle temperature. The girl sat upright, but did not splash her hands in the water or start to smile. A bath was supposed to be a relaxing activity. It had always relaxed Lily. But the girl turned to her with a sudden wide-eyed fright, and opened her mouth as if she were about to scream or cry, though no sound came out. She brought those small fists like little lug wrenches to her eyes and began rubbing mercilessly. But she was filthy, and she smelled of feces and some other indefinable, hospital-like smell, and she had to be bathed. Lily proceeded as cautiously as he could, dowsing her head with water, building up a lather, avoiding the girl's eyes—as if any soap could reach them behind those fists!

But when she began to rub a yellow washcloth against the child's smooth, flawless back, she felt perverse. This was, after all, another person's child, and bathing was a sort of intimate act, and the girl's pubic region was so hairless and frightening. It was nothing like a soap commercial, where adult and child bathe together, and it is all giggles and flotation toys and soap bubbles springing in the air.

Lily took a few days off work, but then was forced to hire a babysitter. She found a local Vietnamese woman who looked old enough to be a grandmother, and whose English was so spotty, Lily thought she wouldn't be able to question anything out of the ordinary. Even so, she felt the need to explain to the woman how her fictitious sister's humanitarian work had called her out of the country for an indefinite time, and how Lily had had to step in and take care of her niece. The woman just nodded and smiled as though she were any other nervous mother, and Lily didn't know what, if anything, had been understood.

At work she was busy, which she normally welcomed, but with the girl at home she could hardly concentrate. She caught herself stenotyping her own thoughts instead of what was being said in the room. Instead of *My client doesn't dispute this* she'd stroked *You can't just keep her.* It'd been years since she'd made that kind of blunder.

"Excuse me," Lily said, erasing her previous line. "Technical glitch." Everyone stopped to look at her, as though they'd only now realized she'd been there at all. It was a divorce deposition, and although the couple was well-to-do, even the smallest appliances and household items had become battlegrounds. Presently, they were discussing the value of their 800-watt microwave after depreciation had been factored in, and whether it was an even trade for a set of chef-quality knives. She remembered that the attorney for the husband had protested, "The microwave is five years old," and the opposing attorney had responded, "My client doesn't dispute this."

She hated interrupting. It was no good for proceedings, disrupted the organic development of things. But she knew the husband and wife started to speed-talk when they got emotional, and she could feel it coming on. She needed a moment to remember what the lawyer had said next. Even though she'd been distracted, a part of her had still been listening. "It's the estimated value that's at issue," she remembered him say, as clearly as if she'd rewound an audiotape in her head. She corrected the line. "All fixed," she said.

Reporting required a unique kind of concentration. A good reporter couldn't focus too hard, trying to capture each word individually as it flew by. That was like putting your face right up to a painting to get a better look at it. It was exhausting to report that way and far too slow. But a reporter couldn't miss a single detail, either, and had to be listening perfectly. Most people didn't realize what shabby listeners they were until they tried to record something verbatim. When Lily first started taking her classes, she couldn't believe how easily her mind wandered, what an effort it was to nudge it back into place. Like meditation, it required patient practice. Part of what made her an excellent reporter was that she was quickly able to direct her mind into this particular zone, and once there, she went on automatic.

Later, the deposition became heated. The wife pushed her chair back, then the husband stood, then everyone was on his or her feet except Lily, who was busy trying to capture the stream of obscenities that overlapped, until she wanted to call out *One epithet at a time, please!*

She was back at the office proofing her transcription when Alan, one of the administrative clerks, found her at her workstation. He was a bookish kid, interested in court reporting, or maybe in her, she wasn't sure.

"I brought you coffee," he said. He could be servile and she didn't know what to make of it.

"That's all right," she said.

"It's not from this morning," he said. "It's fresh." He put the ceramic mug down next to her left hand.

"How was your dep?" he asked, leaning against the cubicle wall.

"R-rated," she said. "There was practically a brawl."

"How do you manage that?" he asked. "I mean, keep recording, when it gets crazy like that?"

She looked up at him to see if he truly wanted to know. He looked like he did.

"You can't make any judgments," she said. "The second you start to think about what they're saying, you're lost. Even when it's gruesome. Or tragic. You can't be reacting while you're getting it all down. The second you start thinking about the witness' credibility or the defendant's innocence, you're lost. You've missed something. You can't have an opinion," she said. .

"That's right," said one of the other court reporters who was making her way to her own desk. "Lily's the best. Doesn't have a thought in her head."

Alan looked like he might leap to defend her, but Lily shook her head at him.

"Just kidding, of course," the woman said.

Lily ignored her, and she moved on to her own machine.

"Now that I'm looking over the transcriptions, it's different," she said. "I can see how unreasonable the wife was during the deposition. How she baited her husband. And the whole thing is really sad." When she was actually recording she was able to suspend it all. There had been a few exceptions, moments when a verdict she was sure was wrong had come down, and her hands had hesitated, as though if she didn't record it, it might still be reversible.

"Don't you ever want to interfere?" he asked her, leaning forward. "To say something or do something?"

"Yes," she said, but not how he meant, not in court or in a law office. At work she soaked it in without resistance, and it was the end of the day that she started to feel it leak, when she could hardly stand not to do something.

Two weeks passed. Lily and the girl were asleep on the vast white couch, each drooling over an opposite arm. Lily hadn't intended to fall asleep; she'd been tricking the girl, closing her eyes in the hopes that she would take a nap. She'd discovered that the girl would only eat or sleep or dress herself when Lily wasn't watching.

The doorbell rang. In the year she had been living in the apartment, no one had ever come to her door unexpectedly, and she feared it could only be Mr. Neskovitz.

"Shh," Lily told the girl, although she hadn't yet said a single word.

It was not Mr. Neskovitz, but Alan, the clerk from work. Through the peephole his face looked horsey and wide.

Against her better judgment, she opened the door. Alan was holding a small houseplant with striped leaves and yellow flowers.

"It's a zebra plant," he said.

"Interesting," Lily said, not realizing it was meant as a gift.

"Do you like it?"

"Oh," she said, "it's very green."

Truthfully, Lily *did* like the plant, but she was hesitant about the intentions that might accompany it. He was a nice boy, a gentle-faced enthusiastic type; she imagined he spent long hours in the library, even though he was not hermitic. He was younger than she was but seemed unnaturally interested in all of her *preferences*. He asked her what kind of movies and books she liked, what kind of weather she preferred, whether or not she used chopsticks. She tried not to let him make her self-consciously aware of what she wore or what her hair looked like. She would not, she told herself, begin that sort of thing.

But now she took the plant from him and placed it on the table and he welcomed himself into her living room. She wondered how he knew where she lived.

"It's so white," he said, surveying the room. The monotony in color soothed Lily; it made her breathe easier.

The girl was peeking her head over the back of the couch.

"And who is that?" he said, bending down to face the child at eye level.

"That's my daughter," Lily said, quickly. She hadn't planned it, but it seemed like just the thing to scare him off.

"A daughter?" he asked, beaming. "You never told me you had a little girl. She must look like her father."

"I wouldn't know," Lily said, and Alan looked at her, clearly surprised. "It was that sort of time in my life," she added. Now she was a single mother *and* harlot; surely this would be discouraging.

But Alan did not seem the least bit put-off; in fact, the glow of interest in his eyes only seemed brighter, as if a sordid and secretive past made Lily more fascinating.

"What's your name?" he asked the girl.

"It's Daphne," Lily said. She had recently been trying it out in her head, and in the moment decided it was right.

"Ambitious for such a little girl."

"I think people grow into their names," she said. She'd decided the child had probably been named something like Libby or Patty or Molly, names that were fine for someone else but not appropriate for this child. She needed something striking to bring her out of herself.

Alan sat on the couch while Lily stood uncomfortably beside it, hoping he'd at least announce the reason for his visit. To her surprise, Daphne climbed right into his lap.

Alan said that the girl's moss green dress was beautiful. It was certainly better than the white sweat suit she'd found her in. "It's hemp," she said. Lily had taken the girl shopping for two days in a row. She'd bought her alphabet books, a See 'n Say, and a stuffed puffball sheep. She'd avoided the tempting coordinates at the Baby Guess and Baby Gap or any other unconscionable retailers. She had almost been overwhelmed by their cuteness—little cardigans, pink and orange striped knits, fuzzy skirts. The girl may not have known the difference, but Lily did, and she wouldn't have felt right dressing the child in a shirt made by god-knows-who-earning-god-knows-what in Guatemala.

It felt wonderful to spend money on someone else. She had done well in her job, and she was paid for it. She knew the other court reporters were not fond of her, and she did not participate in their luncheons or after dinner drinks. And once, when Lily was taking a break in the bathroom stall—quietly reading a novel—she'd heard two of the women talking about her. "Jesus," the woman in navy pumps had said to the one in suede boots, "she's an open wound."

But Alan liked her, and here he was, sitting in her apartment, though Lily wanted nothing more than for him to leave. Perhaps he, too, was some kind of simpleton.

"Let me cook you dinner sometime," he said. Lily thought that was an awfully passive-aggressive way to put it, and she was about to tell him that she wasn't hungry when there was another knock at her door. Jesus, Lily thought, when it rains. In the brief moment before she reached the door, she imagined the police had discovered the child's whereabouts and had used Alan the coworker as a convenient decoy. That would explain all this interest.

But this time it was Mr. Neskovitz.

"Still babysitting?" he said, eyeing the girl on the couch. Lily told him that no, she was done; Alan was here to pick up his daughter. But Neskovitz had just come by to tell her the water would be shut off for two hours the next afternoon.

Alan raised his eyebrows and grinned. Lily told him it was a long story.

The next day, Lily's mother called to announce that the family Doberman had committed suicide.

"Suicide?" It didn't seem like the sort of thing her mother would readily conclude.

"In the pond," she said. "He drowned himself."

That did seem *odd*. Hardy was a fantastic swimmer, could beat the current on the river where her father went rafting, and the pond at the end of their property was only a couple of feet deep.

"He was your dog," her mother said. "It figures."

But Hardy was not Lily's dog: it was her mother who'd brought him home and named him Hardy, and it was her father who took him on camping and hiking expeditions. When Lily had tried to take Hardy to Boise with her years before, her parents had both objected, trying to use him as leverage to keep Lily at home. That was the strangest thing, she thought—no matter how much her parents complained about her, they'd wanted to keep her living at home indefinitely.

"I thought you'd be hysterical," her mother said, as if she were disappointed.

"I am," she said flatly.

Daphne, who'd been playing with blocks on the floor, stood up and hit her head on the edge of the coffee table.

"What was that?" her mother said.

"I'm babysitting." Daphne hadn't hit herself hard, but she looked shocked. Lily rubbed her forehead, blew cool air on her face.

Her mother laughed. "For who?"

"A friend. Look, I should go."

"What sort of friend?"

"A friend. A friend from work."

"Male or female?"

"Female," Lily said, to avoid any romantic conclusions her mother might draw.

"A lesbian? I've heard about lesbians with babies over there. Though I'm sure you don't know any of that sort."

She wanted to tell her mother that she didn't have any friends, let alone lesbian ones.

The girl was crying.

"Well," her mother said, "it doesn't sound like you're doing too well."

Her mother was good evidence, she thought, that a person's biological parents shouldn't necessarily raise them. "Right?" she said to Daphne. She was sad about Hardy, but he was an old dog and she couldn't blame him. She wouldn't want to live with her parents, either. It was just a fluke, she told herself, the strange kind of thing that sometimes happens. Nothing prophetic. But she still made a mental note to buy those plastic prongs and put them on all her electrical outlets.

Lily put a Band-Aid on Daphne's head, even though it wasn't cut. The girl smiled; her cheeks puffed out and her small lips disappeared. In her hand she clutched the gray dishtowel to which she'd become recently attached; Lily had tried to get her fixated on something else, but she wasn't having it. She took the dishtowel everywhere, and Lily let her.

Lily had *wanted* to return the child. She'd even gone so far as to walk by the police station, holding tightly to Daphne's hand. But at the moment she'd passed the front doors, two officers were hauling in a pantless, hairy man, who was shrieking about crop circles and the grassy knoll. Daphne had hid behind Lily's legs.

She checked the newspapers and watched the television news (something she normally avoided because of the panics it might inspire) for a story about a lost child. But when she found nothing, she could not quell her suspicion that Daphne had not been lost but abandoned. Just the possibility made her feel it was morally unacceptable to take the child to the authorities. If she were abandoned, Lily was as suitable a caregiver as any, and if fate should chance the child upon her, she was not going to resist such forces. She'd read exposés on foster care: children shuffled between families, so they only learned fragments of multiple languages and constantly switched schools or were put to work as household maids—or worse. She knew all about children growing up to be desperate types sure to use drugs and then rob and prostitute to get those drugs.

She looked down at Daphne—who at the moment had a stain of purple Kool-Aid circling her lips—and pictured her in twenty years, running into an aging Lily in an alley somewhere and stabbing her in the gut.

So she'd procrastinated, hoping some evidence would surface, a televised plea from Daphne's parents begging for their daughter's return. But now that two weeks had passed, she couldn't just bring the child to the police. They'd be suspicious. Law enforcement officers weren't famous for their sense of understanding. She'd have to drop the girl off outside the station, instead, and then she'd be alone, on the sidewalk, in no better shape than Lily had found her. And then what would be the point of having rescued her at all?

A few nights later, Lily was having a fitful sleep—she kept dreaming about the girl's mother, who looked unerringly like Martha Stewart, except that her teeth were larger and protruding. She dreamed there were always fresh cut flowers in their home, large, intricately frosted cookies, and child and mother made handmade soaps and sachets together. She was a perfect mother (if a bit cold) and Lily had taken the child from that temple of domesticity into her horribly bare, urban apartment.

Lily woke with the awful sensation that there existed a place of perfect order and control, a place religiously guarded from the rest of the world.

When she rolled over to touch the girl's head, she was gone. This had happened before—Daphne would get up in the middle of the night and Lily would find her asleep on the floor or playing with toys in a wilder, more unreserved way than she ever did during the day.

Lily found her sitting on the kitchen tile, facing the sink, all the bottom cupboards flung open and foodstuffs scattering the ground.

She had found a bag of stale gingersnaps, which were now crumbled across the floor, and had taken everything off the bottom shelf of the refrigerator. "What are you *doing?*" Lily laughed, then saw a bag of baby carrots between Daphne's legs. She had two little fistfuls of carrots and was stuffing them into her mouth. She looked up at Lily, caught. "You're eating *carrots?*" Lily said, but the girl stopped, and her face went completely still. She brought her hands up to her neck, but didn't cry out. Oh God, Lily thought, oh shit. She wasn't coughing—that was bad. Lily grabbed her, ran to the dining room table, and threw her over her lap as if she were going to spank her. She thumped, right between the girl's shoulder blades, and kept thumping, with the heel of her hand. It took five times, but a full carrot came falling out. The girl wailed and started coughing. Lily turned her around, holding her to her chest, and rubbed the girl's back. "It's over," Lily said. "Shh. It's over." And it was, just like that.

"Boo-boo," the girl said. It was a word, sort of—the closest she'd come.

Yes, Lily said, that was definitely a boo-boo. When she put the girl to bed and tried to go back into the kitchen, the girl started crying for her, holding out her arms. Lily climbed into bed and brought Daphne close to her.

The next day, she found a substitute for work, and they went shopping again, not just for small things this time but for a dresser, a potty training seat, a new comforter and sheets for the bed (yellow comets and stars), pictures for the walls, a miniature-sized rocking chair.

That afternoon, Lily and Daphne had high tea with animal crackers and the little porcelain tea set they had just bought.

"Isn't this grand?" Lily said to her, pouring them each an imaginary cup. "I just love jasmine tea." Daphne watched Lily closely, picking up her cup a little clumsily with both small hands, and took a pretend sip. "Can you say thank you?" she said, and to her surprise Daphne did—*tank wu*, she said. Lily was surprised. "What else can you say?"

"Fun-ny," Daphne said. "Fun-ny." Lily wondered how many other words the girl knew; perhaps she'd merely been bashful.

The girl gave her new drink-and-pee doll a sip out of a plastic doll bottle. Lily told her that now the little doll would pee, and they took her to the doll potty chair, which looked conveniently like Daphne's real potty chair.

"Pee-pee," the girl said, and a stream of water fell out of the anatomically strange hole in the little doll.

There was a knock at the door. Maybe Alan had come back, and for a moment, Lily realized she welcomed the thought. She had almost stopped worrying about the authorities, about her parents, about all the potential people to whom she'd have to provide an explanation for the child.

Through her peephole she saw it was Mr. Neskovitz, and there was no use pretending she wasn't at home. He looked peeved that he'd been forced to leave his couch and lumber up two flights of stairs.

She opened the door without realizing she was still holding a miniature porcelain teacup.

"That kid," he said. "You know the rules. It's in your lease agreement." And then, "These are singles. That means you live *alone*."

Lily just nodded assiduously as if she were at a lecture and the speaker had just said something that resonated with her.

"By the end of the week," he said, making a snort that sent a wave of menthol her way. Walking away, he turned around just as Lily was closing the door and said, "And I knew about those fucking dogs and cats."

Lily should have felt panicked, but she didn't. In fact, she hadn't felt anxious in days, and she hadn't even noticed that she didn't feel nervous, even though her life was clearly more dangerous, more unpredictable than it had ever been before.

Lily sat down on the couch, in the middle of her small living room that was now consumed by wooden letter blocks and stuffed toys. The girl was playing with her See 'n Say. *What does the cow say? Moo. What does the cat say? Meow.*

"Meow," the girl giggled. "Meow. Meow."

The girl was not a cat or a dog. Lily could not drive her out into a deserted field and let her make her way among the weeds. She was almost thankful Mr. Neskovitz had come. She couldn't "babysit" the girl for the rest of her life—Lily had to do something decisive. The girl's choking had made her realize that. What if she'd swallowed Drano or split open her chin or done anything else that required a visit to the emergency room? The girl had no *papers,* and without papers, she did not exist; she could not go to school, she could not go to daycare, and she certainly could not become an adult, not without a birth certificate, a social security number. She knew there was a black market for this kind of thing—some cavernous, melodramatic place with one naked bulb casting brutal shadows in a corner of the city where they could forge a false identity for this girl.

She'd been a court reporter for a fifteen years now. She knew these kinds of things happened every day. But she'd never been on trial, never had to defend a suspect or pass judgment. She wasn't a part of the world of actors, and from the margin, that world had seemed overwhelming. Now that she had taken a step in, she wasn't so sure. It was like the horrible way the darkness seemed in the glare of her headlights, and how different it felt when she was actually outside at night.

"What do you think?" Lily said.

"Quack," she said.

"Yeah. I think so, too."

Just that week, Lily had discovered that Daphne had a dimple when she laughed. She looked so happy, now, learning animal sounds and training her doll to pee. Lily walked over to her, kneeling down. Her pudge oozed out of the sleeves of her little tie-dyed dress and Lily wanted to bite her. Daphne stuck her finger in her nose.

Growing up in Idaho, the world had seemed to revolve around sustenance, all season and cycle. Squash grew in the pinprick of autumn and deer were shot and butchered for venison; green beans and broccoli sprouted in spring and strawberries fattened in summer.

But ever since she began court reporting, madness had seemed like the world's ruling principle. For a while, she had grown obsessed with the statistics of violence—a murder every twenty-five minutes, a rape every five, an assault every thirty seconds. She knew that these acts were not, in reality, balanced out so incrementally. There were witching hours in which crimes were concentrated—but she could not stop thinking about it at all hours of the day. She would wake in the soft white light of her bedroom, and for a moment she would breathe easily before she remembered that someone, somewhere was being raped. And when she thought about the entire world, her country only a small, dangerous corner, she calculated that something horrible must happen every second. A friend had once tried to comfort her by saying that she was statistically more likely to be struck by lightning than experience any of the things she feared. But it wasn't about herself, she'd tried to explain. It didn't matter if it was happening to her, but that it was happening to *someone,* and she didn't feel right calmly flipping through a magazine with articles on new eye shadow shades when she knew what was happening elsewhere.

Lily had often wondered how other people seemed able to quiet their minds. But now she began to consider that they kept the noise out by letting something else in.

In her rush to find a new place to live, she nearly missed Thanksgiving. But it was her first holiday with Daphne, and she thought it was important to establish a ritual, something that would give the girl a sense of security. It was an improvised meal with a tofu turkey that neither of them ate, but which Lily had set prettily on a platter dressed with sprigs of rosemary. She propped Daphne up on phonebooks so she could sit at the dining table and served sparkling cider in amber-glass goblets. Daphne ate the corn, a few spoonfuls of stuffing, a soft roll, and several helpings of cranberry sauce. The cider kept making her burp, and the burps made her giggle.

Lily was in the kitchen scrubbing out the Corningware when her mother called.

"Happy Thanksgiving," her mother said. "Nice of you to ring."

"I was just about to call," she lied.

"You could have come home, you know," she continued. "I'd convinced your father that you were to going to surprise us."

"What did you do that for?"

"I just had a feeling," she said. "Your father says hello, by the way. He's disappointed. What with Hardy gone this year."

"Why? I thought Hardy was *my* dog."

"He was *our* dog," she said. "All of ours." Sometimes Lily wished she had transcripts of their conversations. She always knew exactly what her mother had said and wanted to be able to read it back to her.

"So," her mother went on, her voice brightening, "What do you have to be thankful for this year?" It didn't matter how Lily responded. It was a setup, and her mother would get to the punch line eventually.

"I'm thankful that I'm safe," Lily said.

"Well how you can feel safe living in that city makes no sense. No sense at all," she said. "You always were so concerned about being safe. I used to have to tuck you in up to your neck. Do you remember that? I'd have to pull the sheets in so tight or you couldn't sleep."

"I remember."

"It's a wonder you can get to bed now, without someone doing the tucking," she said. "Unless, of course, there *is* someone doing it."

"And what if there is?" she said. She thought of Alan, of living like sitcom people, in separate bedrooms, with an adopted daughter and a convoluted backstory to explain it all. "Why are you so interested?"

"I called to tell you about your grandmother. Just in case you care. She's taken a turn for the worse. Just babbles on. Word salad, really. Did I tell you she thinks she wrote the song 'Love Is a Many-Splendored Thing' for your grandfather? She insists someone stole it from her and put it on the radio. Now she wants credit. No royalties, mind you; she says she's too generous for that. Just appreciation. I had to pretend to write a letter to the editor of the local paper in complaint. Never mind that she hated Grandpa. But I'm glad I can at least visit her twice a week. That's what children are for, Lily. Old age. And social security won't be around for your generation. You should think about it."

"Mmm-hmm."

"Anyway, I'm thankful my mother is still alive."

Silence.

"Are you glad *I'm* still alive?"

"Mother."

"Because I'm not opposed to ending it early. I don't want to be pathetic someday. And I know you're not going to spoon feed me, I can see that much already. I could leave you a bit of a nest egg, I suppose. That is, if you needed one."

"Happy Thanksgiving, Mom," she said. "Tell Dad I say hello and love."

"Can I tell him to expect you at Christmas?"

In the living room, Daphne slept soundly on the couch. The sun had gone down and the light from the television illuminated her face. Lily went to the linen closet and brought out a nubby lap blanket that she draped over her. She wondered if her own mother had once experienced the kind of gratitude Lily now felt, watching her chest rise and fall with her breath, marveling that she was there at all.

Lily stood by the bare bay window, running her fingers along the metal piping that separated the diamond-shaped panes. The listing had said the apartment had "romantic details throughout." There was crown molding, an aluminum sconce in the hallway, and an old ironing board that folded out of the wall near the refrigerator.

"Look!" she showed Daphne. "People used to iron in the kitchen."

Children liked romantic details, she thought, even if they didn't know it. She would remember these touches when she was grown.

The one bedroom overlooked a street of similarly slanted townhouses, not unlike the San Francisco of her imagination, if a bit shabbier. It was too far from the courthouse, and outrageously expensive.

"The local school is excellent," the realtor said. They always said that, Lily thought, but it reassured her nonetheless.

She followed Daphne like the girl was a divining rod; Lily watched to see if she would find water, declare this a place worth settling. Daphne dragged her favorite gray dishtowel in her left hand, picking up dust from the parquet floor.

There was a little alcove that she could set off with curtains to make a room of Daphne's own. She thought it would be good for her. In the short time they'd been together, she seemed older, like she was starting to transition from toddler to little girl.

There was good water pressure, a washer and dryer in the unit, and even communal storage space downstairs. But she asked about lead paint and flood zones and retrofitting, of all the ways they could be hurt.

The realtor wore textured tights underneath her straight skirt, and Daphne kept reaching out for the woman's legs, running her small fingers along the raised swirls of the nylons. She was not the same child who would not stop rubbing her eyes with her fists.

"She's sweet," the realtor said, though she brushed her away from her leg. "So curious."

Lily liked the way that sounded. An inquisitive child was a bright child, and she was responsible for teasing this curiosity out of Daphne. This is how people would see them, as mother and daughter.

"It will go quickly," the realtor had said, and Lily replied, "Yes, they grow so fast," before she blushed, realizing the woman had meant the unit.

Daphne smeared her hands and dishtowel across each wall and lower cabinet, every surface she could find, which Lily could only assume was her feral toddler's way of claiming sovereignty over the space, of saying *mine*. She told the realtor she would sign the lease. And when she was finishing the application and Daphne emerged from a closet proudly wielding a rusty hanger, she pried it from her hands, ignoring the look of offense on the girl's face, and placed it safely out of reach.

ACKNOWLEDGMENTS

THE PUBLICATION OF THIS BOOK OWES A GREAT DEAL TO A great many people: the writers and teachers who have offered encouragement and brought their wisdom to bear on these stories and more, including Tom Barbash, David Borofka, Anthony Doerr, John Freeman, Anthony Marra, Lou Mathews, Kevin McIlvoy, the late Hubert Selby Jr., Marisa Silver, Maxine Swann, and Nancy Zafris; Linfield College professors Lex Runciman and Barbara Drake, who took a young writer seriously; the fellow writers I have met at Tin House, Lit Camp, and Valerie Fioravanti's workshops, who have all offered their close reading and camaraderie; graduate school friends who have been cheerleaders, astute editors, and more; steadfast readers Shahan Sanossian and Rachel Earle; Writing Between the Vines, which provided valuable time; the literary magazine editors who work thanklessly to bring short fiction to readers, with special thanks to Hannah Tinti and the crew at *One Story;* Linda Swanson-Davies and Susan Burmeister-Brown at *Glimmer Train;* Speer Morgan and the wonderful editors of the *Missouri Review;* Oscar Villalon, Laura Cogan, and the team at *Zyzzyva;* and many, many others; my family for providing entertaining material; the doctors whose work has inspired many of these pages; Kirby Kim at Janklow & Nesbit; the entire team at the University of Pittsburgh Press; my wife for putting up with all the things someone who lives with a writer must; and my son, my good-luck charm.